Call of the
Jersey Devil

Aurelio Voltaire

SPENCE CITY

Spencer Hill Press

Contact: Spence City, an imprint of Spencer Hill Press,
PO Box 247, Contoocook, NH 03229, USA

Please visit our website at www.spencecity.com

First Edition: May 2013.
Aurelio Voltaire
Call of the Jersey Devil: a novel / by Aurelio Voltaire—1st ed.
p. cm.

Summary:
Four Goth teens and a washed up musician get stranded in the Pine Barrens and discover that New Jersey really is a gate to Hell—and if they don't do something, being banned from the mall is the least of their worries.

The author acknowledges the copyrighted or trademarked status and trademark owners of the following wordmarks mentioned in this fiction: AAA, Bauhaus, Björk, Black Sabbath, Bondo, Boone's Farm Wine, Brookstone, Chrysler Building, Converse, Cracker Jack, Denny's, Depeche Mode, Depends, Diet Coke, Domino's Pizza, Doritos, Eagle Rock Diner, Foot Locker, Forever 21, Formica, Funions, GameStop, General Motors, Ghostbusters, Google Maps, Gothic Beauty, Happy Meal, Hot Pockets, Hot Topic, iPod, Iron Maiden, Jack Skellington, Jedi, Jell-O, Jenga, Jersey Shore, Limelight, Lord of the Rings Ents, Macy's, Master Replica, McDonald's, Mountain Dew, MySpace, Old Spice, Oreos, PayPal, Piercing Pagoda, Prada, Rasputina, Richie Rich, Rollaboard suitcase, Ronald McDonald, Rubik's Cube, Sears, Spencer Gifts, Star Wars, The Body Shop, The Breakfast Club, The Golden Girls, The Number of the Beast, The Pogues, The Price is Right, Uzi, Vaseline, Victoria's Secret, VNV Nation

Cover design by Aurelio Voltaire
Cover art: Michael Komarck : www.komarckart.com
Interior art: Paul Carrick : www.nightserpent.com
Interior layout by Marie Romero
Chapter Animation by Aurelio Voltaire
Independent Proofreader: Audrey Lawrence Greene : ickackeek.com

All art (c)2012 Aurelio Voltaire Hernandez

For more of Aurelio Voltaire's books, music, films and toys,
please visit the official site at www.voltaire.net

978-1-939392-00-8 (paperback)
978-1-939392-01-5 (e-book)

Printed in the United States of America

For Mars, who braved the darkness
of the Pine Barrens with me while
searching for the Jersey Devil.

Chapter 1

THE PINE BARRENS OF NEW JERSEY
OCTOBER 13th
THIRTY-FIVE YEARS AGO

Hell had erupted in the forest. Twisted black trees, seemingly miles high, contorted and swayed at the mercy of ghastly winds. Normally, they'd have disappeared against the deep, black sky that smothered the woods, but not on this night. On this night, all that was foul and terrible, all that reeked of charred flesh, all that was made of pain and suffering crawled out of a chasm. The light that burst from this wicked portal was a glowing red thing, crimson, like a translucent heart throbbing with the passion of a million demons on the horizon. It lit the sky so that the trees were black giants dancing in place. Winds howled like millions of tortured souls, finally released from their bondage, as they whipped through the trees, tearing at the eardrums of any who would listen to their laments. Above the pines, against the red glow of the sky, hundreds of black silhouettes appeared—they resembled a flock of birds, or a colony of bats. Or worse.

One thing was certain: all Hell was breaking loose.

In the center of a clearing, in the maelstrom of the storm, was the only soul who could hold it back. This time wasn't her first. Not even her tenth. But she was old now. Seventy? Eighty-something? She had stopped keeping track of birthdays long ago. Her life had become this—waiting for Hell to break its bounds and then pushing it back, over and over again.

War-weary and battle-scarred, she was once again answering the call. But this time was different. She knew it in her faltering heart and in her creaking bones. She felt weak, and she knew there was more to lose this time—not just her life, not just the safety of the world. This time she was afraid for the child at her side, for her granddaughter.

"Caroline, stay close to me." She pushed the eight-year-old girl behind her. With the child hidden in her shadow, she held up the amulet and opened the ancient book. She read aloud as winds battered her weathered face.

"Spirits of evil, unfriendly beings, unwanted guests, be gone! Leave us! Leave this place, leave this circle, that the Goddess and the God may enter. Go, or be cast into the outer darkness!"

An unearthly howl issued from the black belly of the forest, causing the eyes of both old woman and child to widen. A thrashing, like a giant jackrabbit caught in a briar, crackled through the trees. The two froze. Then, as if the thing in the darkness had suddenly found a way to escape, there was silence—but only for a moment. Next came the sound of giant wings flapping in the night. The woman and the girl, generations apart, scanned the sky with a shared fear. Caroline clung to her mentor's cloak as the old woman continued the incantation.

"Go, or be drowned in the watery abyss! Go, or be burned in the flames! Go, or be torn by the whirlwind!"

A light caught Caroline's eye. In the old woman's hand, the amulet was starting to glow. A look of wonder washed over the child's face. The old woman's voice grew stronger, urged on by the emanating light.

"By the power of the Mother, we banish you! We banish you!"

Suddenly, with a great thud, a winged demon crashed to the ground before the woman. It stood there cocking its head from side to side, examining her defiantly with big, black eyes. Caroline squeezed her eyes closed, cowering behind her mentor, but when the demon hissed, curiosity roused her to steal a glance. There, before her, was the most unbelievable thing she had ever seen. The beast was twice the height of a grown man. Its face was long and skeletal. Big, black eyes were set on each side of its skull; one end held rows of razor-sharp teeth the length of steak knives, and the other was covered with a mass of pointy horns. Some of the horns were short and straight; others were long and curled like the horns of a massive ram. Its body was muscular but spindly. The arms, bulky at the shoulders, led to long, bony fingers, each ending in a curled, shiny black talon. Its legs ended at hairy cloven hooves like that of a goat. Between them, a barbed reptilian tail lashed from side to side like a hungry snake.

Caroline looked up to see it spread its wings. A sickly, translucent skin stretched over great, hand-like bones. They spread for a moment, then abruptly closed as it barked into the old woman's face. Caroline snapped her eyes shut again and desperately buried her face in the old woman's robes. The mentor had no less fear than the child, but she kept hers at bay. Struggling to maintain her composure, to hold her ground, she stretched her arm toward the beast and thrust the amulet forward. Her hand stopped mere inches from the monster's fangs.

"*Be gone, foul beast!*" she cried. "*Get... thee...*"

The amulet glowed brightly, blinding all in its path.

"*Back to…*"

Slamming the book shut with one hand, she began to utter the last word of the incantation.

"*Heh…*"

With a mighty wave of its clawed hand, the creature cut her head clean off of her body. Blood shot straight up from the older woman's neck, like short bursts from a fountain. Caroline screamed. The beast let out an unbridled roar that echoed throughout the forest and beyond. Caroline clung desperately to her mentor's robes as the body within dropped to the ground. She was left standing like a carriage driver, holding the reins of a corpse. A beat later, the head dropped and hit the moist grass of the clearing with a dull thud. It bounced once or twice and rolled in a semicircle, coming to a stop at Caroline's feet. She whimpered, looking down at the head in dismay.

The beast turned its attention to Caroline. Leaning toward her, it opened its drooling, toothy maw and roared, blasting her little face with hot, rank breath and saliva. She fell to the ground instinctively, picked up the amulet, and without a moment of hesitation, belted out the last phrase of the incantation:

"*Get thee back to Hell!*"

A bright light burst from the gem-encrusted bauble, causing the beast to cover its eyes. From a distance, a loud sucking sound was heard. This cacophonous din grew louder, echoing through the trees like a tornado of screams. The wind, the eerie red glow, the black silhouettes of creatures in the sky, all began moving away, moving toward the sound, caught in a hellish whirlwind. Like Saint-Saens' "Danse Macabre" playing in reverse, creatures flew backward through the red sky. As if against unseen hands, the monster before Caroline struggled to stand its ground. But it, too, was defeated, swept up and off of the very ground on which it stood, sucked with great force with the rest of its ilk through the air and back into Hell. Its anguished cries faded into the abyss.

And suddenly, there was silence in the forest.

Caroline looked down at the body of her grandmother, her mentor, at her feet. Finding herself alone, she began to cry. It was the sort of cry you hear from a child when she first realizes she is lost, a passing train of sniffles and meek whimpers. She knew it was not becoming for a female of her lineage to behave this way, and a wave of anger rushed through her, directed at the culprit behind her pitiful situation. Turning her face to the black sky, she screamed through her tears.

"You're an asshole, Jersey Devil!"

Chapter 2

NEW JERSEY, PRESENT DAY

Heavy metal music filled the air. Candles flickered. A Satanic ritual was underway.

"Rise up you dark gods, and open the gates of Hell. Rise up from the darkness, rise up from the pit."

Squatting on the floor, a young man waved his pale hands over the scented smoke, its source a metal incense burner before him. His name was Aleister, and to any soul willing to listen, he would proudly profess himself a powerful Satanist and conjurer of demons. The ritual at hand was not new to him, and he knew in his mind that he was no novice. In fact, he had performed this ritual many times before, in this same dark corner of this, albeit unlikely, hallowed room. He'd gathered, as he'd done in the past, the occult objects needed for the task, and with great confidence in his skills, he continued his nefarious pursuits.

He clasped a small, metal pentagram between his thumb and index finger and held it before him over the smoke.

"Ancient demons of the void, I call out to thee. Hear my plea that you may do my bidding.

Come forth Hecate, Come forth Belial!

I command thee, I implore thee!"

He placed the pentagram beside him and reached for the ceremonial dagger. A gargoyle gazed down at him with a frozen look of concern. He rolled the black cape off of his forearm, revealing a mesh of cut marks on his pale flesh, most of them healed. With a quick swish he made a new one. He held his arm out over of the incense burner. A drop of blood fell through the air, hitting the charcoal with a hiss.

"Rise! Rise up you demons, and open the gates of Hell!"

He closed his eyes and saw a red light growing in the darkness. It widened and stretched, forming a rift, a glowing red portal to Hell.

"Bring forth the destroyer!

Bring forth… the BEAST!"

Suddenly, a shadow appeared over his left shoulder.

"What the hell are you doing?" The clerk yelled at Aleister. "Jesus! Are you burning incense back here?"

"Silence, mammal! You're disturbing the dark Gods!"

"That's it! I'm calling mall security! I mean it." The clerk snarled, spinning on a heel and marching off. He had every right to be angry. The back aisle of a Spencer Gifts store was no place for a Satanic ritual.

Elsewhere in the same mall, AJ and Prudence were deep in conversation as they strolled between Macy's and Sears. It was a Saturday, and the Maplecreek Mall was abuzz with people, mostly ones who took issue with weirdos, freaks, and other non-conformists. So, it came as no surprise to the pair when, as they passed Forever 21, snickers and jeers shot from a group of teenage girls within. AJ was used to it—being Goth was bad enough, but being black and Goth in a town dominated by close-minded, suburban white folk made it all the more challenging. Nevertheless, AJ had long since stopped caring about what people thought of him. He had bleached his short-cropped frohawk white and wore clothes covered in patches depicting logos of his favorite bands, as well as the occasional acerbic slogan. These accents gave him an appearance that leaned more toward Punk—Punk had always seemed a bit more threatening than Goth, and that occasionally came in handy. Moreover, he'd always suspected that whites in general had a deep-seated, perhaps subconscious, fear of blacks, and he played to that when it suited him. It didn't save him all of the time, though. He'd had his share of scuffles, but more often than not, people resigned themselves to limiting their condemnations to disapproving stares and mumbled insults, for fear the black Goth might "pop a cap in their asses" or "bite them on the neck" or both. He was uninterested in doing either, of course, just as he was uninterested in what people thought of him in general.

Prudence, in sharp contrast, was very concerned about people's perceptions of her, but was generally too busy admiring herself in a mirror to actually notice what they were. Slim, pale and naturally beautiful, she would have been considered extremely attractive by most mall Neanderthals if not for the Gothic façade. Her skin was milky white, her hair was black like the feathers of a raven, and her eyes were like blue gems. She was stunning and she knew it. Or so it appeared. Her makeup, which she never left the house without, was immaculate and seemed at all times to be the work of a consummate professional. She amplified her paleness with a foundation a few shades lighter than her already snowy complexion, and her eyes were rimmed with deep black liner that branched into ornate spider web-like designs at her temples. In her black leather corset and flowing black gossamer skirt, she struck the image of a wicked enchantress or an evil queen regally strolling among her subjects— even if her subjects happened to be the denizens of a single New Jersey mall.

Prudence craved attention and affirmation, primarily from men, and felt that anyone who did not find her attractive must be the victim of some brain-eating bacteria. She was the very embodiment of the term "high maintenance," a fact that AJ had discovered very quickly during their brief attempt at a romantic relationship. She was as difficult as he was easy-going, as vain as he was comfortable in his own skin. They were very much alike in another way, however; they were both strong personalities, choosing to live against the grain. Despite the disapproval of their families, their peers, and most of the world around them, they were dead set in their determination to be *Goth*. It was, perhaps, for all of these reasons that they decided to remain best friends, and nothing more.

AJ glanced over his shoulder at the jeering and disapproving pack of girls. He stared at them blankly for a moment before turning back to Prudence. Nonchalantly, he recalled a slogan from a T-shirt he'd once seen. "'They laugh at us because we're different. We laugh at them because they're all the same.'" It was a bit cute to be a mantra, but he believed it with all of his heart.

"Whatever," said Prudence, "those girls have *zero* style. Probably out buying some bargain-basement turquoise prom catastrophe for their *big night* in the city."

"Yeah, *Atlantic* City," scoffed AJ. "Those girls have got *Jersey Shore* written all over them."

"Forever 21." Prudence pondered, shaking her head. "They should be shopping at 'Forever 16' since they will be mentally sixteen—*forever*!"

"I seem to recall you being sixteen not too long ago." AJ smiled slyly.

"Yeah, hello! That was, like, a year ago! And anyway, we're the same age, asshole."

AJ primped his frohawk. "Yeah, but I'm a mature seventeen-year-old. You know, on account of being on my own and stuff."

Prudence snorted. "Ha! That's a good one. You live with your Grandma!"

"Hey! I may live with my Grandma, but I have a job, and I make my own money."

"Please! You never have any money! You don't have a phone or a car or anything!"

AJ spun to face her. "And do you know why that is? Because ever since my mom died, I've had to man up fast. I walk to my job, and I work all week and every cent I make goes to paying the rent and taking care of my Grandma. You can think it's 'gay' or 'stupid' or whatever you'd call it, but she depends on me. So, I do whatever I have to, and I go without some of the niceties of life that you're so familiar with. You know what that's called?" He stroked his chin and pursed his lips. "It's called being mature for a seventeen-year-old."

Every muscle in Prudence's face tightened. "I'm mature for my age. All of the college guys tell me so."

"Uh, newsflash, they say that to all the young girls they wanna bang. Well, the ones who are gullible enough to believe it, anyway."

"That's bullshit!"

"PS, where's *your* car and cellphone? You said you walked here, and I'm sure you'd be texting up a storm if you had your phone on you."

"My parents took them away from me."

"And do you know why that is?"

"Because my parents are dicks?"

"No, because you're immature." AJ's laugher rang through the halls of the mall.

Prudence brooded for a moment. Then, an evil snake of a grin slithered across her lips. "You didn't think I was immature at the prom. Remember, in the parking lot? In the back seat of my car?"

"Dude! You made out with, like, eight guys at the prom!"

"Oh my God, no I didn't!" She contemplated for a moment. "I only made out with two guys, including you."

"You were my girlfriend!" screamed AJ.

A chuckle frolicked out of her mouth. "You're so cute when you're jealous."

"Pru, seriously. You need to get this insecurity thing in check."

"Insecure?" she cried. "I'm not insecure! Please, I'm like, the prettiest girl in this whole mall."

"See, that's the problem right there. If you really believed that, you wouldn't say it. You sure as hell wouldn't try so hard to prove it." She looked away. "Seriously, it's like you need every guy in the world to like you. It's not healthy." He placed a hand on her shoulder. "Pru, really, you have to reel it in. It's going to lead you to a bad place."

"I don't know what you're talking about." They walked in silence, gazing in opposite directions into the shops. AJ awkwardly attempted to maintain a feigned interest in the interior of The Body Shop. Prudence did the same, peering into a Brookstone. "Damn, I didn't realize you were still so sore about the prom."

"I'm not mad. I'm over it. Way over it." He shook his head. "But yeah, I gotta say, it was way out of line. And well, we both know how that ended."

"Whatever, I didn't even want to go to prom. It was *your* dumb idea!"

AJ smirked, sarcasm pouring from every word. "I seem to remember you having a magical time at the prom."

"Please! I only went because I thought I was going to get to see the prom queen covered in pig's blood."

"Come on! You should know better. I told you he wouldn't do it."

"Aleister is *crazy*! You don't know what he might do!"

"He's not crazy. He's a moron. And he's only got three settings—he talks mad shit, he loses his head, and he talks mad shit."

"Speak of the devil." Prudence gestured into the gaping mouth of the Spencer Gifts store. Aleister, in full Satanic priest garb (his term for a black cloak, leather gauntlets, and a Black Sabbath T-shirt) was in the middle a full-on pointing and screaming match with the sales clerk.

"Come on," said AJ. "Let's bail out the weirdo... again." Prudence and AJ proceeded toward the store. Without turning his head and with a mischievous grin growing on his face, AJ asked Prudence, "By the way... didn't *you* wear a turquoise dress to the prom?"

"As if." Prudence growled, rolling her eyes.

"You're in big trouble this time, mister!" screamed the clerk. "I mean it!"

The clerk was trying with every fiber of his being (and there were many fibers) to project the image of authority bestowed upon him by his "manager" badge. However, everything about him communicated, "I'm an impotent thirty-year-old who lives in his mother's basement." The Hawaiian shirt he wore might have looked alright if it were a size 3XL (known around those parts as a "Trekkie Small"), but instead, this poor rag was a good two sizes short of fitting the clerk's Hot Pockets-engorged frame. It inspired an image of someone taking Hawaii on its absolute ugliest day and then trying to make it cover the entire continental United States.

"You don't understand," yelled Aleister. "There is great power in that aisle. I can feel it!"

AJ and Prudence entered the store. AJ marched straight to the young Satanist. "Man, are you with this *Dark Gods* shit again? Why you gotta do this shit at the mall? Do you not have a home?"

"Yeah!" cheered Phil the Clerk. "Tell your friend he can't come in here and do this crazy stuff anymore! He's gonna burn the place down!"

AJ looked at Aleister and narrowed his eyes. "Dude, how *old* are you? This shit's stupid."

Aleister glared at AJ. "You don't understand the ways of the darkness!"

"Bitch, I *am* the darkness!" AJ reached for a Master Replica lightsaber from a nearby display.

"What's *his* malfunction?" Prudence gestured toward Aleister.

AJ turned to her, lightsaber in hand and, in a fluid samurai-like motion, he brought the blade up toward his face. He flicked the switch. The lightsaber made its signature powering-up sound and lit up, glowing a deep red. In his best James Earl Jones voice, AJ answered, "*Aleistah doesn't know the true powah of the dahk side!*"

Prudence shook her head dismissively.

Aleister lunged at AJ with a red Master Replica lightsaber of his own. Sabers met, the red lights reflecting off of their faces. Aleister struck, but AJ swept down, blocking the blow. Lightsabers crackled and fizzled as they made impact again and again. *Crackle! Swoosh! Tzzzzzt!*

"Hey! Wait! No! You can't... you can't do this in here!" Phil the Clerk pulled at what was left of his hair.

With one last lunge, AJ knocked Aleister to the ground. Aleister rolled out of sight and disappeared behind an aisle, his lightsaber left buzzing on the carpet floor. AJ scanned the room, lightsaber still in hand. He looked toward the blacklight posters, then toward the row of resin gargoyles. Nothing. Silence. Suddenly, from behind a cardboard cutout of Justin Bieber, Aleister emerged holding a massive double-ended dildo.

"Prepare to feel the force of my flesh saber," warned Aleister.

Prudence shook her head. "You guys are *so* gay."

The lightsaber versus sex toy battle continued, albeit sloppily.

"Stop it! Stop it!" The clerk waved his hands at them—from a safe distance. "This is total bullshit! You guys are going to..."

As if on cue, Aleister swung the rubbery appendage, knocking a couple of lava lamps off of a shelf. They shattered to the ground.

"That does it!" screamed the clerk. "You guys are *really* in trouble now!"

It was obvious to all involved that it was time to go. In one motion, AJ turned off his lightsaber and returned it to the display. He straightened himself up, and the three began to leave the store.

"Get out, and don't come back," yapped Phil the Clerk. "I swear, I'm really gonna call mall security. I'll do it! I mean it!"

As AJ passed the clerk, he channeled Arnold Schwarzenegger. "I'll be back."

Behind him, Aleister muttered under his breath, "You'll be black."

AJ elbowed Aleister in the gut without even turning around. Aleister grunted and cradled his stomach as the trio walked out the door.

Phil the Clerk glared at them with disdain. He looked at the shattered lava lamps and the general disorder they had caused. Thirty-something years of frustration bubbled up in him. He could contain it no more. He released it in the only way he knew how— by punching the life-sized Justin Bieber cutout and shouting, "Fuckin' losers!"

Chapter 3

Mixed into the pastel-clad horde of Maplecreek Mall zombies, three Goths in black struggled upstream to put more distance between them and the Spencer Gifts store.

AJ and Prudence walked along with Aleister, who was lagging a foot or two behind. AJ addressed him without turning, "They sell double-ended dongs at Spencer Gifts?"

"Nah," answered Aleister, "I brought it from home for my ritual. Whatever. They can have it. I got what I needed out of it." AJ and Prudence looked at each other with a mixture of confusion and repulsion. Knowing they didn't really want the details, they let it go.

Prudence stopped abruptly, frozen like a deer in headlights. AJ looked at her, then around the mall for the source of her sudden shock. "What's up? You okay?"

"Did you see that creepy guy?"

"What creepy guy?"

"That guy with the frizzy hair and glasses."

AJ scanned the mall. "I don't see anybody like that."

"Oh my God, he was staring right at me! He was like some creepy rapist!"

AJ signed. "Pru, not every guy in the world wants to bang you."

"I do!" cried Aleister from a few feet behind.

AJ raised an eyebrow. "Yeah well, that's hardly a surprise coming from a guy who had anal sex with a poodle."

"That's bullshit. It's just a rumor. I vehemently deny these anus allegations!"

Prudence leaned in towards AJ and whispered in his ear. "I think he did it."

"Me too," whispered AJ.

"It's just a rumor!"

"So, dear Prudence," asked AJ. "What's on the agenda for today?"

"We're meeting Stuey."

"Ah, the illustrious Count Stuey!" AJ proclaimed with a flamboyant twirl of the hand. "When are you going to leave that poor kid alone?"

"What are you talking about? He's my friend."

"Right. He just wants to be your friend." Sarcasm dripped from AJ's tongue.

Aleister, who'd been hanging back, suddenly found reason to catch up. He craned his neck toward Prudence. Sounding like a perverted little imp, he panted while punctuating his words with pelvic thrusts. "Yeah, he wants to rub his little vampire wiener all over you!"

"You're disgusting." Prudence snarled with a curled lip.

AJ smirked. "You conned that sad little bastard into buying us all lunch again, didn't you?"

"Please," said Prudence, "he can afford it. That boy's got more money than God."

Aleister earnestly added, "Yeah, I heard his uncle gives him shitloads of money to, like, touch him and stuff... *inappropriately*."

AJ turned to Aleister. "You're not right, you know that? You've got serious problems."

"It's true!" demanded Aleister, adding, "Ask him yourself!" as he pointed upwards.

The threesome stopped. At the top of the escalator was their friend Stuey. He had, no doubt, just left the Hot Topic on the second floor. He was not alone—at least, not exactly. Just behind him, one tier up on the escalator, were two towering jocks who looked like they had just walked off of the set of MTV's *Jersey Shore*. They had dreadful tans, the kind of glowing, radioactive color one could only get from a can. They wore brightly colored polos, one chartreuse and one teal. Against the color of their orange skin, these shirts made one's retinas vibrate like those green and orange optical illusions designed to drive monkeys mad. Their collars, popped of course, stood at attention, as did their short, stalagmite-like hair (which was more gel than hair). They had clearly gone to great lengths to achieve a look that, for better or worse, the majority in these parts had deemed "cool."

In sharp contrast, Stuey was the very embodiment of haplessness. He was chubby, he had curly hair, he was a ginger, and he was a Goth. He had a genuine appreciation for all things vampiric, but no matter how earnest his desire to dress like the Vampire Lestat was, he always ended up looking like Rip Taylor or Jonah Hill on his way to a Halloween party. He was a true connoisseur of dark and alternative music, a dedicated fan of the genre, and one of the sincerest and kindest people one could ever hope to meet. Of course, that meant nothing to the two fellows behind him. To them, he was just some short, fat "faggot" in a frilly shirt, deserving as much punishment as they could dole out. And so, they took turns pushing, shoving, and slapping his head as they descended on the escalator. Stuey, in turn, did his best to laugh it off.

Slap. "Hey!" *Shove.* "Heh heh, okay guys! Very funny!" *Poke.* "Ha ha, easy fellas! We're on an escalator here! It's kinda dangerous!" *Punch.* "That's enough. Heh heh, okay. I get the picture."

And so it went all the way down. When they arrived at the first floor, the two jocks broke off toward Foot Locker.

"See ya later, faggot!" yelled one.

"Yeah, see ya, homo!" mocked the other.

Stuey waved jovially. "Alright guys, be cool! Catch ya later!"

AJ, Prudence, and Aleister stood frozen, locked in horror as Stuey came running up to them.

"Hey guys!"

"You okay?" offered AJ.

"What, you mean *those* guys?" Stuey gestured toward the jocks. "They're harmless. Honestly, they're just mad at the world or something. I mean, a person has to be pretty damaged and hurt to feel anger for total strangers. I feel sorry for them, I really do. They're probably in love with each other or something, and can't show it. Can you imagine how awful that must be?" The trio stared at him blankly. "Okay, well, who's up for lunch?"

Aleister, Stuey, AJ, and Prudence began a slow crawl to the food court. Stuey made small talk.

"So, what have you guys been up to today?"

"Well," said AJ, "Aleister nearly burned down Spencer Gifts while trying to summon Cthulhu. And then we had a lightsaber battle."

"With a giant dildo," added Prudence.

"And we were subsequently banned from Spencer Gifts for life," concluded AJ.

"So, in other words," added Aleister, "business as usual."

Stuey chuckled. "You guys are insane!" As he laughed, something caught the corner of his eye.

"The guy who works there," laughed Aleister, "has threatened to call mall security on me, like, a million times. He never has and he never will. He is a giant, fat pussy!"

"Oh my God," muttered Stuey. "Guys!" He suddenly broke off from the pack. The trio looked at each other apprehensively and started after him. They found him stopped by a column near the Piercing Pagoda, where he was reading a flier. Peeling the flier off of the column, Stuey waved it at them. "Oh my God! You have to check this out!"

"What's that?" asked AJ.

"There's a huge Goth festival going on *today*!" bubbled Stuey, "and the greatest Goth singer of all time is going to be there!"

"Give me that!" A.J snatched the flier out of Stuey's hand. "'Featuring Raised by Bats lead singer, Villy Bats, in a special solo appearance'," he read aloud. "Who the hell are 'Raised by Bats'?"

Stuey exploded. "Oh my God! You're killing me! They're only the *greatest* band ever! Hello?" He pulled open his frilly shirt to reveal a black T-shirt underneath. On it was an image of a bat carting off a baby carriage, and spooky Gothic text spelling out the name of his favorite band, Raised by Bats.

"Never heard of them." AJ spoke in a monotone.

"Yeah," said Prudence, "when you said 'greatest Goth singer,' I thought you were going to say Peter Murphy."

"Or Robert Smith," added AJ.

"Or Andrew Eldritch, or someone like that," said Prudence.

Aleister cut in. "Andrew Eldritch is not Goth."

"Says who?" Prudence sneered at him.

"Says Andrew Eldritch."

"Whatever."

"Okay!" Stuey broke up the exchange. "Not everyone's heard of him. But his band, Raised by Bats, was one of the best bands to come out of the whole third wave Goth scene, early nineties—you know, March Violets, Rosetta Stone, The Sisters."

Prudence placed her hands to her hips and looked at AJ and Aleister. "Does anyone have any idea what he's talking about?"

"Yeah, shit, Stuey!" AJ laughed "You sound like a fuckin' indie rocker!"

Aleister, doing his best Emo imitation, brushed his bangs to the side and cooed in a mocking tone, "My favorite band is so obscure, they've never even heard of themselves." He laughed along with AJ and Prudence.

Stuey grew more animated and desperate. "Come on guys, this means a lot to me! We *have* to go to this show. *Please*?"

AJ looked at the flier again. "Come on, dude, this shit's in the Pine Barrens. You gotta be kidding me!"

"Okay. Fine." Stuey feigned indifference. He spun on a heel and turned to leave.

"Where are you going?" asked AJ.

Stuey turned back to his friends and announced matter-of-factly, "I'm going to the food court. I'm going to get some lunch. And then, I'm going to a Goth festival in the Pine Barrens to see my favorite performer in the whole world."

"What about us?" asked Prudence. "I mean, I thought we were having lunch?"

Aleister craned his head into the conversation. "Yeah fucker! You promised to feed us! I mean, I think. I heard that somewhere."

Stuey replied in a haughty tone, "Whoever is coming with me to the Goth festival is welcome to be my guest at lunch." He turned and began to walk away. Two steps later, he stopped, but did not turn around. "Furthermore—you have to beat me to the food court." With that said, Stuey walked off on his own.

Aleister was not pleased. "The fucker's got us by the balls!"

AJ turned to Prudence. "Looks like your boy just freed himself from your icy grip."

Prudence narrowed her eyes. They all stood motionless watching Stuey walk further away.

"Well." AJ, greedily rubbed his hands together. "Who's hungry?"

Aleister needed no further prodding. "One, two, three, GO!" He yelled and off they went, racing toward the food court shouting at the top of their lungs. They overtook Stuey in mere seconds, leaving him behind. Stuey smiled widely, like a child on Christmas morning.

The food court at the Maplecreek Mall was packed, as it generally was on Saturdays, and it was only by some small miracle that they found a table. Stuey gleefully munched on a souvlaki sandwich from the Greek place, white tzatziki sauce dripping from the corners of his mouth. Across from him, Prudence sadly pushed the pieces of iceberg lettuce around in her salad, as if she hoped she might find a hamburger hiding under a leaf. Beside her, Aleister had already plowed through his McDonald's Happy Meal, as evidenced by the pile of golden arch-covered detritus before him. Now, he furiously fiddled with a small box that looked something like a Rubik's cube. This odd cube, however, was gold and had strange markings on it, as if made by some ancient or alien race.

AJ arrived at the table and placed a tray of Japanese food down in front of him. Captivated by Aleister's manic manipulation of the cube, AJ froze, staring at him for a moment. "What are you doing?"

Prudence answered with the slightest condescending curl in her painted lips. "He's trying to summon the Cenobites."

AJ snatched the cube from Aleister's hands and slammed it forcefully down on the table. "*This is a toy.*" He leveled his eyes at the Satanist. "It's a child's plaything from a goddamned toy store! It does not have magical powers." He turned to Prudence and Stuey. "I swear this kid is retarded or something."

Aleister sat with his head bowed, glaring up at AJ through his contorted brow. "You laugh now!"

"I laugh *now*? Shit!" countered AJ. "When you're around, I laugh *always*!"

"So." Prudence interrupted, trying to lighten the mood. "How are we getting to this festival? None of us has a car."

Aleister raised an eyebrow. "*You* have a car."

"Her parents took it away from her because she's immature," grinned AJ. Prudence replied with a single finger and turned to the Satanist.

"Where's *your* car?" She purred in a catty tone.

Aleister lowered his eyes to the strange cube. "I'm not allowed to drive anymore. Long story."

AJ filled in the details with a smile. "The incident in question took place in Middlesex County. It involves a dead goat, a copy of Iron Maiden's *The Number of the Beast*, and a bottle of Boone's Farm Wine."

Prudence's jaw went slack. She marveled at the Satanist with mixture of disbelief and disgust. "Oh my God, really?"

Aleister fiddled with the cube for a moment, avoiding the question. Then, his head shot up like a pop-up turkey thermometer. "Hey! What about Richie Rich over here? Why don't you have a car? I bet you could get your, um… uncle… to buy you one."

Stuey sat up firmly in his chair. "My parents are perfectly able to buy me a car. They just... won't. They don't think it's safe for me to drive."

"Lame," growled Prudence through half-closed eyes.

"I think they're just afraid that if I have a car I'll leave. Go places. Move out."

"Lamer."

"Well, anyway, it doesn't matter because I've got that all worked out," said Stuey, fidgeting with his cell phone. "I'm texting Ari as we speak."

"Oh, hell no! That bitch is crazy!" AJ folded his arms and shook his head emphatically. "We went on a date once and she didn't say a word. Not *one* word the whole time!"

Prudence perked up. "Oh my God, you went on a date with that weird new girl who came to our school senior year? Jeez, how pathetic are you?"

"Don't play yourself, she's plenty cute... in a Björk kind of way. But yeah, she does *not* speak. I asked her what movie she wanted to see... Nothing. What flavor ice cream she liked? She just cocked her head like a goddamn cocker spaniel. It was the freakiest shit *ever*!"

"She creeps me out," hissed Aleister.

Prudence's eyes widened. "Somebody creeps Aleister out? Now, *that's* rich."

AJ continued, "Seriously, she doesn't talk, like, *ever*. She doesn't talk at all!"

"Maybe she's autistic or something," said Stuey.

Aleister leaned in conspiratorially. "I heard she doesn't talk because she killed her father."

"What?" his audience exclaimed, practically in unison.

"Yeah," Aleister continued. "The word is that she was angry at her dad because he wouldn't buy her something, so she said, 'I wish you were dead!' And a minute later he died. He dropped dead right on the spot. She cursed him with her words, so she vowed never to speak again."

"That's ridiculous," said Prudence.

"Yeah, well, that's what I heard," said Aleister. "She has powers. It gives me the willies."

"*Kreeeeee!*" A shrill peeping reverberated from Stuey's phone.

Aleister jumped. He looked around at his friends and, feeling a bit embarrassed, straightened himself up.

"All *I* know is that she's no fun to be around," said AJ. "She doesn't communicate."

"Oh, I disagree entirely," sang Stuey. "She communicates perfectly." Looking at his phone, he began to read her text aloud. "'Not really doing anything today. Pine Barrens sounds nice. Count me in. Pick you guys up at three in front of GameStop.'" He looked up and smiled at the gang. His grin was met with a communal sigh, but their lack of enthusiasm did nothing to stop the excitement building up in him. "Oh my God! I'm going to get to see my favorite singer of all time! This is so amazing! He never performs anymore, you know. He's become kind of a social recluse. I read in a magazine that Villy got tired of being famous, so he bought the steeple of the Chrysler Building. He lives there, now, in the tower and raises giant bats."

That last part got Aleister's attention. He popped up in his chair and excitedly beamed. "Oh! It must smell like fuckin' crazy in there! Bat shit." He turned to Prudence. "It's called guano." Prudence rolled her eyes, but Aleister wasn't deterred. "Bat shit smells really bad, and they say that if you smell it for too long, you go completely insane. You go bat shit crazy! That's why they call it that—bat shit crazy!"

"What's bat shit crazy," declared AJ, "is that you ass-clowns actually believe he raises giant bats in the fuckin' Chrysler Building. That's just stupid."

"It was in *Gothic Beauty*!" Stuey shook his fists.

AJ shook his head. "I don't know. It just doesn't add up. He's super famous…" He paused, weighing the facts. "But none of us have ever heard of him?"

Prudence raised an eyebrow. "And he's a social recluse?"

Stuey shrugged his shoulders.

Suddenly, Aleister said something that didn't involve summoning devils, feces, or anal rape—and he actually made sense. "If he's such a social recluse, then why the hell is he playing a huge Goth festival in the Pine Barrens of New Jersey?"

The four friends looked into the distance as if contemplating an answer to that question (though, it was just as likely that all involved, Aleister included, were simply wondering if they had actually just heard something sensible come out of his mouth).

Then, Aleister's lips parted again, and the spell was broken. "Do you think he, you know, does it… with those giant bats?"

The answer came in the form of a simultaneous triple facepalm.

Chapter 4

ONE WEEK EARLIER

The sound of a church organ filled the air. Low, sustained chords bellowed —the kind that conjured images of ruined castles and Eastern European vampires rising from their crypts. A harpsichord joined the sonic landscape, weaving an arpeggio through the thick pads of the organ's moaning. And then came the drums, and then the guitar. This was no symphony. This was Deathrock. The crowd cheered. A man's voice soared over the music. "This one's for the spooky kids!" he proclaimed, causing the cheering to surge. And then the volume *really* kicked in, drums pounded like cannon fire, and guitars rhythmically chopped out crunchy power chords.

All in all, it was a lively affair. But not so was the image of the man before the crowd. With microphone in hand, he was poised on the edge of the stage like a hungry vampire, ready to pounce upon his followers. In spite of this action-pose, he remained motionless, completely still, as did the lights, and the audience, and the other band members. They were all frozen in time, frozen in the past. It didn't make for much of a show, but it made for a fine poster.

Upon closer inspection one could see that the poster, with the words "Raised by Bats" scrawled along the top in some nearly illegible font, was not hung on a wall. This grand image of Villy Bats and his cohorts, performing at one of the few Raised by Bats shows that had ever taken place, was ingloriously affixed to the outside of a cardboard box. Inside of that same box were many, many more of these posters, rolled up and standing at attention like an army awaiting orders that had never come.

The music was real enough, though. It came from a TV hooked up to a DVD player. On the screen was footage of the very same show depicted in the poster, an event that took place at the legendary Limelight club in New York City circa 1995. The TV sat on a shelf cluttered with skulls and action figures, Raised by Bats memorabilia, and other artifacts of a young Goth's life—but the abode that housed these things was not that of a young person. The resident of this tiny East Village studio apartment was a forty-something-year-old man.

He bore a resemblance to Villy Bats, minus the makeup and the highly coiffed hair; also missing were the glamorous, vampiric garb and svelte physique. In their place, this man sported an unkempt head of hair hidden under a cap, and the beginnings of a beer belly which jutted out slightly from his skull-emblazoned black T-shirt and matching black underwear. He sat, legs folded, on a convertible futon couch across from the screen, staring intently and eating instant noodles from a ceramic bowl.

If you squinted, you could tell that this *was*, in fact, Villy Bats. But he had been the victim of the world's most common crime—his youth had been kidnapped by a thing called time. It had likely also been raped, dismembered, and buried somewhere, never to be seen again.

The younger Villy on the screen swayed to the music and crooned about darkness with a sinister, sultry pout on his face. The present-day couch-ridden Villy sang along and resisted the urge to mirror the expressions on the taut face of his younger self. Instead, slurping at the bowl of noodles in his lap and keeping the DVD remote by his side, he reminisced and relived his past glories.

The phone rang. Peter Murphy's voice could be heard only barely warbling from somewhere under Villy's thick thighs. He put down the bowl and searched for his cell phone among the folds of the comforter he had been sitting on. The king of Goths sang on as the search grew more intense. Liberated and no longer muffled, the ring tone—a tinny rendition of "Bela Lugosi's Dead" by Bauhaus— chimed through the room. He answered the call in the nick of time.

"Hello, this is Villy Bats." His voice was deep and aristocratic. A beat later, his shoulders dropped, his belly extended to its normal size, and his voice returned to its usual, unassuming tone. "Oh. Hi, Mom."

From the phone speaker came an awful, garbled, incomprehensible chattering.

"What's that?" responded Villy. "Yeah? Listen, I'm kind of in the middle of something."

More chatter came. He reached for the DVD remote.

"I'm... mixing a record." He turned up the volume on the TV.

The tinny cacophony continued.

"Yes. I got the box of instant noodles. Thanks."

His mother persisted.

"I don't know. I haven't figured that out yet. I'm still five hundred dollars short—but all things considered, my landlord isn't completely unreasonable. He's just going to have to wai..."

The chattering on the other end got louder.

"Oh, please don't start that again!" Villy sprang off of the futon, noodles in hand, and stomped to the tiny cubicle that passed for his kitchen. "Look, if I could get a job, I would, but…"

He was interrupted.

"I don't teach guitar lessons anymore."

A noise came from the phone that resembled the sound of a howler monkey having an ice cube inserted into its rectum.

"It's complicated." Villy spat as more telephonic barking came in response. "No, I *can't* walk dogs!" wailed Villy, rolling his eyes. "It's an image thing— you couldn't possibly begin to understand."

The chattering took on a different tone, lower and deeper.

Villy slammed the bowl down onto the counter and stormed back to the couch. "Stop! Okay? Just stop. It's not like I'm sitting on my ass doing nothing." He reached for his laptop and waved it around toward the window, hoping to pirate an internet signal. "I really am looking for a job of some sort. I'm online all day, and I always have my eyes open for…"

The screen on the laptop changed as the webpage refreshed and updated his GothMail.com account. He had picked up a signal! A noise sounded from the laptop reminiscent of a bell tolling. *"Gong!"* It was followed by a creepy recorded voice. "You've got Mail!" said the cheesy Transylvanian accent, then maniacally laughed, *"muahahahahahahah!"*

One particular subject line caught Villy's eye. He read it aloud to himself: "Goth Festival booking request." He clicked on the message and began to scan the email, no longer paying attention to his mother's heated rant. A moment or two passed.

"What? Yeah. Yeah, listen, I have to go. I think I just got a lead on a job."

One last exclamation issued from the cell phone speaker.

Villy sighed. "I love you, too."

Villy hung up the phone and began frantically dialing the number listed in the email.

"But I'd love you more," he thought aloud, "if you'd just send money and get off my ass."

He hit *send*. The phone on the other end began to ring. Someone answered. Villy straightened himself up and cleared his throat. Again, he spoke in his more affected voice. "Hello. Is this… Henry Berger?"

There was a pause.

"This is Villy Bats. I'm calling about your email."

There was excited chatter on the other line, sounding not unlike his mother in pitch, tone and cadence.

"Oh, come on. I'm not *that* famous!" Villy beamed, smiling broadly.

There was another blast of digital squawking.

"Absolutely. I'm free on that date, and I think I can fit this show in."

A strange squeal squeezed out of the phone.

"Listen," Villy said cautiously, "about that modest $500 fee…"

There was a long pause as he treaded carefully into the home stretch.

"… can you do PayPal?"

The Saturday after that fateful email and call, Villy packed his guitar. He coiled his lucky golden cable and slipped it into the outer pouch of his guitar case. He slung the case over his shoulder and reached for the small Rollaboard suitcase he'd filled with merch. He'd forgotten to ask Mr. Berger how many tickets had been sold, or how many people were expected to show up at the festival. Standing there at the threshold of his apartment, Villy wondered if he'd packed enough stickers, CDs, and buttons to sell to a large festival audience. Knowing wouldn't have helped. He hadn't played a show in a few years and had long since been unable to afford pressing more CDs and printing more band memorabilia. As such, he packed whatever he had left, which all fit comfortably in the small carry-on. Still, he wished there were more. Pausing for a moment, Villy glanced at the box of posters by the front door, considering their salability at the show. Unfortunately, between the guitar and the suitcase, his hands were full. Carrying the box was out of the question, as he'd be walking forty city blocks to meet Mr. Berger. He would have to leave it behind.

Of course, Villy could have had the promoter pick him up right in front of his home, but that would have meant revealing that he lived in a tiny studio apartment in a dilapidated, pre-war tenement in the East Village. That would not do. So, keeping up appearances, he told Mr. Berger that he lived in the steeple of the Chrysler Building, where he presumably raised large bats, just as circulated in rumors.

The walk from the East Village to the Chrysler Building was long, and somewhat slowed by the guitar on his shoulder and the suitcase in tow. It was October in New York City. A cold breeze heralded the first signs of autumn. Villy, as usual, wore a long black mourning coat over a hand-knit skull sweater, making the otherwise pleasant stroll something of a sweaty endeavor despite the chilly air. With his black, spiky hair and long, black-clad extremities, he struck the image of a lanky, Gothic spider crawling through a gray city of metal and stone, cathedrals and spires. "Marian" by the Sisters of Mercy pumped directly into his brain from his iPod. Gargoyles stoically looked on as he passed.

He eventually reached the Chrysler Building. Striking some mild curiosity from a doorman, he positioned himself and his gear in the mighty mouth of the famed edifice. He didn't need to wait long—within minutes, his ride arrived. A car horn sounded as the vehicle came to a halt directly before him. It was a dilapidated jalopy from the late nineties. The outside was so covered in dents and half-hearted fixes that the registration papers must have listed the color as "Bondo."

A jovial voice bellowed from the driver's side window. "Villy Bats?"

Villy nodded.

"I'll be your chauffeur for the day! Let me give you a hand with your stuff!"

The thing that emerged from the driver's side door was a sight to behold. A glance just north of his stocky frame revealed a patchy but bushy beard peppered with all manner of crumbs, dried egg yolk, and other mysterious food-like particles. This hairy net was apparently the first sieve in an obstacle course for food on its way to the finish line that was his once-white T-shirt. The perennial winners, if the stains served as evidence, were Doritos, Mountain Dew and something resembling caked-on blood, probably sauce from a Domino's Pizza mishap. Peeking from beneath his beard was a big, friendly—if perhaps goofy—young face with glowing patches of red on his cheeks. He wore thick, black-rimmed glasses that could have easily passed for protective eyewear from the '50s, with lenses so thick that a quick glance toward the sun would instantly fry the back of his skull. They distorted his eyes in a manner that was not the least bit reassuring. His silly countenance was framed with a frightening shock of frizzy brown hair that burst out from under an oversized, green top hat. When matched with the mundane white T-shirt and jeans, the enormous hat made of cheap imitation velvet gave him the appearance of a crazed, nerdy, pedo-clown on his day off.

The young man darted out and around the vehicle and bee-lined past Villy toward the rear of the car. "Wow, Villy Bats! Awesome!" he beamed as he opened the trunk.

Villy loaded his suitcase and guitar into the mostly empty trunk. He waited for a lull in the waves of yellow cabs weaving past Grand Central and quickly swung around to the passenger side. He opened the door and was stopped by a horrifying pile of fast food wrappers and empty soda cans. Villy stood for a moment, wondering how to (or whether to) get in. He gingerly lifted a leg and tapped the cans around, as if he were dipping his toe in a pool to test the water. Eventually, a yellow cab gave Villy the impetus he needed. As the taxi zoomed past, blasting its horn, Villy leapt into the passenger side, where his feet disappeared into a clanging pool of rubbish. He sat stiffly on the edge of his seat, poised like a cat in a bathtub about to be filled with water. His cell phone beeped to alert him that it was running out of power. "You care if I plug my phone in?"

"For you?" exclaimed the driver. "Anything! You don't even have to ask!" He then glued his meaty, red hands to the wheel and merged into the flow of New York City traffic while stealing a glance at his cargo. "Wow, Villy Bats! In *my* car! I've never had any famous people in my car before." He beamed and then laughed nervously.

Villy rolled his eyes.

"Well, except for that one time I was in Saddlebrook, New Jersey, picking up my roommate at the train station, and he had that guy with him from that reality show. You know—the one where people go on, like, some kind of a race around the world or something? I don't remember his name. My friend didn't know him or anything. He just met him on the train, and I guess he needed a ride. Weird. You would think someone famous like that would have a limousine waiting to drive him everywhere. Then again, was he *really* famous? I mean, he wasn't famous like you. He was just on some reality show, so basically he was just some normal guy who happened to have a camera on him all of the time. He wasn't really a celebrity *per se*. You know what I mean?"

Villy sat for a moment, agape and staring at the babbling fool to his left. "No." Villy answered flatly and turned to look out the passenger side window.

After a moment of contemplative silence, the eager fellow with the machine-gun mouth posed a question. "So, what's it like, anyway?"

"What's what like?" Villy continued gazing out the window.

"Being famous, silly!" chuckled the driver.

"Uh, I don't know." Villy suddenly wished he had a rehearsed reply.

"You're being modest," smiled the hobo hobbit in the top hat, which was now crushed between his fright wig and the ceiling of the car. "Wow, and you really live in the Chrysler Building! I heard that somewhere before, but I thought it was just a rumor. Oh, I'm sorry! I should have met you inside or something. It must suck for you standing on the sidewalk. I mean being famous and all, on account of all the people who come up and talk to you and stuff. That must be really weird."

Villy fumbled for a reply. "You get used to it... I guess." Something had to be done to get this immature ignoramus off this moronic line of questioning, so Villy took a stab at changing topics. "So." Villy turned to the untidy imbecile behind the wheel. "You are Henry's assistant?"

The driver began to laugh, harder than was really necessary, harder than one would expect from someone who wasn't truly mentally deficient.

"Oh, God no!" He guffawed. "Jeez, I'm such an idiot!" With great force, he slapped his ham-like hand flat on the center of his face. "I'm so sorry! I didn't even introduce myself. *Duh*!" He looked down at that same fat hand for a moment and outstretched it toward Villy. "I'm Henry."

Villy was incredulous. "You're Henry?"

Henry let out a bubbling geyser of moronic giggling. "Hehe, hehe, yeah."

Villy turned his face away, buried his chin in his shoulder and muttered to himself, "Oh, God."

They drove south through the city toward Tribeca. Henry continued his incessant blathering, only stopping on occasion to hurl an uninspired insult at a fellow driver. "Hey buddy! That's a car you're driving! A car! C-A-R. You know what that is, right? Those things that go? You know, with the engines and the wheels and stuff? Sheesh!" He turned to Villy. "You'd think he got his license out of a Cracker Jack box. Am I right, pal?"

Villy shook his head dejectedly as Henry laughed at his supposed wittiness.

Upon seeing a sign up ahead that indicated they were approaching the Holland Tunnel, Villy struggled against his growing desire to jump from the car. Henry was, as far as Villy could tell, a complete weirdo, possibly a psycho of some sort, or, at best, mentally retarded. This moment was Villy's last chance to escape from Henry's vehicle and still be able to walk home. Once through the Holland Tunnel, Villy would be in a different state, and should he have any revelations that remaining in the car would result in irreparable damage to his sanity, or that Henry might try to ass-rape him in the woods of New Jersey, it would take a very expensive cab ride to get back to civilization. And Villy simply didn't have the money. He thought of the five hundred dollars he'd been promised. He thought of the Goth festival and of the possibility of reliving a bit of his past glory. His mind was a jumble, and that prevented him from leaping from the decrepit automobile.

Out of the blue, however, Henry said something that got Villy's attention and pulled him out of his maelstrom of thought. "So, you haven't made a record in, like, what? Fifteen years?"

Turning to Henry, Villy faced him for the first time without a look of befuddlement or horror. "Actually, Raised by Bats only ever made one record. That was in 1990."

"That was *The Belltower*, right?"

"Yeah, that's right." Villy, somewhat surprised, thought for a moment. "How do you know about my band? I mean, no offense or anything, but you don't look like someone who would listen to my music."

Henry chortled. "Yeah, I guess I look about as Goth as Ronald McDonald, huh?" His inane giggling rose and dipped so sharply in pitch that he sounded like a machine gun shooting a round of effeminate sheep at a Jell-O-filled water bed. Villy stared at him blankly. "Heh heh. Anyway, when I decided to put on a big Goth festival, I asked a friend of mine who's a Gothic to suggest some names. I wanted someone like The Cure, or someone like that, but he said it would never work.

He said they're too commercial. He said I should get someone more, you know, *underground.*"

"So, your friend's a fan of my music?" asked Villy.

"No, not really. But he said that, for five hundred bucks, the best I'd be able to get was someone like you. You know, like, a minor local celebrity."

Villy tried his very best not to look horrified. He cradled his head in his hands and looked out the window. He thought again of his plan to throw himself from the vehicle. But it was too late—they were entering the Holland Tunnel.

"Oh, there's no toll," noticed Henry. "It costs twelve bucks coming into Manhattan, but I guess it's free going back to New Jersey.

"That should tell you something," said Villy, crestfallen.

Henry glanced at him like a confused puppy.

"You know—that you're leaving civilization and entering the bowels of Hell. Look, there's proof." Villy pointed at a sign up ahead. It read, "New Jersey," and had an arrow pointing forward toward the tunnel.

Henry rolled his eyes. "That's silly!" He sighed heavily and smiled. "So, I don't look Gothic, eh? What about this top hat, huh? Tell me this baby isn't Gothic."

Henry pointed at the florescent green, faux-velvet top hat on his head. Only then did Villy notice the shamrock pattern and the "Erin Go

Bragh" embroidery—not that it really mattered anymore at that point.

"Seriously, though, I thought about being Gothic," mused Henry. "Gosh, that was a while ago. Seventh grade, I think. But my mom wouldn't have had it. '*No way, José!*' That's what she would have said. I went to a Hot Topic once. It was okay. They have some cool stuff in there, I guess. There's this girl at the mall I like. But you know, I'm not a Gothic, so…"

The darkness of the tunnel enveloped them. After what felt like five minutes to Henry and like eight weeks to Villy—and was ten minutes in reality—they exited the unholy mouth of the Holland Tunnel on the New Jersey side.

"… they threw me in the pool," ranted Henry. "That wasn't very nice. So I kind of figured I shouldn't go to any of their stupid Gothic parties anymore. That's when I thought that maybe I should throw my own damn party. You know what I mean? Besides, maybe then she'd like me because—you know how women are. They like guys in charge. Am I right, buddy? Am I right?"

Villy pressed his face against the passenger side window.

"You okay there?"

"No," tolled Villy, like a big, dull, rusty bell. "I'm pretty sure I'm in hell now."

"You're not in hell, silly. You're in New Jersey."

Villy was so defeated at this point that he simply couldn't find the energy to yell, "SAME FUCKIN' THING!" at the top of his lungs. He resigned himself, instead, to getting satisfaction out of just a sneer. It was a good sneer, though. It was the kind of sneer one would get from a hipster when asking for directions in Williamsburg, Brooklyn, or the kind that has accompanied pretty much anything Alan Rickman has ever said, on- or off-camera. Nevertheless, it didn't put off the inanely jolly Henry.

"So, where was I?" Henry bubbled, unsolicited. "Oh yeah, I was just about to tell you about how I got into promoting. It's kind of a long story, really. You sure you want to hear it?" He giggled to himself.

"Oh, I can hardly contain my fluids." Villy put on his headphones and turned on his iPod.

"Well, it's a funny story," said Henry. "Gosh, where do I begin? Well, for starters, I hardly even know what I'm doing. I mean, this is, after all, my first event…"

Villy's music kicked in and successfully drowned out Henry. His lips were still moving, but now all Villy could hear was "Tear You Apart" by She Wants Revenge, loudly. Very loudly. Villy closed his eyes and went to sleep. He dreamed he was playing at a huge Goth festival, admired by hordes of adoring fans. He dreamed that money was raining from the sky. His lips stretched into a peaceful smile. He dreamed that this very day, in the Pine Barrens of New Jersey, his life would be changed forever.

Chapter 3

The outside of the Maplecreek Mall was the very portrait of suburban civic planning. Well-paved parking lots led to an orderly beige sidewalk that wrapped around the entirety of the monolithic temple to consumerism. Immaculately trimmed landscaping, a tree here and there, a shrub or two every few feet—it all formed a neat ribbon of green that hugged the sidewalk on one side and the mall walls on the other. This grassy moat was only three or four feet wide at any point, making it useless as a park, and dogs were certainly not allowed on it. As such, it was clear that its only purpose was to remind the arriving shoppers of nature and beauty—presumably the same nature and beauty that had been struck down, killed, and removed to make way for the mall itself.

The outside walls of this sprawling structure were high, made of some sort of poured stone, and painted—no doubt by written mandate—in non-colors deemed by a highly paid psychiatrist to elicit feelings of calm.

Given those considerations in construction, it came as no surprise that on that sunny, Saturday afternoon this masterpiece of planned pleasantness and saccharine civility managed to keep up its untarnished image. Something had upset the beige beast. The mouth of one of its many heads opened and spat out something unclean and foul. Out rolled four Gothic mallrats.

"And don't come back!" The security guard, a puffy, pinkish man in a beige uniform, spoke with the authoritative tone of a righteous mall cop. "You're lucky we didn't call the police. And you…" He pointed menacingly at Aleister. "I'll be calling your mother tonight. Someone's gonna pay for this damage!"

AJ, Prudence, Stuey, and Aleister stood there looking back at the guard. Aleister shook his fist at the man. "A pox upon your ancestors!"

The guard just shook his head, reentered the mall, and shut the door behind him.

"I think you mean, *descendants*," said AJ.

"Whatever. What's the difference?" The young Satanist balked, making Prudence roll her eyes. "I still can't believe that fat gimp from Spencer Gifts actually got the balls to call security!"

AJ shook his head. "Dude, your mother is gonna kill you."

"Are you kidding me? Have you ever spoken to my mother? She's insane. Seriously… insane! She thinks that Spider People live in the cistern. They come out when she's sleeping and hide the TV remote and her glasses and shit. Seriously, she's deranged. She leaves peanut butter and jelly sandwiches under the couch as an offering so they'll leave her alone."

"Gross." Prudence frowned at the implication of festering piles of rotten sandwiches.

"It used to be worse. They used to be tuna fish sandwiches. It was rank at my house, let me tell you. I had to start hiding the cans of tuna any time she bought them. Of course, she thought it was the Spider People and just got worse, but luckily, I was able to convince her that they'd prefer PB and J."

Stuey placed a hand to the side of his head. "Oh my God, that's so sad. Then you have to go and throw out the sandwiches when she's not looking?"

"Throw them out? I *eat* them! You think this crazy bitch cooks?"

AJ looked truly concerned. "She needs to get some help, dude."

"She did! She has pills she's supposed to take, but she thinks there's poison in them, and the only thing that kills the poison is whiskey. So, she chugs, like, a gallon of whiskey a day. It's the only way she'll take her pills. So basically, my mom's crazy and hammered at all times and communicates in an incoherent stream of obscenities and gibberish. I can't wait for that cop to call! He's gonna call my mom, and she's going to scream at him to shove his own buttered fist up his pooper to stop the Spider People from riding monkey boats at the toilet party."

AJ, Stuey and Prudence stared at each other in disbelief. Aleister then spun on a heel, putting his back to the mall. "Ah! I'm blind! I'm sunshine blind!" He threw his arms up, shielding his eyes from the blazing sun.

The other three friends turned and followed suit, drenched by the rays of the big, yellow, hurty thing in the sky. Stuey cut away from the pack and scampered to the edge of the sidewalk. He scanned the parking lot for Ari's car.

"Where is she?" His voice held a mild desperation. "She said three o'clock."

Behind him, Aleister clutched his throat, sinking to the ground like the Wicked Witch of the West. "'I'm melting! Melting!'"

AJ lovingly placed a foot on Aleister's rump and helped him the rest of the way to the ground, then moved to Stuey's side. "Relax," he said. "It's only 3:15. By female standards, she'd be half an hour early."

Prudence perked up. "What?"

"Come on," said AJ. "Women are never on time for anything! I've never met a woman who wasn't perpetually late. *You're* never less than half an hour late."

"That's not true!" protested Prudence. She flipped her long, black locks over a shoulder.

"What time did I tell you to meet me today?" AJ smirked.

"Twelve."

"And what time did you show up?"

"I don't know. 12:10?"

"Try 12:45. I'm telling you, it's just female nature. It's biology. Women are in constant pursuit of a mate. So, they feel they have to make themselves attractive all of the time. That's why you all sit in front of a mirror for hours and change your clothes fifty-three times before you can leave the house."

"That's bullshit!" spat Prudence.

"I bet you tried on a minimum of five outfits before you settled on this lovely ensemble." AJ gestured to her outfit like a Price is Right hostess would to a set of flatware the audience was expected to *ooh!* and *ahh!* over.

Prudence crossed her arms and turned away.

"And that's just to hang out at some busted mall on some broke-ass Saturday afternoon. Well, that is until we got kicked out on account of this idiot over here." He gestured at Aleister who was still lying on the ground.

"Don't mention it." The supine imp smiled, punctuating it with a wink and a pistol-shaped hand gesture.

"And the *best* part," continued AJ, laughing, "is that you always end up wearing the first outfit you put on anyway!"

"That's fuckin' bullshit!" Prudence violently smoothed the wrinkles in her skirt.

AJ turned to Stuey. "If we spent as long as they did in front of the mirror every day, *we'd* be the pretty ones."

Aleister popped up, adding with a sincere tone, "It takes me about an hour to do my makeup."

AJ shook his head incredulously. "I'm not even going to get into all of that."

Just then, a car horn blew.

"It's Ari!" Stuey smiled and waved.

A large, white minivan swung through the parking lot and came to a stop in front of them. A bumper sticker reading "Proud Parent of a Mountain High School Honors Student" marked the vehicle as belonging to her mother. Needless to say, a friend with wheels, borrowed or otherwise, was good to have.

Ari hopped out of the minivan and ran around to the passenger-side door. She was small and meek, and a glance under her long bangs and slightly bowed head would have revealed that she was quite pretty. She was Eurasian. Her mother was Japanese, and her father, God rest his soul, was of European descent.

She fumbled with the handle on the passenger side door. It was apparently jammed. She gave a few good pulls, took a deep breath, then rammed her somewhat inconsequential weight into it once or twice. After a tug or two, it swung open, almost throwing her to the ground. She stumbled for a moment, got her balance, then righted herself. She stood awkwardly before the group of friends, bashfully brushing a long strand of hair away from her face and sheepishly smiling. There was silence. Then Stuey, as if coming out of a trance, burst forward, lunged at her with a giant bear hug, and proclaimed, "Hi Ari! Thanks so much for giving us a ride. We really appreciate it!"

She nodded as the others chimed in with cautious hellos.

"Hi," said Prudence.

Ari meekly smiled.

"Hey, Ari." AJ spoke gently.

Ari lowered her head and began to turn.

"Ari," called out AJ. He hesitated for a moment. "I'm sorry about your dad. I didn't know." Ari nodded her bowed head and scampered toward the driver's side door.

Aleister craned his neck to get a glimpse at her ass. There wasn't much to see, but he pursed his lips anyway and nodded his head in approval.

"Nice." Prudence punched the pervert in the arm. "Ow! What's your problem?"

"And don't say anything stupid about her not speaking." The pale-faced girl with the spider webbed temples leveled a deadly glare.

"I wasn't going to say anything stupid!" Aleister spat back indignantly.

"Come on, move!" Prudence pressed, motivating Aleister to jump into the single back bench seat of the minivan. Prudence and AJ followed. Stuey climbed into the front passenger's seat.

"Shotgun!" He yelled gleefully, despite having no competition.

The passenger's side door closed with a slam, the side door of the minivan closed with a swish, and they were off. As no one was keeping track, there was no way of telling just how long they had been driving before Aleister broke the awkward silence. "So," he said to Ari, "why don't you speak?"

Prudence elbowed him in the ribs.

Stuey jumped right in to change the subject. "Ari, have you been to the Pine Barrens before?"

She shook her head no.

Prudence looked mildly concerned. "Are you sure you know how to get there?"

Without even turning around, Ari produced a piece of paper and held it in the air.

Stuey took it from her hand and read it. "Google Maps!"

"So," continued Prudence, "where is this thing exactly?"

"It says here," said Stuey, "that it's in some place called *Gatter der Hölle*."

Prudence was instantly alarmed. "Gator Hole? Oh, hells no! There's gonna be alligators?"

Stuey gently laughed. "I think it's pronounced '*Gahter dare Holeh*.' It's got, like, an umlaut on the O. I think it's Dutch or something. It's some kind of campground in the woods near Leed's Point."

Aleister sprang to life. "Leed's Point? Oh shit! We're going to see the Jersey Devil!"

"What?" AJ rolled his eyes.

"Leed's Point," continued Aleister. "That's where the Jersey Devil is from."

"What's that?" asked Prudence.

Aleister shot her a look of shock and disbelief. "You have got to be shitting me, right?"

AJ turned to Prudence. "It's like some kind of giant devil-bat. The local people made it up." AJ adopted a ridiculous Southern drawl. "To scare off the city folk!"

Aleister grew angry. "That's bullshit! First of all, it's real! Secondly, it's not a bat. It's a demon. The legend states that long ago, in a town called Leed's Point, there was a woman named Mrs. Leeds—"

"Well, that's redundant," said Prudence.

"Wait!" Stuey shushed her, intrigued. "Let him talk."

"She had twelve children." Aleister took on the tone and posture of someone telling a fireside ghost story. "She could barely manage them all."

From the faraway look on his face, it was clear to all that Aleister could see the events unfolding in his imagination, as if he himself were there witnessing the ghastly events of that night.

In a rundown cabin, on a dark night, in the middle of the Pine Barrens, a very pregnant Mrs. Leeds was tending to her twelve children. They were dirty and hungry, and at least two of them were crying.

"And she's pregnant again, with her thirteenth child." Aleister gave a wide-eyed look to his audience, describing the scene as he saw it in his mind.

Mrs. Leeds offers the last bit of bread to one of her hungry children when another steps up gesturing for more. "There's no more," states Mrs. Leeds.

"But I'm hungry," cries her child.

"*That's all there is,*" she barks back. "*There isn't any more!*" The child begins to cry, joining the already mind-splitting cacophony. Mrs. Leeds' desperation turns to rage. "*Stop it! Stop it! There isn't any more, I said! There's just not enough!*" She feels an intense pain in her womb. Her unborn child is also complaining. "*And another on the way!*" She cries, "*Damn you!*" She makes a fist and hits her belly. "*Damn you!*" she screams at her unborn child.

"She couldn't take it anymore," conveyed Aleister to his audience, "so, she cursed him." He closed his eyes and envisioned Mrs. Leeds mouthing the words as he uttered them. "And then she says, 'I hope this child comes out a demon!'"

"That's stupid!"

Aleister pictured one of Mrs. Leeds' children speaking to him, but upon opening his eyes, he realized it was just Prudence.

"Who would say that?" she continued. "You're basically cursing yourself. I mean, if you give birth to a demon, it's going to hurt like hell coming out. Am I right?"

"Yeah." AJ nodded in agreement. "It would tear up your va-jay-jay pretty good."

"I didn't make this stuff up!" exclaimed Aleister. "That's the way the legend goes."

"Well, it's stupid." Prudence shrugged and turned up her nose.

"Yeah, well, you should know what stupid looks like, considering how often you look in a mirror," countered Aleister.

She contorted her face and stuck her tongue out at him.

Ignoring her, Alesiter continued his tale. "Anyway, one night she went into labor…" He closed his eyes and let the vision take form again in his mind.

It's night in the Pine Barrens. Inside of the cabin it's dark, save for the flickering yellow light of the fireplace. Mrs. Leeds lies on the kitchen table, legs spread. Several dirty-faced and frightened children huddle in a corner, cringing as their mother howls in pain. She is in her cabin, by the fire, giving birth.

"When the baby comes out, she can tell right away something is wrong." Aleister's voice dropped to a hissing, yet hypnotic, whisper, as the others more actively listened, despite themselves. "The child emerges. It's slimy and covered in afterbirth. It looks all deformed and shit. She thinks it's like a hunchback or something. But then she notices the tail!"

Mrs. Leeds' eyes widen as she notices the unholy appendage. And then the thing stands up in front of her. It has a long hideous face, bat wings, and cloven hooves.

"Because she cursed it, it came out all fucked up. It was an actual demon!" He gazed intently at each of his audience members, narrowing his eyes for effect.

The hideous creature stands between her legs and lets loose a pained, primordial birth cry. It looks right at her with its big, black eyes and then spits in her face! She flinches, her eye full of sebaceous demon goo, but she's too shocked to move. The beast loses its balance and clumsily falls off the table, tearing the umbilical cord. Mrs. Leeds cries out. Her children huddle closer together. Some cover their eyes. Blood squirts from the umbilical cord. Mrs. Leeds wants to cry out, but her fear far

outweighs her pain. She remains glued to the table, nervously scanning the room.

And then she sees it. Standing on the floor by the fireplace, only a few feet away. It starts flapping its wings. They are veiny, translucent, and sticky, as if covered in molasses. With every flap, though, they become stronger. It stands, shifting its weight in the flickering firelight, lashing its little tail, flapping its wings. It turns to the children. They gasp in terror, and it releases an angry, little cry—an anguished bleating, like that of a goat getting its throat slit. It turns to Mrs. Leeds and narrows its eyes. She holds her breath.

"And then, it just tears up the chimney, screaming into the night." Aleister shot his head upward as if watching the demon soar into the sky.

The Leeds children all start crying. The monster gone, Mrs. Leeds collapses onto the table and bursts into desperate, breathy sobs. From outside, they hear a noise, like trees rustling. They freeze once more in silence, some placing hands over their mouths. From the forest, the creature lets out a horrible shriek that fades into the distance. Mrs.

Leeds peeks out the window. All that can be seen are the dark and foreboding Pine Barrens.

"People say," continued Aleister, "that if you are in the Pine Barrens at night and you listen closely…"

Stuey, AJ, and Prudence leaned in, eyes wider than they'd want to admit, and their breathing more shallow.

"… you can still hear…" Aleister paused for dramatic effect. There was a long silence.

Suddenly, AJ let out an ear-splitting, bloodcurdling scream. "*Aaaaahhhhhhhhhhhh*!!!! The Jersey Devil! It's real!"

Aleister nearly jumped out of his skin. "Jesus-H-fuckin'-Christ! What the hell is wrong with you?"

Everyone but Aleister laughed. Even Ari silently chortled into her hand.

"Aw, I was just messing with ya," AJ said, still laughing. "Come on, you don't actually believe any of that Jersey Devil crap, do ya?"

"It's real, you dumbass!" Aleister was livid. He folded his arms, took a deep breath, and jerked violently toward the window. Looking out at the passing landscape, he growled through his teeth. "You'll see. You'll all see."

Chapter 6

The Pine Barrens of New Jersey has a nature and character all its own. This forest of pines, pygmy pines, oaks, orchids, and carnivorous plants stretches for roughly forty miles along the coastal plains of New Jersey and inland for about twenty. There are state roads that traverse the length and width of it, and an unfathomable web of dirt roads and unmarked trails weaves through it. Though very sparsely populated, people do live there. Once, they were derogatorily called "Pineys." In recent history, however, locals have embraced the term proudly, perhaps because it distinguishes them as people who continue to live and thrive where so many others have tried and failed.

The great majority of the over one million acres that make up the Pine Barrens is rife with dense forest and bogs. It doesn't take long after turning off a main road for one to be nestled deep in the thick of these woods. It is said that, unless the moon is shining, no forest gets any darker, and that the sounds that issue forth from this darkness are enough to drive a man mad. Perhaps, then it's no surprise that these woods should be the birthplace of such a thing as the Jersey Devil, or some of the other creatures and ghosts whose stories were born amid these trees.

For a couple of centuries, different industries have tried to get a foothold in the Pine Barrens, with limited success. Iron is plentiful there, and has been for centuries. Iron mills thrived for some time back when the United States was still a collection of English colonies. The tawny red metal that sprang forth from those mines furnished the colonists with weapons and cannonballs used to fight the British. Later, these same iron mills supplied soldiers in the War of 1812 and in the great Second Barbary War. In fact, it's said that the iron bogs there yield so much of the red stuff that there are rivers in the Pine Barrens that run like blood.

Nevertheless, as has happened there again and again, industries are pushed out as if by the forest itself. The iron mills eventually moved to Pennsylvania where, presumably, the land was more willing to give it up. The towns that were built around the mills were left abandoned, and were eventually reclaimed and swallowed up by the Pine Barrens. Spending enough time in the Pine Barrens, one would stumble upon countless ghost towns buried in thick brush.

Perhaps it's the ground itself that wants interlopers out. Strangely enough, unlike in other forests where the ground is primarily dirt or clay or covered in underbrush, the ground in the Pine Barrens is sand. This aspect is perhaps the most distinguishing feature of this mysterious woodland. It's not just any sand, but an acidic and largely nutrient-deprived powder the locals call "sugar sand." Despite its sweet name, it was found to be unfriendly and infertile by the early Dutch and English settlers, hence traditional agriculture never had a chance to develop in this place. In all fairness, it must be stated that the sugar sand does not always reject outsiders. Sometimes, it has quite the opposite effect. Some say that, when it rains, the puddles on the sandy roads can get so deep as to swallow a car whole.

Whether it wants you to leave or wants to consume you, one thing is for sure—once you find yourself at a crossroads where the security of a paved road leads to a sandy one extending into the darkened wood, it's best to tread carefully, because then you are truly in the thick of it. Once you happen onto a sugar sand road, you are plunging into the very heart of the Pine Barrens.

Of many such crossroads deep in the Pine Barrens, there is one of special interest. A turn-off from Route 30 narrows after five or so miles, and eventually leads to a crossroads with a dilapidated wooden sign. The old sign was hand-painted over a hundred years ago; in now-faded red paint, it reads, "*Gatter der Hölle*." On the upper left part of the sign is an arrow that beckons the intrepid traveler. It gives them two choices—ignore it and stay to the left, sticking to the comforts of the asphalt road, or follow it and make a slight right onto a sandy path that leads up into what appears to be a dark and hungry mouth of the forest.

"We're here, buddy! This is it!" Henry patted Villy on the shoulder.

Villy wearily opened his eyes and groggily surveyed the scene around him. He was gently jerked as Henry's car turned off of the main road and onto the sandy path leading to the campground. Towering pines on each side of the narrow road leaned in toward them like an honor guard of Tolkenian Ents, forming an archway of crossed wooden swords. They proceeded, bobbing and rocking on the sugar sand road through the veritable tunnel of trees. Villy marveled at how dark it had become while driving through the womb of pines.

The light returned as the car was borne into a large clearing. Before them stood a log cabin. Off to the side of the cabin was a picnic table nestled on the edge of a large field of grass. It was the kind of grassy expanse where one could imagine hosting a soccer match or an elementary school's field day, or perhaps a huge Goth festival in the Pine Barrens of New Jersey. Surrounding this placid and picturesque field were woods, woods, and more woods.

They got out of the car. Henry began removing Villy's guitar and suitcase from the trunk. Villy came around, took the guitar from Henry, and slung it over his shoulder. He glanced into the trunk, which was practically empty save for a small canvas bag; unlike the interior of the car, it was immaculately clean.

"Damn, your trunk is spotless," he said. "I should have ridden in there." Henry smiled awkwardly. "You should maybe toss those soda cans in here to, uh, you know, clear out some room in the car."

"Hm, not a bad idea." Henry cocked his head to one side.

Villy left Henry to drag the suitcase. He headed toward the cabin, not entirely sure of where he was supposed to go. He mumbled to himself, "Of course, you could just throw them in a fuckin' garbage can or recycle them or something."

Henry scampered toward the edge of the field. He spun around and threw his hands into the air as a look of euphoria washed over his face.

"Isn't this great?" exclaimed Henry. "This is going to be amazing!"

Villy stopped, turning to see Henry standing at the edge of the field like a conductor facing an invisible orchestra.

"We're going to put you..." Henry waved his arms like a melodramatic turn-of-the-century film director while surveying the grounds. "Over there! Everyone can sit here on the grass. They'll have a great view. People can park their cars," he continued, turning back toward where he'd parked his vehicle, "there!" He turned to the right. "That's my aunt's cabin. She said I can use it, so if you want to freshen up or get changed or..."

"Wait a minute," demanded Villy. "This is it? This is where the festival is taking place?"

"Um, yeah." Henry burped, caught off guard.

"Am I missing something? I mean, the festival is today, right?"

"Of course, silly!" Henry smiled. "I wouldn't drag you all of the way out here if..."

"What time did you say this thing was taking place?" The edge on Villy's voice was getting sharper.

"Well," blubbered Henry, "I guessed we'd start around six. I mean, unless you think..."

"Henry! It's 5 o'clock *right now*! People should be showing up already, don't you think? Did you do any promotion?"

Henry nodded his meaty, pumpkin-sized head. "Yes, of course!"

Of this, Henry was confident. The promotion he had done was still fresh in his mind—as are most things one does only a few hours prior. He thought back to earlier that day when he was at the mall. He always went on Saturdays because that's when *she* was usually there. This girl, the object of his desire, was gorgeous. She was slim and pale and naturally beautiful. Her skin was milky white, her hair was as black as the feathers of a raven, and her eyes were like crystalline blue gems. She was stunning, and she knew it. She dressed in flowing gossamer gowns of black, and she was Goth. She spent much of her time at the mall with a very handsome, African American punk rocker and a strange, though not unattractive, young man who looked like a Black Metal musician turned Satanic priest. Henry had come to know that the girl's name was Prudence. She, on the other hand, didn't know Henry was alive. But Henry knew he could change all of that. If only she could see him in a different light, see him as someone important in the Goth scene, then he would have a chance with her. To that end, he'd saved all of his holiday gift money in order to put together a Gothic festival in the Pine Barrens of New Jersey. Admittedly, he hadn't been entirely sure of what that entailed, but he had known that he needed to book a band, and he'd done that part. He'd also known that he had needed to make a poster, and he'd done that, too. Perhaps most importantly, he'd known that, before running off to New York City to pick up the talent, he had needed to give that poster to the girl who had inspired him to do all this.

That was how he had found himself standing across from the Spencer Gifts store earlier that day, clutching the one poster he'd made, ready to give it to the girl of his dreams. He almost had too, except that suddenly she and her punk rocker friend had disappeared into the store. He had patiently waited and hoped that she'd emerge alone—it would have been easier to talk to her that way. Moments later, however, she had emerged with not only the punk rocker but their Satanic priest friend as well. Time had been slipping away, and Henry had needed to get going to pick up Villy Bats on time. He'd summoned all his courage and had decided he would just march right up and give her the poster, but then she had turned toward him, and their eyes had met. He could have sworn she'd looked right at him. He had frozen like a deer in headlights. But then she had looked away and had continued onward with her friends. Henry had struggled to get his courage back up and had nearly decided to approach her again when, suddenly, a fourth friend had joined them. Henry'd felt like it was getting ridiculous, and he'd known that if she didn't ridicule him, her friends surely would have.

A moment had passed, the foursome was walking toward the food court, and that was when Henry'd had an idea. He had run ahead of them, careful to go unnoticed, and had taped the poster to a column near the Piercing Pagoda—directly in their path. There, he'd known they were sure to see it! And surely enough, moments later, his plan had paid off. One of her friends had spotted it, and before long, they had all agreed to go. Henry'd done his job. At least four people were definitely going to be at the event (although, to him, only one really mattered)! And more people were certain to come, Henry had been convinced. That hadn't been the only promotion he'd done, of course. He'd also created an event on MySpace, which he'd figured had to be good for something.

"Don't worry!" he assured Villy. "People are going to come. You're overreacting. Everything is going to work out just fine, I promise."

"Overreacting?" bellowed Villy. "It's five o'clock and the stage isn't even set up!"

"Well, I didn't think we needed a sta—"

"Are you fucking kidding me?" Villy's pale face turned to increasingly darker shades of crimson. "I mean, what are you thinking? I'm supposed to just stand in the grass and everyone is going to be able to see me? I mean, for that matter, where are the lights? The mixing board? Shit, do you even have electricity out here?"

Henry grew increasingly unnerved. He looked around frantically, as if trying to imagine all of the gear Villy was describing. It hadn't occurred to him that he needed any of those things, or perhaps he had just been preoccupied with more personal concerns. Either way, he was *not* good at being yelled at—it exacerbated his *condition*. Moreover, and to make things worse, he'd forgotten to take his medication. As Villy screamed, Henry began nervously grabbing at his pants and violently scratching at his head.

Villy looked around the campsite incredulously. "Shit, man! I mean, Christ! What am I supposed to plug my guitar into? A fuckin' tree?"

He was completely unaware of the mental breakdown Henry was having just behind him. And it was getting worse.

Henry began biting his hand and intermittently hitting himself in the leg with a clenched fist. Years ago, he would have lashed himself with a violin bow, as a sadistic teacher had trained him to do upon committing the slightest error. His parents had made him quit the lessons when they discovered the scars on his calves and forearms, but by then, the damage had been done.

"This is just a nightmare!"

Henry heaved as if about to start crying. "There's a… generator… in the cabin… I think."

"You think?" hollered Villy. "Oh, that's just fuckin' great!" Villy threw his hands up into the air, and when they came down, they cradled his head. He stood there for a moment, rocking his face in the palm of his hands. He took a deep breath and centered himself. "Shit. Okay. Alright." Villy calmed himself down. "Do you have an amp, at least?" He turned to Henry and finally noticed the young man's deteriorating mental state.

"Um… yeah. I'll get one." Henry blubbered while alternately tugging at and punching his pant leg.

"You'll *get* one?" asked Villy, wondering what he meant.

"Uh, I mean, I have one. I'll get it. It's in the car." He stood there for a moment and, with his giant, ham-hock hand, he slapped himself repeatedly in the face grunting, "Stupid! Stupid! Stupid baby!"

"Alright. Alright," said Villy. "Just go get the amp. We'll figure something out."

Henry turned stiffly, his demeanor like that of a nervous three-year-old. He gripped the fabric just below his pants pockets and seemed to be guiding his legs like a puppeteer as he shuffled toward the car.

Villy watched, astounded by his odd behavior. "Jesus, what a weirdo!"

He went back to looking around the campground, dejected. It was starting to set in that he would *not* be performing to a large crowd at a *huge* Gothic festival as he had thought, as he had hoped. He was beginning to wonder if anyone would show up at all. And why wouldn't they? Did no one want to see him perform? Had he been forgotten? Certainly *someone* would have bought a ticket to come see him. He consoled himself with the thought that it was the promoter's fault. It certainly didn't seem like Henry had done any promoting—or like he knew what he was doing at all, for that matter. Hell, at that moment Henry seemed to be having a complete mental and emotional breakdown. Villy figured it was up to him to make this show work. He just needed to think. He needed electricity, he needed a microphone, and he needed an amplifier.

He looked over to the car to check on Henry's progress. Henry was by the rear of the car, the trunk half-open, just standing there. Like a creepy statue, motionless, one hand on the trunk, Henry awkwardly stared back at Villy.

A chill went through Villy Bats. It seemed in reaction to the sheer creepiness of it all, but there was something more, something that Villy's subconscious realized before the rest of him did. Suddenly, it bubbled up to the surface. He saw in his mind the inside of the trunk. He'd seen it earlier. It was immaculately clean and, most importantly, it was practically empty. There was definitely no amplifier in there.

"Henry!"

Spooked, Henry started crying and shaking in place. He slammed the trunk closed and frantically scampered to get into the driver's side door.

"Hey, wait a minute!" yelled Villy. "Wait!"

Henry hit the ignition. The car roared like a rusty tiger.

"Oh God, no! Wait! Wait! Wait! No!" Villy screamed as he ran toward the car. "No! No! My phone! At least give me my phone!"

The car spun wildly like a pork-filled dreidel on Yom Kippur and screeched toward the sandy road that led through the trees to the main road. Villy ran as fast as he could after it, but it was too late. The reddish jalopy was tearing away from the *Gatter der Hölle* campsite. In a matter of seconds, it was gone from sight. Villy was left at the crossroads, stranded in the heart of the Pine Barrens. He stood there bent over, heaving, out of breath. He strained to hear the engine of Henry's car, but there was only silence. He looked at the empty road ahead and sighed.

"Okay, now that's fucked up."

Chapter 7

It had been a while since Aleister had told his macabre story and was subsequently enraged by AJ stealing his thunder. His sulking and the awkward silence of the others made it seem like days had passed on the long, straight road. The tedium was only exacerbated by the endless miles of trees on either side of the highway. It had been a while since the passengers had seen an exit or a building or any other sign of civilization. One thing was for certain—they were far from any city or suburb and, quite possibly, a town of any sort as they could be. It surprised them all when Ari turned the vehicle sharply, heading off the road.

"What's going on? Where are we going?" Prudence looked up, her face colored with mild alarm.

Stuey glanced at the dashboard and turned to the backseat riders. "We're low on gas."

"Oh," exhaled Prudence.

The minivan pulled into a small one-pump station that looked like a throwback to the 1950s. The rusty pump was from a bygone era, and the small general store just behind it looked more like an abandoned house in the bayou than a gas station convenience store. Whatever color it originally had been was hard to tell, as it certainly hadn't been painted or cleaned in decades. The paint was peeling and cracked. The warped wood underneath showed the kind of wear seen when the elements batter and beat a plank, stretching the grain wide open as if to suck out its very soul.

"Man, this place is creepy." Stuey frowned, looking out the window.

"Yeah," continued Aleister, "this is definitely the place to go if you want to get ass-raped by some retarded, toothless, inbred Piney!"

Suddenly, a horrifying scream came from just outside of the minivan. "*Aaaaaaaahhhhhh*! Run while you can!"

The kids all turned and choked down screams of their own—there, pressed against the glass just next to AJ's head, was the weathered face of an old man. His eyes bulged in a manic expression of terror. Aleister noticed his nearly toothless mouth and cringed.

The deranged old coot croaked again, his voice sounding like broken glass on a chalk board. "You girls sure do have purdy mouths!"

Frighteningly enough, he was not looking at the girls when he said it. He had one of his eyes on Aleister and the other one on AJ. The teens stared, mouths agape; those who did talk were unable to find any words. They sat, frozen, as the wild man shifted his crazy eyes from side to side, scanning the interior of the vehicle. After a moment, he stood up and calmly began wiping his hands with a rag.

And then, in the most normal of voices, he calmly uttered, "So whaddya kids want? Gas?"

"Jesus Christ!" protested Aleister. "What the hell's wrong with you? You scared the crap out of us."

The old man, Malechai by name, if the embroidery on his coveralls was to be trusted, gently laughed. "Well, you're in the Pine Barrens now, boys, and you know there are *some* people…" He put heavy emphasis on the word *some*. "… who think all of us Pineys are… what was it now? 'Retarded, toothless ass-rapists'."

Aleister hadn't realized the man had heard him earlier, and he withered a bit in his seat.

"But you know," Malechai then said, "as that band Depeche Mode always seems to be sayin', 'people are people'. So, uh, as I see it, as long as folks are polite with each other, it don't much matter where you're from. Am I right?"

"Yes, sir." Stuey lowered his eyes meekly.

"So, uh, what are you all doing out here?" Malechai continued to wipe his hands with an oily rag. "Are ya lookin' for the Jersey Devil?"

Aleister practically jumped out of his seat. "You know about the Jersey Devil?"

"Sure!" said Malechai. "Everyone 'round here does."

"So, it's real then!" exclaimed Aleister.

"Nah, it's not real. It's just some nonsense the locals came up with to scare off you city folk."

AJ looked over at Aleister and smirked victoriously. Aleister showed him one of his fingers in response.

"It's just that when people come 'round here looking like you guys do," said Malechai, "well, there's a better than average chance you're on some kind of hunt for ghosts or the Jersey Devil or some such nonsense."

AJ raised an eyebrow. "And how *exactly* is it that we look?"

Malechai very conspicuously surveyed everyone in the vehicle, his eyes wandering over each piece of skull-adorned clothing, each spider ring, and each bat bracelet. "You know—like you worship the Devil. No offense."

Aleister smiled wryly. "None taken."

"Well, what's it going to be, then?" asked Malechai.

"Gas," said AJ.

Malechai nodded, and an exodus began. Ari jumped out of the driver's side. Stuey hopped out of his side of the minivan and stretched.

"Let me out," said Prudence to AJ. "I have to pee."

AJ slid open the door to his right and motioned for her to hop over him. She begrudgingly did, landing smack dab in front of Malechai. She looked up at him. "Do you have a ladies' room?"

"Yeah, it's around the back."

Prudence smiled and slinked past him, squeezing between him and the gas pump. The greasy old coot turned, craning his neck to get a glimpse of her ass as she strutted to the far side of the building.

"It's open," he called out. "You don't need a key!" He seemed to be saying anything he could think of to prolong their interaction.

She looked over her shoulder at him and smiled.

Malechai's brief moment of paradise was shattered by Stuey. "You got snacks?"

"Yeah," said Malechai, mildly annoyed. "They're inside." Stuey gave him a thumbs up, then bobbed up and down like a hobby horse as he chugged toward the front door of the shop. "Lard ass," hissed Malechai under his breath.

As Malechai turned back, he was slightly startled to find Ari standing right in front of him. She had come around the front of the minivan and had taken Stuey's place by the passenger's side door. "You want me to fill it up?"

Ari shook her head no, but offered nothing else.

"So, how much you want me to put in?"

Ari fumbled through her pockets, eventually producing a twenty dollar bill. She held it out in front of her. He gingerly took it from her hand and looked at it.

"Twenty bucks?"

Ari nodded yes.

"You want me to put in the whole thing or you want change or what?"

Ari stood there motionless, unable to communicate what she wanted. The look on Malechai's face was becoming increasingly pained. Growing more and more uncomfortable, Ari shifted her weight from side to side and looked about nervously. Finally, she simply turned, following Stuey into the store. Malechai was naturally confused.

"Damn kids," he said to himself while grabbing the pump. "They play so many damned video games they forget how to talk." He forcefully jammed the pump into the gas tank, looked up at the gathering storm clouds in the sky, and shook his head.

Inside the minivan, Aleister and AJ sat in silence, watching the whole exchange between Ari and the gas station attendant. After a moment, Aleister spoke.

"You ever fuck her?"

AJ responded, still looking out the window, "I told you, I only went on one date with her."

"You think she moans?" continued Aleister. "You know, when she's gettin' it?"

AJ turned to face him. "Dude, I don't know!"

Aleister was never any good at reading people's expressions, hence he was even worse at understanding when to stop.

"I mean, is she physically capable of moaning? You know, like deaf people—they can't hear and shit, but they sure as fuck can make sounds. Funny fuckin' sounds! Wouldn't that suck? I mean, 'cause she's hot and all. If you were doin' her, and she sounded all retarded?"

He pantomimed having sex with her, reaching out and placing his hands around her imaginary waist, then pumping the air in front of him. He was grinding away with his tongue out and a cartoonishly pained look on his face. Then, he imitated her by flailing his arms around and bobbing his head in circles and making noises, the kind he imagined would be made by a mentally retarded person having an orgasm.

"*Whuuuuuugh! Gaaaaaaaagh! Geh geh geh! Gleeeeh geh gehgie!*"

Suddenly, there was a telltale clicking noise from the driver's side door. Ari was getting back in the car. AJ noticed and smacked Aleister over the top of his head.

Aleister angrily froze in place. Indignantly, he spat, "I'm just saying. Does one choose not to, or is one physically incapable? It's a scientific question."

Annoyed, AJ shook his head and went back to looking out the window. "Man, just let it be."

"I'm just saying," reiterated the young Satanist.

AJ leaned over to him and whispered. "PS: everybody sounds like that. You just don't know because you've never had sex... with a human female."

"I told you, it was just a stupid rumor!"

They sat there in silence for a while, AJ took to staring out the window. "Where the hell's Prudence?"

The slamming of a screen door drew their attention to the shop. Stuey was chugging toward the minivan holding a bag of chips.

"I left a dollar on the counter!" he told the attendant.

Malechai nodded, but looked completely disinterested. Stuey popped into his seat, slammed the car door shut and victoriously displayed his bag of chips. "Funions!"

No one said anything.

"Alright, let's go! I'm ready to rock!"

Still, no one responded. Nobody moved.

"Where's Prudence?"

"She's in the shitter," answered Aleister.

Malechai walked over to the van, removed the hose from the gas tank and slapped the side of the vehicle. "You're all set!"

"Thank you!" Stuey yelled, craning his head out the window as the attendant disappeared behind the car.

Ari hit the ignition. The minivan revved triumphantly, ready to take on the world. And then they sat—and waited for Prudence.

"Man, what is taking her so long?" growled AJ.

"She's probably making a number two," said Aleister. "You ever see a girl making a number two? It's weird, dude. They refuse to sit their prissy asses on the toilet seat, so they crouch up on it like a gargoyle, then they get all hunkered down and…"

"Will you shut the fuck up?" AJ shook his head in his hands.

The ladies' room at this remote one-pump station was a dirty, dingy mess. Had Prudence glanced into either of the toilets in the two doorless stalls, she would have certainly thrown up the salad she'd eaten for lunch. Luckily, she had not gone to the bathroom to relieve herself in any physical sense. She had simply wanted to fix her makeup.

Though cracked and spotty, the mirror in the ladies room was suitable for the job. She placed a small makeup bag on the edge of the sink and removed a black lip-liner pencil. Leaning into the mirror, she pursed her lips and outlined them carefully. She examined them—the coloring was perfect. Satisfied, she dropped the pencil back into the case.

She moved on to the spider web designs at her temples. These were difficult to keep pristine. While she wished with all of her black heart that it wasn't the case, Prudence was quite capable of sweating, and the dewy drops that had developed on her temples during the long car drive had wreaked havoc on these dainty designs. She retrieved black liquid liner from her bag and delicately filled in the places where the makeup had flaked or smeared. For good luck, she added an additional character to the web on her right temple. This miniscule, two-stroke design might have been a bat, but more than anything, it resembled a tiny letter V.

"'"Step into my parlor," said the spider to the fly.'" Her lips curled into a mischievous grin.

Prudence stood up straight. She inspected herself in the mirror again, this time admiring her entire physique. She turned to the left to examine her profile. Her eyes swept down from her neck to the small of her back toward her bottom. She never did feel her bottom was as ample as she would have liked, and so she arched her back, jutting her buns out a few extra inches. With a languid sweep, she ironed a fold from her skirt with the palm of her hand. She glanced up at her hair. With a middle finger, she parted her black locks, tucking a strand behind her dainty, pale ear. She smiled. She turned to the right and repeated the ritual almost exactly, first admiring her ass, then sweeping some static from the folds of her skirt, and then fixing her hair.

She turned once more to face the mirror straight on. She smiled. She stopped smiling. She smiled again wider. Then, she pantomimed a laugh without making a sound. Though completely silent, it was a vivacious and hearty laugh that ended with her throwing her head back and letting it roll, coming to a stop with her right cheek pressed coyly to her shoulder. She looked at the mirror intently and she held out her hand.

"How do you do?" she said quietly. And then she did it again. "Hi, nice to meet you." She held out a hand for an imaginary suitor to kiss, this time trying to look casually beautiful. After a moment, she shyly giggled, as if reacting to a compliment she'd just received. She leaned in toward the mirror, and inches from the glass, she stared into her own eyes for a moment. She blew herself a kiss and whispered "You are the most beautiful girl in the world."

Her eyes shot open, as if startled by her own words. Her lips moved with a mind of their own, repeating the phrase. "The most beautiful girl in the world." The phrase surprised her like being called a secret name known only by one other person. Her mother... her mother used to tell her that. "The most beautiful girl in the world." Coming from her, these words meant... everything. Staring into the mirror, Prudence let herself get caught up in the memories.

Prudence's mother, Kate, was a beauty queen in the true sense. She had always been particularly fetching. Her parents entered her in a pageant at a county fair when she was just ten years old. She went home with a giant ribbon that made everyone burst with pride. It was the first of many wins on the pageant circuit. It became a hobby, and the hobby became a career of sorts. As graceful as she was physically beautiful, Kate had little trouble finding her way to a blue ribbon or a sash or a diamond tiara. She did just that, many times over. She was admired and courted by many young men, but having a weakness for bad boys, her heart melted at the first site of Frank. He was a swaggering Rockabilly Romeo covered in devil tattoos, who smelled of Old Spice, yesterday's beer, and cigarettes. He played double bass in a band called The Hellcats Are Go—when he wasn't fixing cars at the auto body shop. She knew he wasn't the marrying type, but it wasn't long before they walked down the aisle and even less time before she was pregnant with Prudence. They seemed blissfully happy...for about six years. But of course, motherhood meant responsibilities. There was little time for pageants, little time for exercise, facials, pedicures... little impetus for

dieting. Over time, while still gorgeous, Kate looked less like a beauty queen and more like... a loving, doting mother. Prudence was her pride and joy, and she took great pleasure in dressing her up, putting ribbons in her raven-black hair. "You are the most beautiful girl in the whole world," she told her precious, little one. "The most beautiful girl in the whole, wide world!"

Prudence loved hearing it, but she knew she was but a mere spark compared to the raging inferno of beauty that was her loving mother. To Prudence, there was no woman on God's good Earth as beautiful as Mommy. It made it all the harder for her to understand when her father stopped coming home. At first, her mother told her Daddy had gigs out of town, that he was on tour with his band, but she remembered the fights like they were yesterday. On the nights when he did come home, she could hear the muffled sounds of their yelling. Through the daisy-covered wallpaper of her room, she was tormented by her mother's agonizing words. "Is she prettier than me? Is that what it is, Frank? Is she younger? Thinner?"

"You're the prettiest, Mommy." Prudence cried into her pillow, smothering it with her little face, wetting it with her tears. "You're the prettiest mommy in the whole world!" Those nights were Hell. Prudence often sobbed herself to sleep.

Mornings were always surrealistically sunny. Kate was always well put together and chipper, waking Prudence with a big smile and a delicious breakfast. The smells of blueberry pancakes or waffles filled the house. She never mentioned the fights, never brought up the reason Daddy wasn't coming home any more, but Prudence knew. She knew everything. Daddy wasn't coming home because he had found someone prettier.

The month that followed was devoid of late-night fights. Prudence's mom would often invite her daughter to sleep with her, to keep her company. "We're having girl's night tonight," she'd say with a huge, bright smile. They'd watch David Letterman together in bed and eat some ice cream. And they'd snuggle to sleep. These blissful times, some of Prudence's happiest moments in her six years of childhood, were often shattered when she'd awaken in the middle of the night to the sounds of her mother's sobbing. Prudence would lie in bed, frozen, afraid her mother would know she was awake, a witness to her suffering. One night she dared speak. She reached out her pale, little hand and placed it on her mother's trembling shoulder.

"Are you okay, Mommy?"

There was sudden silence. A moment later, in a startled tone, her mother stuttered. "I-I was... having a bad dream, dear. I'm sorry I woke you, darling."

"It's okay, Mommy. It's okay." Prudence patted her mother's shoulder. She tried to be strong for Mommy, but she simply couldn't hold back the flood.

Her eyes welled with tears, her throat tightened and finally, she burst into relentless sobbing. "I'm sorry, Mommy." Her mother joined her. That night, they held each other tightly and cried until they both fell asleep.

Over the weeks that followed, little Prudence fell into a routine. She didn't forget her father, but she stopped expecting him to walk through the door or to call. Her mother bought her a turtle she named Stanley, with whom she played in the kiddie pool in the back yard. Despite the occasional crying at night, it was an August like any other. And then came the fateful day.

It was her seventh birthday, and when she returned from Sunday school, her mother greeted her, swinging open the front door of the house. She was gorgeous! She wore a silver-green sequined dress that hugged her hourglass figure. Her luxurious hair cascaded onto her shoulders in loose curls like a butterscotch waterfall. Prudence looked up at her and thought she looked like a beautiful mermaid. Mommy was a vision to behold. She looked just like she did in those photos on the mantle, just like a beauty queen. The only things missing were the sash and the tiara. "I have a surprise for you, honey!" Her mother was radiating love and excitement. "We're meeting Daddy for lunch... for your birthday!"

Prudence barely had time to register what she'd been told before her mother snatched her by her

*hand and raced her to her bedroom. "Come on,
we are going to get dressed up!" She rummaged
through Prudence's closet, uncharacteristically
tossing clothes all over the room. "Oops, I'm kind of
making a mess!" A giddy glow shined from her eyes.
Finally, she settled on the little blue dress Prudence
had worn on Easter, white tights, and shiny black
Mary Janes. Next, Mommy did her hair, combing it
out into pigtails and finishing it off with her prettiest
blue ribbons. She even let Prudence wear a little
makeup! The birthday girl was exhilarated at the
thought of wearing a little lip gloss; it felt taboo and
adult and like all rules had been suspended for the
whole day. "We have to look good for Daddy. We're
going to show Daddy how pretty we are." Mommy
smiled while gingerly applying just a touch of rouge
to the girl's cheeks.*

*"Can he come home to meet Stanley?" Prudence
looked up at her mother with her big, blue eyes.*

*"Of course, sweetie! We'll ask him." She turned
Prudence to look at herself in the mirror. "Look at
you. Just look at you! How can he say 'no' to the
most beautiful girl in the whole world?"*

*They met Frank at the Denny's on Route Ten
near Cedar Grove. Looking back, Prudence could
no longer remember seeing his face. What she
remembered was the watch on his hairy wrist. He
looked at it a lot through lunch. When not checking
the time, he gazed out the window as if there was
somewhere else he needed to be. She remembered*

her mother. She was so beautiful. She vibrated in her seat, lobbing conversation starters into the air that Frank let drop to the ground like unreturned serves. That's what Prudence remembered most: her mother's desperate attempts to climb a cold, harsh mountain that stoically sat there, refusing to be climbed.

And then, "Honey... Prudence has something she wants to ask you." Prudence told Daddy all about Stanley and the kiddie pool and asked if he could come home to meet him. She could no longer recall her father's words, only that they were some sort of noncommittal mumbling that meant the same as no. Seconds later, he was gone.

She never saw her Daddy again.

She didn't realize it right away, but in time, she came to understand that her mother had driven her father away. She could have tried harder; she could have been prettier for him. In essence, she let another woman take him away, and more importantly, take him away from Prudence. She never forgave her mother. In the years that followed, her mother did what she could to find a husband, find someone who could support her and Prudence. Eventually, she did. What little love Prudence had for her mother vanished the day she brought home Phillip ("with two l's, two i's and two p's") Winthrop. He was an old, wrinkly toad, twenty years Kate's senior. But he was rich. My mother's a trophy wife, *thought Prudence.*

"He's a good provider, and he loves us, Prudence. He loves us, both. He really cares about you and wants the very best for you." Her mother did everything she could to soften her daughter's heart, but it was all for naught.

"When I think of you in bed with that disgusting, old monster, I just want to puke!"

Her mother expressed to Prudence she was just being an emotional teenager, and that in time she'd see the light, but maybe... it was something else.

Prudence glared into the mirror. "That will *never* happen to me. I can have whoever I want, and they would *never* leave me." She leaned in and cocked her head from side to side. She admired the spider web designs on her left temple. "And do you know why that is?" She took a step back and admired her feminine frame. She glanced seductively at the mirror over her right shoulder. "Because I'm the most beautiful girl in the whole world."

In the minivan, AJ tapped the back of the chair in front of him. "Stuey, honk the horn."

Stuey reached over and gave it a generous push.

Prudence was mid-pose when the abrasive horn bellowed. Startled, she jumped as we all do when caught doing something horrifyingly embarrassing, like defecating, or masturbating, or perhaps practicing being charming while having fake conversations with imaginary people. She frantically zipped the makeup bag shut and whipped toward the door. Swinging the door open, she was shocked again. Before her, Malechai blocked her exit, straddling the doorway. She jumped back. He stood there menacingly, still wiping his dirty hands with that greasy rag.

"Everything okay in there?" he asked. "Can I give you a hand with anything?"

"*Ew*, sick!" spat Prudence. She gathered herself and pushed by him.

"Your friends were going to leave without you," he called out to her as she stormed off. "I told them to wait!"

"Yeah, right!" Prudence marched angrily away from him, heading toward the minivan. "Asshole!" she yelled, without turning around. She reached the minivan and climbed in, crawling over AJ to her middle seat. Once she was settled in, AJ slid the door shut.

Prudence was noticeably irritated and perhaps a bit shaken. "Come on, let's go!"

"What's up with you?" asked AJ.

"That creepy, perverted fuck practically raped me!"

"What'd he do?" asked AJ valiantly.

"Just the way he looked at me," said Prudence. "He was fuckin' gross."

AJ laughed to himself knowingly and settled back into his seat. "See, this is what I'm talking about. You think all guys want you."

"Really? Really?" She was practically yelling. "He was watching me in the bathroom, and when I came out, he asked me if I needed *help* in the toilet! What kind of help would I need in the toilet?"

Stuey craned his head back. "Okay, that's pretty rapey."

"Do you?" Aleister perked up in his seat. "Need help, I mean, you know, wiping and stuff, because if you do, I would totally…"

"Shut up, you pervert!" Prudence cradled her head in her hands.

AJ proceeded *very* cautiously. "Do you think you might have led him on?"

"What?" Prudence was completely incredulous.

"Well, I mean, did you smile at him or wink or something?"

"I might have smiled at him earlier. So?"

"Well, I'm just saying, you know, sometimes the way you treat guys, it gives the wrong impression."

That did it. Prudence exploded. "Oh, so if I'm nice to a guy, that means I want to have sex with him? I deserve to be raped because I smiled at someone?" Tears were now streaming down her powdered face like ski trails on a virgin mountain. "So, what am I supposed to do? Am I supposed to be a bitch? Is that what I'm supposed to do, huh, be a bitch? Jesus, I swear, I just can't win!"

"Come on, relax." AJ put an arm around her. "That's not what I'm saying."

Aleister leaned back and locked eyes with AJ. He placed an outstretched index finger to his temple and rotated it in a circular pattern while mouthing, "cuckoo". AJ shooed him off with a grimace. He pulled Prudence closer. "It's just… you have to be careful *how* you smile at some guys. Look, I'm just lookin' out for you. Seriously. You know I care about you. I'm just lookin' out for you."

Prudence leaned into AJ's warm chest, calming down. She dug through her bag and liberated her compact. She was not pleased when she saw the water damage to her immaculately made face. "I hate you guys sometimes, you know that?"

AJ giggled. "Yeah, I hate us too."

Between sniffles, Prudence nestled against AJ and fixed her face. "This festival better be good!"

Stuey craned his neck back to meet her eye. His mouth was overflowing with Funions. "It's going to be amazing!"

They laughed as the minivan pulled out of the station and hit the road.

Malechai stood by himself watching the minivan tear off. He looked mildly bewildered. "Well, God damn!" he said, honestly perplexed. "I thought Goth chicks were supposed to be easy." He shrugged his shoulders and went back to watching paint peel at that lonely gas station.

The minivan trekked down the road for a while in near silence. The only sound was the hum of the wheels on the black asphalt. Stuey thought it might be a good time to break the monotony, so he slipped a CD into the car stereo and turned it up.

"What is this playing?" asked Prudence after a while.

Stuey was visibly excited. "It's Raised by Bats! This is Villy Bats singing! He has such an amazing voice. This is my favorite song of his. It's called 'Never'."

"Yeah, well, that's perfect because I *never* heard of it!" Aleister laughed at his own supposed wit.

Stuey was not one to be easily deflated. He'd learned over the years that the best way to stop a bully was to engage one, to remain unflappable, to get his attention and appeal to his desire to talk about himself. "What's *your* favorite song?" He asked to Aleister.

"What, by *this* band?"

"No, I mean in general."

Aleister threw up the devil horns sign and banged his head while singing at the top of his lungs. "'*Generals gathered in their masses! Just like witches in black masses!*'"

AJ laughed in approval. "Ah, 'War Pigs' by Black Sabbath! Good one," he chuckled.

Prudence was less impressed. "Black Sabbath? That's not even Goth!"

"It's *totally* Goth!" demanded Aleister.

"Yeah, I've got to go with Aleister on this one," said AJ. "That shit was Goth before Goth was Goth."

Stuey turned to AJ. "What about you? What's *your* favorite song?"

"I don't know," said AJ, "I couldn't pick a favorite. I like a wide range of stuff—Danny Elfman, Rasputina, The Pogues. I don't know. I guess anything that's dark, but doesn't take itself too seriously."

Prudence was eager to share her opinion. "I like VNV Nation!"

"They're not even Goth!" exclaimed AJ. "They're techno!"

That ruffled Prudence's feathers. "No they're not! They're E.B.M.!"

Stuey was legitimately intrigued. "What does *that* stand for?"

Aleister couldn't resist. He started doing the robot and, in a robotic German accent, stuttered, "Excruciating... Bowel... Movement!"

Prudence was quick to correct him. "It's 'Electronic Body Music'!"

"Come on!" huffed AJ. "Only some German techno DJ could have come up with a term as gay as…" He switched to a German accent. "'Electronic *Body Music!*'" He liked the way that sounded, so he decided to create a little E.B.M. song of his own. He arched his back and began rubbing his nipples while gyrating like a gay Scandinavian go-go dancer and repeating, "*Electronic Body Music! Electronic Body Music!*" Prudence scowled. Then, just as suddenly as he had begun, AJ straightened up and continued in his normal voice, "Seriously, that shit is gay, and I don't mean that in the *good* way."

"Preach it, brother!" howled Aleister, laughing.

"Seriously," continued AJ, "think about it. Drum machine." He mimicked the sound of a drum machine. "*Oonce! Oonce! Oonce! Oonce!* Electronic beeps and whirs." He mimicked those, too. "*Bleep! Boop! Bleep! Boop!* Glowsticks? It's fuckin' techno! You can call it whatever you like. It's fuckin' techno."

Prudence was not pleased. "Whatever! I didn't make fun of *your* favorite music!"

"No one's making fun of you," soothed AJ. "You're entitled to your opinion."

Aleister was quick to cut in. "Yeah, however wrong it may be!"

Prudence elbowed Aleister in the ribs.

"I didn't say it was bad," continued AJ. "I'm just saying it's not Goth. That's all."

Prudence did not like being criticized. Whenever criticized, her instinct was simply to hit back. "Danny Elfman isn't Goth!"

"Alright, whatever," said AJ.

"Well, he's not!" snapped Prudence.

Aleister jumped in. "Right! He's just the voice of Jack Skellington, that's all!" He contorted his face.

"Just forget it," said AJ.

Again, the conversation came to a halt. From the CD player, Villy Bats was crooning, "Never! Never!"

Aleister broke the silence, clapping his hands together loudly. "Well, what do you guys think is Ari's favorite song?"

Everyone in the van stiffened.

He continued menacingly, "Let's see. Shit. What was the name of that song? Who was it by, now? Depeche Mode, maybe?" He stroked his chin as if pretending to remember. "Hmm."

The air in the minivan grew thick. Ari glanced nervously at him through the rear-view mirror. AJ looked over at Aleister, narrowed his eyes, and shook his head from side to side as if to advise him not to continue on this track. Aleister ignored them all.

"What was it called?" He tapped his face with one finger while glancing into his brain. "Oh yeah! I remember!" There was a long, pregnant pause. Then, he threw his hands up and exclaimed, "Enjoy the Silence!" He cackled manically.

"Come on," reprimanded AJ, "stop being an asshole."

"What?" Aleister offered his version of an innocent blink. "She's perfectly fair game. So she doesn't want to talk. So, what does that mean? I have to pretend that's not weird or something?"

"Maybe she *can't* talk," whispered Prudence.

"Well, that's just it, isn't it," said Aleister. "Nobody knows. I'm just trying to get to the bottom of it, is all. Does one choose not to speak, or is one physically incapable? It's a perfectly good question. I say she can and just doesn't feel like it!"

Ari's eyes could be seen by everyone in the back seat via the rear-view mirror. She was getting more and more upset.

"You're being a total dick!" Prudence glared at Aleister.

"Yeah man, why do you have to be that way?" asked Stuey. He glanced at Ari, who looked like she might cry. He turned back to Aleister. "It's not funny. Cut it out!"

"Come on." Aleister took on the tone of a flamboyantly arrogant trial lawyer. "It's a fair question. Can she make sounds, or does she just choose not to? I don't see why it's wrong to ask this."

Through the mirror, Ari glared at him with watery eyes. She reached over and turned up the volume on the CD player.

"Does she sing in the shower when no one's around?" He sang in a mocking tone. "Can she cry? Does she laugh?"

Stuey turned to Ari; she was on the verge of tears. He whipped around to face Aleister, shooting him an angry look. "I said stop!"

"I say she can laugh." Aleister turned his attention directly toward Ari for the first time. "Come on!" He spoke in that silly voice people reserve for children and small animals. "I know you can laugh. Come on! Laugh for daddy. Come on!"

"Dude!" scolded AJ. "What the fuck?"

"Yeah, stop it!" Prudence slapped Aleister repeatedly on his shoulders, but he persisted.

"Come on!" He directed in baby talk. "Let me hear you laugh! I know you can!"

Ari reached for the volume control again, and turned it up, desperately trying to drown him out. The music was getting louder and louder, everyone was yelling, and Prudence kept slapping Aleister again and again. Still, he wouldn't relent.

"Come on!" Aleister lunged over the middle seats, digging his fingers into her sides and tickling Ari's ribs.

Ari let out a shriek. Everyone in the minivan screamed as the car swerved. There was a jolt and the sound of crunching steel and shattering glass as they crashed into a tree.

Chapter 8

The teens were all in shock. Nobody spoke or moved for what seemed like minutes. Suddenly, Ari sprang from the minivan and swung around to the front to survey the damage. It was bad—really bad. The front of the vehicle was completely wrapped around a tree, as if holding onto it for dear life. The grill was in pieces on the ground. The clear plastic domes covering the headlights were smashed to bits; all that remained of them was a handful of clear and colored jewels on the ground, hinting at the source of their existence. The bulbs themselves seemed intact. The front windshield hadn't shattered, but it had a giant crack that snaked from one end to the other with smaller fissures veining out in several directions. White smoke billowed from what was left of the engine.

Ari stood before the wreck. She heaved as if choking. The noxious smoke was not the cause—she was choking back an overpowering desire to burst into tears.

Inside the van, Stuey turned to the inhabitants of the back seat. "Is everyone okay?" No one answered as they grappled to understand what had just happened. When reality set in, anger came first.

AJ turned to Aleister, shooting daggers from his eyes. "Man, what the fuck is wrong with you?" he yelled.

Aleister was uncharacteristically embarrassed and humbled. He spoke slowly and softly. "I just wanted to see, you know, if she could actually make a sound. I was just trying to make her laugh."

"You're an asshole!" yelled Prudence. She stared at him for a moment waiting for his usual retort, but Aleister, surprisingly, said nothing. Disgusted, she turned away and crawled between the two front seats of the minivan, exiting the vehicle from the driver's side door.

"You're fuckin' unbelievable." AJ shook his head incredulously at Aleister. He then turned to Stuey. "Come on, Stuey," and he exited the minivan.

Prudence joined Ari in front of the battered vehicle. She placed a hand tentatively on Ari's shoulder. "You okay?"

Ari's eyes welled up with tears. It was clear she was teetering on the very precipice of uncontrolled sobbing. She nodded yes and abruptly broke off, briskly walking down the road by herself.

Stuey was emerging from the minivan when he saw her hurrying down the road. "Ari, wait!" He was mid-step, about to run after her, when AJ stopped him. AJ placed a hand on his shoulder.

"Let her go," he told Stuey.

"But…"

"Where is she going to go out here?" AJ asked. "Let her be. She just wants to go find somewhere to cry where no one can hear her."

Stuey solemnly nodded in agreement.

"Come on. Get the map," said AJ. "Let's start walking."

Stuey reached into the minivan and retrieved the map, then he, AJ, and Prudence proceeded down the road slowly, keeping a respectful distance from Ari. A moment later, they were joined by Aleister scampering up from behind.

"When you think about it…" he began.

AJ spun around and quickly forced out a palm as if to magically push Aleister through the air. "You know what, dude?" he spat at the Satanist. "Just don't fuckin' talk. Okay? Just… don't… talk."

With that, they all turned and continued walking down the road with Ari leading the way. With every step, she put more space between them, getting farther and farther ahead.

Before long, dusk was upon them. The sun had not yet set, but it was tucked behind the thick woods so that the only evidence of it was the diffused bluish light it cast over everything. It was quiet. Despite there being four people in the party, the walk was devoid of conversation. No one spoke. They marched in silence, examining their strange surroundings. Aleister's gaze was drawn more than once to the mournful cawing of a crow somewhere in the trees. When a clap of thunder rumbled in the distance, the pay-off was a murder of crows taking flight against a backdrop of ominous storm clouds. Aleister smiled and muttered quietly to himself, "These are the moments…"

AJ peered with narrowed eyes into the dense woods. They were perfectly illuminated along the road, but just a few feet into the trees was pitch dark. He craned his head from side to side, trying to penetrate the darkness. Prudence just sighed a lot and occasionally glanced into her compact mirror.

Stuey had been walking for a long time with his eyes transfixed on the edge of the road. He was intrigued at the light-colored sand, not dirt, where the forest began. He had looked around him once or twice, trying to imagine a beach nearby, but it just seemed so unlikely. He knew, geographically, the shore couldn't have been too far off, but it was still so incongruous to see this powdery white sand where he expected dirt and pine needles. He glanced at the map and finally broke the silence. "The entrance should be just up here somewhere."

"It seems Ari's already found it." AJ pointed ahead.

Stuey looked up, and there at a crossroads was Ari. She was sitting under a sign that read "*GATTER DER HÖLLE* CAMPGROUND". There was no telling how long she'd been there, patiently awaiting the arrival of her friends. Stuey jogged toward her, and she stood to greet him. He placed an arm around her and they smiled at each other. Without a word, they proceeded up the sandy road that led to the campground. The other members of their fellowship followed behind.

It was dark as they walked through the tunnel of trees that led into the forest—and it was quiet. It was as if the trees blocked out all sounds from the outside world. At the same time, however, this womb of branches seemed to magnify every little sound within. Every twig snapping underfoot crackled like fireworks, every breath became uncomfortably audible. The sand underfoot made swishing sounds beneath their sneakers and boots, as if shushing them to keep quiet as they walked the isolated path into the woods.

They were near the end of the path, and overcast light was slipping through the branches as they became less dense and far less entwined, like a woven straw basket coming undone. A light ripple of thunder echoed through the tunnel. And then they were out. They stood at the edge of a clearing. Before them was a simple log cabin and, off to the left, a large field. It was the kind of grassy expanse one could imagine hosting a soccer match or an elementary school's field day activities on—or perhaps a huge Goth festival in the Pine Barrens of New Jersey. At the edge of the field was a picnic table. Sitting at that picnic table there was a man. Spindly and clad in black, he looked like an overgrown spider draped over the table. His head was buried in his pale hands so that his spiky black hair emerged like a sea urchin held in a porcelain chalice. Upon seeing him, Stuey froze.

"That's him!" Stuey exclaimed. "Oh my God, that's him!"

Stuey tore off from the pack and ran as fast as he could across the field. In moments, he was standing, albeit winded, before his idol, beaming like a child on Christmas morning. He hovered before the picnic table trying to catch his breath.

"Oh my God! It's you!"

Villy looked up at him with a face devoid of expression. Stuey bent over with his hands to his knees and breathed in and out a few times.

"It's really you! Wow, you have no idea what an honor this is, Mr. Bats." He took a deep breath and let it out. "I'm your biggest fan in the whole world.

Gosh, I can't even believe I'm actually talking to you. Man, I hate to do this to you, but can I have an autograph?" He righted himself, still out of breath. "Hold on, I have something to write on somewhere."

Stuey manically fumbled through his pockets. He was so excited to meet his idol that he never once noticed that Villy was completely motionless, staring blankly. The rest of Stuey's friends were just now arriving at the spot with AJ leading the way. It was only then that Villy snapped to attention. He sprang to his feet and stood before them, looking at AJ intently.

AJ was taken a bit off guard. "Hi."

"How did you guys get here?" countered Villy Bats curtly.

"We… drove." AJ cocked his head in surprise.

Villy perked up considerably. "Can you guys give me a lift into town? It's kind of a long story, but I got stuck here, and I really have to get back to the city."

"We crashed our car about a mile down the road." AJ jerked his thumb behind him.

The man's face fell, conveying it was not what Villy wanted to hear. "Shit! Do you have AAA? Maybe we can get them to come and pick us up or something?"

AJ looked at Ari who communicated with the shaking of her head that she had no such AAA membership. Villy got the point.

"Well, do you have a phone, at least?"

AJ motioned to Stuey, who had just managed to find a scrap of paper, which he held out with a pen for Villy to sign.

"Here," said Stuey, oblivious of the conversation that had been taking place. "You can sign this wrapper." Stuey looked up to find Villy staring intently at him. He looked about to find all eyes were on him. "What's going on?"

"Give him your phone," commanded AJ.

Baffled, Stuey reached into his pocket, dug out his phone, and handed it to Villy. Villy fumbled around, desperately pushing buttons. He grew more and more frantic until he finally gave up. His arms dropped lifelessly to his sides; the phone dropped to the ground.

Ari pulled her phone out of her pocket and examined it closely. Crestfallen, she shook her head. She handed it to AJ, who in turn held it up for Villy to see. "No bars."

This only exasperated Villy further. "There's no signal up here. We're in the middle of fuckin' nowhere!" He spun around and hatefully examined the scenery. "That's great. That's just fuckin' great! Now we're *all* stuck up here!"

Stuey was still a bit perplexed as he reached to pick up his abandoned phone. "What do you mean? What about the festival?"

Villy erupted. "Are you stupid or something? Look around! Do you see a fuckin' festival? Do you see a stage or lights or sound gear? Do you see hordes of adoring fans cheering for an encore?"

That last line got Ari's attention. She turned to AJ and expressed a strong dislike for their new acquaintance by contorting her face. AJ replied in the way of a mild shrug.

Villy continued screaming at Stuey. "There's no fuckin' festival! Do you understand?"

Exasperated, Villy threw his hands up in the air and turned his back on his biggest fan. Stuey looked at the wrapper he held in his hand for Villy to sign, and dejectedly put it back in his pocket.

"What happened?" asked AJ.

Villy took a deep breath and calmed a bit. He took a step toward the picnic table and crumpled onto the bench like a deflated inner tube.

"The guy who booked me. He was, I don't know… an idiot or something. I think he might have been… crazy or mentally deranged. He was definitely an amateur, that's for sure. He knew enough to book me, but that's about all he did. As you can see, he didn't rent any gear or anything. I don't think he even promoted the event."

"We saw a flier at the mall," said AJ. "That's how we knew to come here."

"Yeah, well, that was probably the only one he put up," countered Villy.

Stuey took a step forward and threw out his chest. "We could still make the best of it, right?"

That was the final drop in Villy's bucket, and it put him right over the edge. "Oh yeah, absolutely!" he sarcastically sang. He rose from his seat and glared at Stuey menacingly. "It's like a goddamned dream come true! It's getting dark! It's getting cold! And I'm going to play a '*festival*'," Villy emphasized using air-quotes, "for *free* to, no offense, five mallrats in the middle of fuckin' nowhere? So yeah, I'm not really sure how we can make '*the best of it*'," he continued, again employing the quotation gesture, "because frankly, Mr. Shankly, I just don't see how this could get any fuckin' worse!"

One beat later, a thick and heavy drop of rain landed smack dab on the end of his nose. Another hit his head with such force that it made a sound. Another hit a shoulder, then a dozen or so hit the picnic table, sounding as if a ghost were practicing typing on the old wooden planks. The clouds opened up, and a veritable stream fell upon them.

Villy looked up angrily at the heavens. Through his fiery gaze, he shot a quiver-full of arrows at God's heart. "And now my hair's ruined!"

His words echoed through the forest, causing birds to take flight and small woodland animals to scamper for cover. The thunder rang out as God clapped his massive hands together in feigned approval.

They all stood there in awkward silence for a moment, then Ari broke off from the pack. She ran through the wet grass toward the cabin, taking refuge under the eaves of the rickety porch. She stood there, hugging herself for warmth and looking back at her friends. They eventually took the hint and ran to join her.

Outside it was cold and wet, but the cabin provided them with a safe and dry place to rest. Prudence found candles, which cast a warm and nearly inviting glow to their impromptu shelter. Ari sat quietly by the back window doodling on some paper and occasionally gazing at the rain-drenched forest. She was only mildly startled by the flashes of lighting that lit the crooked trees on the periphery of the clearing. In the momentary bursts of light, she could see AJ, Aleister and Stuey out back, struggling with the generator. Even in such brief flashes, the unintentional comedy of their bickering was evident. She giggled silently to herself and shook her head. Villy sat by the front door at a big, thick, wooden table, still cradling his forehead in his hands.

"I found more candles." Prudence placed a couple of fat, honey-colored candles on the table in front of him.

"Fabulous," he said disingenuously. "Your friends still outside?"

"Yeah, they're working on getting the generator started." Prudence pressed her delicate chin against her left shoulder and with a middle finger, gently swept a strand of her hair behind her right ear. She offered Villy her hand, offering a coy smile. "I'm Prudence."

Villy just nodded.

Her hand dropped to her side, and she stood there awkwardly for a moment searching for something to say. "So… you're a musician…" She flicked her hair. "I love music."

Villy looked up at her as if she'd just pointed out they both breathe oxygen.

She swallowed, took a breath, and pressed on. "That must be pretty awesome, I mean touring and stuff. I bet you meet a lot of people."

Villy shrugged.

"Is it true, what they say, I mean about the groupies and stuff?"

He remained expressionless.

"I bet you meet a lot of beautiful women."

"I suppose."

"You meet a lot of models, I bet. I always hear about models hooking up with musicians, you know, like Patty Hanson and Keith Richards? Or Seal and Heidi Klum? I've been thinking about getting into modeling." She tossed Villy a sideways glance in the hopes or reading his expression. It remained unchanged. And then she just let took her metaphorical hands off of the safety bar and reached for the brass ring. "Do you think I could model? I mean, because you know lots of models and stuff, you would probably know. Do you think I could be a model? You can be honest."

Villy perked up, though not much, and sized Prudence up and down. "Yeah, you could model."

She nearly erupted. "Oh my God, really?" She bubbled and beamed. "Wow, that's really cool! I mean, you know, getting, like a professional opinion and stuff…"

Villy looked down at her strappy, high-heeled sandals. "You could be a foot model. You have pretty feet."

"What?"

Suddenly, the lights came on. She chortled a little despite herself, more relieved by the sudden conversation changer than by the actual joy of having light. The boys could be heard cheering from outside.

"I guess they managed with the generator," she said awkwardly.

The inside of the cabin was lit up by small, incandescent bulbs that gave off a warmish glow. Just outside the windows, floodlights had burst to life, lighting up the porch and a good deal of the clearing before the cabin.

Prudence took a seat at the table near Villy. She stared down at her feet, closely examining them. She wondered if it was even possible for feet to be pretty. "Well, now we don't have to sit in the dark anymore."

"Hallelujah," said Villy in a tone that revealed no traces of sincerity.

The back door suddenly sprang open, and in marched the dripping-wet Aleister, AJ, and Stuey with a great deal of pomp and commotion. Aleister led the way, throwing his hands up in the air dramatically. "And Aleister said, 'Let there be light', and there was, and he saw that it rocked mightily!" He threw up a devil-horns sign and several droplets of water flew onto the nearby Prudence, who flicked them off as if they were raw sewage.

"As if you helped." AJ slapped him on the back of the head.

"I helped!" insisted Aleister. "I was chanting an incantation under my breath. And I waved my hands." With a raised eyebrow, he greasily added, "I used *the force*!"

AJ shook his head, sighed and joined Villy at the big, wooden table. Aleister and Stuey followed suit.

Stuey turned to Villy and ranted excitedly. "Wow, that was amazing! That generator was all beat-up and stuff. We didn't think it even had any gas in it. But AJ gave it a big tug…" He looked over at Aleister. "And Aleister, he helped, too… and *blam*! It came on!"

Villy sighed deeply.

"Man, this is so crazy! Being in the woods, at night, with Villy Bats!"

Villy rolled his eyes.

"You should write a song about this! That would be so amazing!" Stuey turned away from Villy to address his friends. "Oh my God, can you guys imagine that? We'd be so famous! If *the* Villy Bats wrote a song about this—the weekend we all hung out together in the woods…"

Villy abruptly sprang to his feet.

"Would you just stop? Just stop! Shit! I mean, I'm glad you're having such a swell time and all, but if I were going to write a song about being stuck out here with you guys, it would be called *'Worst Fuckin' Weekend Ever'*! God damn!" He jumped out of his seat. "Seriously. This is total bullshit!"

Across the room came the sound of tearing paper as Ari ripped the sheet on which she had been drawing.

"Maybe you losers have nothing to do," continued Villy, "but I have a life, and I've got better shit to do than hang out with some fools in a cabin in the middle of fuckin' nowhere!"

He huffed toward the door, but Ari beat him to the pass. She grabbed him by the sleeve and passed him a scrap of paper. He held it before himself between his thumb and forefinger.

"A note?" he mocked. "Jesus! What is this, junior high school? If you have something to say, just fuckin' bloody say it!"

Everyone cringed a little. Villy crumpled the unread note in his fist. He tossed it to the ground and turned toward the door—but he didn't get far. Visibly angry, Ari dove to the floor. Picking up the note, she grabbed Villy by his coat and shoved the crumpled paper back into his hand. He shook his head dismissively.

"You guys are pathetic." He stormed out the door, slamming it behind him.

Villy walked out into the humid, yet still crisp, autumn air and took a deep breath. It had stopped raining, and the clouds appeared to be clearing up. He surveyed his remote surroundings. The floodlights on the porch illuminated the great field before him up to the trees on the periphery of the forest. Beyond them, as far as he could tell, lay a thick darkness, miles and countless more miles of it.

He was a long way from New York City with no evident way to get home. He shook his head at the hopelessness of it all. His heart was full of anxiety and dread. He had been feeling like he was in some kind of terrible nightmare since the whole ordeal had begun, and if asked, he'd have said it started when he found himself abandoned in the woods of New Jersey. But that would be a lie. He knew the nightmare had begun earlier—the moment he met the young Henry Berger, the moment he stepped into his garbage-filled car. At that moment, he had realized that he was not working with an industry professional and doubted that he'd be performing for thousands of fans at a *huge* festival. He felt stalked by a black and dreadful monster. It wasn't something external like being lost in the woods, or being stuck in a cabin with some annoying kids. It was something far worse. It was something that devoured him from the inside. But he dared not admit it.

"What an asshole!" declared Aleister.

"Look," said Stuey, "you don't understand. He's Villy Bats. He could be performing anywhere…"

"Villy Bats, my ass!" countered Aleister. "You're the only one who's ever even heard of him! He's a nobody! He's washed up! No one's even heard of this guy, and he acts like a total douchebag, rock-star asshole!"

AJ joined the fray. "I'm sorry, Stuey. I know you're a fan and all, but I have to agree with Aleister. This guy's a jackass! I mean, seriously, even if he were a huge star, that kind of behavior is totally uncalled for." He turned to Prudence for approval. "Am I right?"

"I don't know. I guess," said Prudence. "Still, he's kind of cute. I mean, for an older guy and all."

"He's an ASSHOLE!" Aleister yelled again to make sure everyone got it.

On the porch, Villy was straining to hear the conversation when he realized that all along he'd been clenching his fist. He opened his hand and gazed at it to find, in his palm, a crumpled-up ball of paper. He gingerly loosened it as one would a fortune cookie and read the message Ari had scribbled upon it. The words were unexpected, but they hit home. He crept over to the window and peered in through the curtains. In the midst of the heated debate that was going on inside, Ari had returned to the rear window and was sitting there doodling. Villy was overcome with a sudden urge to kick in the door and tell them all to go screw themselves. And yet…

Inside the cabin, AJ was formulating a plan. "I say we get out of here. There's no point in sticking around. We can all start walking down the road until we get to that gas station we stopped at today."

"That gas station is, like, a million miles away!" exclaimed Prudence. "We're supposed to walk all that way?"

AJ raised an eyebrow. "You have a better plan?"

"What about Villy?" asked Stuey. "What if he doesn't want to come with us?"

"Fuck that guy!" Aleister threw the respective finger in the direction of the door. "He's been nothing but a dick-bag!"

"We can't just leave him up here by himself." Stuey stood his ground.

"Jesus, Stuey, what the fuck?" said AJ. "That guy's treated you like a piece of shit and you still act like…"

Stuey cut him off. "Look. I don't expect you to understand. I know he's a jerk and stuff, but actually, I owe him. He saved my life."

AJ, Aleister, Prudence, and Ari all looked at each other inquisitively.

"I know it sounds weird, and maybe it's corny, but a few years ago I went through a really bad time. I'm not going to get into all of the gory details now, but let's just say that I experienced things no kid should have to experience and it made me feel terrible, worthless, like I didn't want to be alive anymore. And then I heard a song by Raised By Bats called 'Never'. When I listened to the lyrics of that song, I could see that the singer had gone through some of the same things I went through. Just knowing that someone else understood what I was going through made me feel like I wasn't alone anymore. And it was someone like Villy no less. I mean, he was tall and cool and sang in a band, and he'd made it. He was someone famous and successful. It made me realize that I could be someone too, despite whatever had happened to me. It made me want to be alive and to look at every day as a chance to make something good happen— for myself or for someone else. It made me realize that every day there is an opportunity to bring some joy into the world or to do something nice for people, for my friends."

His comrades looked around at each other again, but this time not inquisitively. There was a knowing look on their faces now, as if they could now understand his never-ending optimism. That trait of his that they all secretly thought was due to a lack of intelligence was something deeper, something very conscious—and beautiful.

"Look," Stuey continued, "I know he's being a giant turd and all, but I just think that, deep inside, he's someone who's been hurt and I think…"

The front door opened. All eyes turned to Villy as he meekly entered the cabin.

"Hey." He spoke softly, gently closing the door behind him. "I usually practice around this time. So, if you want, you can listen… I guess. I mean, I'm going to be playing anyway, so, anyone who's interested…"

Stuey exploded with glee. "Oh my God! Villy Bats is playing a private show for us? This is better than any Goth festival could ever be! Oh boy, now I'm *glad* we crashed that stupid car!"

Every eye in the room glared at him disapprovingly.

"Okay, okay, you know what I mean." Stuey made room for Villy, who grabbed his acoustic guitar and took a seat at the table.

"When I was invited to play a big Goth festival," said Villy slowly, "I guess I was expecting tons of people. This is not exactly what I had in mind, but I guess it could be worse." He looked at the five kids in front of him. "There could be *no one* here." He gave a wry chuckle. "Anyway, I'm sorry it took me a minute to realize that I should appreciate the people who actually did show up. So, um… thanks." He looked over at Ari, who was still sitting by the back window. "Especially you."

Villy began strumming the first chord of a song when suddenly there was an unexpected sound.

"You're welcome," said Ari.

Shocked, everyone whipped around to face her. Slowly, she rose from her perch and approached the table. She took a seat directly in front of Villy.

Stuey stared at her wide-eyed. "I thought you couldn't…"

"I can speak," said Ari quietly. "I just… would rather not."

"I told you." Aleister hissed in an obscenely loud whisper.

AJ put up a hand to silence him.

"Why?" demanded Prudence, looking at Ari with a furrowed brow. "I can't imagine not speaking my mind or voicing my opinion on… well, anything."

AJ smirked at Prudence. "Yeah, I can't imagine it, either."

Ari spoke slowly and quietly into her lap. "A couple of years ago, my father got really sick. I went to visit him in the hospital with my mom. Back then, I used to speak," she laughed softly to herself. "You could say I used to talk… a lot. Mostly on my phone. I practically *lived* on my phone. I always got teased that I was using up the whole world's minutes."

"That's kind of hard to imagine," said Stuey.

Ari nodded in agreement. "I was at my father's bedside. My mother had stepped out to get some water for him. I was talking to a girlfriend on the phone. I was going on and on about something—probably something about my parents not being fair because I couldn't go to the mall, or something stupid like that. I remember my father grabbed my wrist at one point. He said *something* to me…" She paused and took a deep breath. "… but I told him to wait a second."

With that, Ari shrunk a little in her seat. Suddenly, she could feel everyone's eyes on her. For fear she might meet any of those eyes and lose her courage, she searched the room for somewhere else to look and finally found a spot—a spider web in the corner of the room by the ceiling. The girl told the rest of her story to the spider in the web.

"I was too busy to listen, I guess. When I finished, I looked up and saw my mother crying." Her eyes began to well up with tears. Through those pools, the people around her blurred and distorted. In that distortion, she could almost imagine she was looking at the horrible image she'd seen in the hospital, forever ingrained in her mind. "He was dead," she cried. "My mother looked over at me. She was in so much pain. 'Your father is dead', she said to me… and she started to cry. She asked me, 'What were his last words?' But I didn't know. I didn't hear him. 'You and that damn phone!', she screamed at me. I'll never forget the look on her face." Ari looked earnestly at the others.

"She never forgave me." Her tears could not be held back any longer, and they streamed down her face. "I don't blame her. I missed my father's last words. I'll never know what he was trying to say to me." She wiped the tears from her eyes, took a deep breath, and straightened up in her chair. "After that, nothing really seemed important enough to talk about."

"That's when you stopped talking?" asked Stuey.

"At first I stopped talking on the phone around my mother, so as not to upset her. The way she looked at me every time she saw me on the phone… it was enough. Eventually, I stopped talking on the phone at all. At some point, I just stopped talking altogether."

Stuey gently wrapped his arm around her. "I'm so sorry. Thank you for sharing that with us though. I know that wasn't easy for you."

They sat in silence for a moment holding each other.

"Talking *is* overrated." AJ broke the silence.

Everyone looked at him inquisitively.

"Well," he continued, "most people spend a lot of time getting all worked up about stuff that really isn't important in the end. Like she said. They forget to look around at what's actually going on around them. That's all I'm saying."

"What about you?" Stuey looked at AJ, who narrowed his eyes.

"What do you mean?"

"I mean, is there something that really bothers you that you never share with other people? You could tell us."

AJ laughed out loud. "Nah, Jack! I'm not about to get all *Breakfast Club* in here."

"You don't have anything personal that bothers you," prodded Stuey, "that you keep to yourself?"

"No, I'm just saying that I don't roll like that," answered AJ. "If I have an issue, I just work it out myself, that's all."

Villy gently cut in, "I think everyone in our scene has one thing about them, maybe—one moment in their lives when they realized that people are not what they seem, that humans are intrinsically evil and out to hurt each other. I think that's what brings us together, draws us to this particular scene. You know what I mean? I think it's what makes us different from the *normal* people."

That word caught Prudence's attention. "I'm normal!"

Everyone turned to her.

"What?" scoffed AJ incredulously. "Come on!"

"I'm serious," said Prudence firmly. "I am."

"Girl." AJ laughed out loud. "If *you're* normal, mankind doesn't stand a chance!"

"Whatever." Prudence crossed her arms and scowled. "I'm probably the only one here who *is* normal."

Aleister leaned his head forward, eager to share. "I secretly like to wear dirty women's clothes," he lasciviously moaned. "Like, pantyhose and stuff… if it's dirty."

"Wait." AJ spun to face him. "What do you mean by dirty? You mean, like Victoria's Secret, like some kind of slutty lingerie?"

"No, I mean dirty. The dirtier the better. Sometimes, when my mom is asleep, I sneak down to the basement, to the laundry basket and go through her stockings…"

"No! No! No! Stop! Stop! Stop!" AJ turned to Villy abruptly. "Alright, look! If you're going to play a song, you need to play it *right now*, 'cause I do *not* need to hear about all of that!" He pointed at Aleister to ensure everyone knew what he was talking about, which elicited a laugh from everyone in the room (everyone except Aleister, of course), including Villy, who chuckled and brought the guitar up to his chest.

"Alright," he began. "Well, here's a song about my moment, if you want to call it that… when I realized that I was, perhaps, not like the other boys."

He began to gently strum the stings. The music was pleasant and soothing. Everyone settled in, as if slowly falling into a trance. He began to sing.

"A long, long time ago, I fell to this place from another dimension, thrust amongst the beasts and they way they behave—it borders on dementia. And now, after all these years, I can barely take it. I don't

think I can make it. Take me away from here. I want to go home. I'm so sick and tired of the..."

The song was interrupted by an ear-piercing, otherworldly cry from the forest. Villy's eyes shot wide open and stayed that way. It was a monstrous shriek, a screeching mournful wail, the likes of which should not be made by anything from this world. Everyone froze for what seemed like an eternity. All eyes crept toward the front door of the cabin.

Stuey was the only one who managed to form words. "What the HELL was that?"

Chapter 9

Villy, AJ, Prudence, Stuey, Aleister, and Ari sat motionless and wide-eyed staring at the front door of the cabin. Besides the tapping of stray drops against the wooden floorboards of the porch, the forest was quiet. They sat frozen on the edge of their seats, waiting for an acknowledgement that what they had heard was real. There was silence. Just when they began to settle back in, the dreadful cry echoed again. They all jumped. It was closer this time, louder and more pained. Villy crept up, gingerly parted the curtains, and peeked out one of the front windows. He craned his head from side to side, trying to find the source of the wretched howl. The rest rose and huddled behind him.

"What is it?" asked AJ.

Villy frowned. "I don't see anything."

Again, the infernal cry filled their ears. It was a long, mournful wail, and this time it was followed by rhythmic bursts and breathy barks, like a mad beast in heat. Villy pushed past the teens and headed cautiously toward the door. The kids followed close behind him. He slowly opened the door, and together, they stepped onto the porch into the cool, humid night. The sounds were now short guttural bursts, like some kind of weird mating call. They scanned the forest before the cabin but saw nothing.

"There!" Stuey pointed to the far end of the clearing. In the distance, *something* was moving just in front of the trees.

"What the fuck is that?" asked AJ.

Together, like a band of Spartan soldiers, they all took two steps forward in unison. In that distant part of the clearing, a strange creature stood in the moonlight. Standing on its hind legs, it hopped up and down, emitting strange shrieks and squawks.

"I knew it! I knew it!" exclaimed Aleister. "Demons *do* exist!" He pushed his way past Villy and the other teens, running off the porch onto a patch of grass and collapsing to his knees. He threw his arms up into the air.

"What are you doing?" Villy barely contained his whisper. "Get the hell back in here!"

Aleister ignored him. "*Oh, dark one, risen from the black abyss!*" He projected loudly into the night. "*Hear my plea!*"

"Are you nuts?" persisted Villy. "Get your ass back in your, you idiot!"

A chorus behind him joined in.

"Come on!" came from AJ, as Stuey demanded, "Stop foolin' around!"

But Aleister wouldn't listen to any of them.

"*Agent of Satan!*" he called out. "*Submit to my will! I command thee! I compel thee!*"

Startled by Aleister's cries, the strange creature in the clearing took flight. The sound of flapping wings echoed through the trees as it disappeared into the night sky. With it no longer in sight, Villy and the kids took tentative steps off of the porch toward Aleister.

"Where'd it go?" Stuey scanned the sky.

Prudence's shaking wavered her voice. "What the *hell* was it?"

No one answered because no one, save Aleister, had any idea. For that matter, no one had gotten a particularly good look at it since it was so far across the clearing, and because it was lit only by moonlight on a misty, humid night. Even then, only seconds after the sighting, the majority of the group were already muttering doubts about their memory of the event.

That doubt quickly disappeared, though, as the sound of flapping wings returned, louder than before, punctuated with a thunderous crash. The creature had landed behind them on the roof of the cabin. They turned to see it.

There was no missing it this time. Merely looking upon it caused their faces to contort into expressions of disbelief and possibly madness. The hideous *thing* right there before them—in plain view—was like no beast any of them had ever seen before. It had a monstrous head with two black eyes that gleamed like enormous, black ostrich eggs. Its hinged mouth had an underbite that revealed a row of teeth of various shapes and sizes. All were razor sharp. Two prominent horns, segmented and curled like those of a ram, took up the majority of the space on each side of its face. The top of its skull was covered in all manner of additional horns, like a grotesque bouquet of antlers from multiple animals, some straight, some curved, all sharp. Wielding this horrible, oversized head was a scaly, snake-like neck. Its upper body was spindly, with sinewy tendons and muscles clinging to a bony frame. From its shoulders protruded two arms almost long enough to drag on the ground, each ending in elongated fingers with curled, black talons. Its legs were goat-like, long, thin and hairy, ending in cloven hooves. From between them emerged a scaly, reptilian tail that narrowed to a nightmarish barb. The unbelievable beast standing menacingly before them was completed by leathery, black wings that sprouted from its shoulder blades.

As though it could sense they doubted its very existence, it reassured them by turning its face directly toward them. It curled its bony back like an angry cat and let out yet another fearsome shriek. All but Aleister jumped and instinctively scurried back under the overhang of the porch for cover.

"Jesus!" exclaimed Villy.

"Oh my God!" Prudence hugged her quivering body.

Aleister remained kneeling on the grass. Shifting on his knees, he turned to face the beast.

"*Submit! Submit! Bow before me, oh mighty god of the fiery pit. Seducer of souls, defiler of innocents!*"

The beast turned directly toward Aleister and roared voraciously at him. That did not deter the young Satanist.

"*I command thee, foul beast!*" Aleister yelled at the top of his lungs.

Seemingly startled, the creature sprang from the roof and disappeared into the dark sky.

Aleister jumped to his feet and screamed at the tops of the trees. "Come back here, you pussy!"

Cowering by the front door of the cabin in terror, his friends implored him to return.

"Come on!" yelled Stuey. "Get over here!"

"Yeah," added AJ. "Stop fuckin' around!"

Aleister turned to his friends, his eyes ablaze like Roman candles.

"Holy shit, man! Did you guys see that? I totally *owned* him!" He clenched his bracer-clad fists, beaming. Everything he'd ever dreamed had just happened for him. Everything he had believed, against all odds, had been proven to be true. A huge smile stretched across his wide, pale face.

In a flash, the creature reappeared. Swooping out of the blackness, it passed Aleister—appearing as a mere streak—flying so close to him it seemed to soar *through* him. This sudden split-second fly-by was so powerful it created a burst of wind. Aleister's friends braced themselves against it from under the porch eaves. Aleister felt it, too, of course. The expression on his face changed to one of awe. It was as if he were experiencing a feeling he'd never felt before—and he was. The cool wind on his rosy cheeks was the last thing he felt before his head rolled off of his shoulders, fell with a dull thud onto his Converse sneakers, and rolled a few feet away. A few small crimson squirts followed from the single spurt of blood.

Villy and the gang screamed in unison. Aleister's lifeless body crumpled to the ground before them. They gasped in disbelief. All asses and elbows, they pushed, shoved, and fought their way through the front door of the cabin like so many clowns squeezing into a tiny car. Somewhere in the black skies behind them, the beast shrieked, urging them on. Once inside the cabin, they slammed the door behind them as hard as they could. Stuey pressed his back against it with all his might. "Oh my God! Oh my God! Oh my God! Oh my God!"

"God, what the hell just happened?" whimpered Prudence. "Did you *see* that thing?"

"Alright," said Villy. "Calm down, everybody! We have to think about this."

"I'm out." AJ proclaimed flatly.

"What do you mean, 'you're out'?" asked Villy.

"I mean, I'm out. I'm getting out of here."

"Are you crazy?" bellowed Stuey. "Did you not see that thing?"

"Yeah," added Villy, "you can't go out there."

"It's like… the Jersey Devil or something." Stuey gripped his hands to his head.

"Look," said AJ, matter-of-factly. "I don't know *what* I saw. Maybe it was, like, a whooping crane or some shit."

"That whooping crane just decapitated your friend!" Villy pointed toward the front door.

"Yeah," continued AJ, "but I ain't Aleister. I'm not trying to sit around talking to the damned thing. I know how this shit goes. Y'all can sit around here and get picked off one by one, but I'm not going down like that."

"What are you going to do?" asked Prudence.

"I'm going to hike down to the car, and I'm going to try to get it to work."

"Are you crazy?" cried Stuey. "The car is totaled!"

Villy jumped in. "Yeah, what if he's right? What if you can't get it to start?"

"Then I'm going to do the only reasonable thing and run like a motherfucker. I'm not stupid. I'm not going to sit around here waiting for more crazy shit to happen. I'm going to get as far away from here as I can." To drive his point home, he then broke his plan down into rudimentary language and gestures. "This place—*bad*!" he said. "Get away from the *bad* place." He turned to Prudence. "You coming?"

Prudence froze in place. "Uh…"

"Prudence, you do *not* want to stay here, believe me." She didn't budge. "Pru," he urged.

She sighed heaving and dropped her shoulders. "I'll go with you."

"You sure?" asked AJ.

Prudence nodded yes and turned to Stuey. "You coming?"

Stuey looked at Villy for an opinion.

"Don't look at me!" exclaimed Villy. "I'm never going outside ever again!"

"Yeah, I'm staying, too," said Stuey.

Ari looked at Villy and Stuey, then over at AJ, then back at Villy and Stuey. Her head swished back and forth, as if watching an imaginary tennis match. She tossed her car keys to AJ and took a step toward the washed-up rock star and his biggest fan.

"Alright," announced AJ. "Suit yourselves."

He and Prudence approached the front door. Stuey cautiously opened it, glancing outside nervously. Prudence and AJ proceeded past the threshold into the cold, moist night.

"Hey!" called Villy.

They turned to him.

"Good luck!" he said.

AJ nodded.

"And if you make it… send help."

"Of course," said AJ.

He and Prudence turned and walked into the darkness. Stuey closed the door behind them and locked it. Villy, Ari, and Stuey all looked at each other in silence. Villy shook his head side to side, as if conveying he feared AJ and Prudence had made the wrong choice, that they would not make it far before encountering that frightful creature. But nothing of his expression showed certainty. He turned and gazed out the window, as if wondering if he'd made the right decision to stay behind.

Outside of the cabin, AJ scanned the clearing. All was quiet. He gestured to Prudence that it was okay to step off the porch onto the sandy road. He led the way down the rickety, wooden steps that seemed to creak and complain more loudly now than he had noticed before. Their postures relaxed when both of them had their boots on the decidedly quieter sugar sand.

Just a few steps away from the cabin, Prudence noticed something strange in the clearing. She tugged AJ's shirt to get his attention and pointed at the spot where Aleister had met his demise. Both Aleister's body and his disembodied head were gone.

Chapter 10

Prudence and AJ stopped for a moment and stared at the spot where Aleister's head and body had been just moments earlier. The rain-drenched grass glistened brightly in the moonlight, save the spot soaked in Aleister's viscous blood.

"Do you think that thing dragged him away?" asked Prudence.

AJ shook his head. "I don't even want to know." He abruptly turned off the sandy path and headed into the woods.

"Where are you going?" whispered Prudence.

"It's not safe to be out in the open... I don't think." He looked toward the sky with anxiety and confusion clearly written on his face. "We should cut through the trees."

Prudence was unsure, but forged forward, clinging to him for comfort. They scanned what they could see of the skies through the treetops. With the threat of being beheaded or eaten or torn to sheds hanging over them, their trek toward the road seemed much longer than they remembered it being earlier. Every creak beneath their feet was an explosion, every breath a screaming invitation to be discovered. Thus, they tip-toed and tried not to breathe. Eventually, they came to the edge of the forest. When they emerged from the trees and their feet hit solid asphalt, they gasped and filled their lungs like divers coming up from the bottom of the sea.

"There it is!" AJ pointed ahead of them.

There, before them, was the white minivan. The vehicle sat diagonally by the road, its hood smashed against a large tree further into the woods. They both jogged toward it. AJ opened the driver's side door and hopped in. He dug through his pockets for Ari's keys and stuck them in the ignition. He gave it a go. The terrible grinding that issued forth from the wounded metal beast was a pained and pathetic cry somewhere between a whimper and a death rattle. Prudence paced nervously outside the vehicle. He tried again. It made no sound at all the second time. It was no use.

AJ poked his head out of the open door. "It won't start."

"Well," whined Prudence, "at least turn the lights on! It's creepy as shit out here!"

AJ reached down and turned the lights on. They worked. They worked *really* well. The lights burst on and illuminated the dense wood before them. Between the trees, just a few feet away, a ghastly, white face was staring, wide-eyed, back into the lights. Somehow, neither of the two noticed the ghostly figure lurking in the trees before them. Like a rare creature of the night, never meant to be seen by human eyes, it continued to stare back toward the lights, shocked for a moment, before coming to its senses. By the time AJ lifted his head to look out of the cracked windshield, the *thing* had crept behind a tree and receded back into the murky darkness.

AJ stepped out of the minivan and stood before Prudence. Defeated, he shook his head. Prudence threw her hands on her hips.

"So what now?" She raised an eyebrow. "We start walking?"

AJ did not answer. He cocked his head to one side and narrowed his eyes as if fine-tuning his hearing. "Do you hear that?"

"Hear *what*?" snapped Prudence.

"You don't hear that music?" asked AJ.

The always sarcastic and caustic Prudence made a face as if to say, "If I heard the damn music, I would have said so," but AJ didn't seem to notice her expression. He remained staring into the air, seemingly transfixed.

"Wait here, I'll be right back!"

Before Prudence could even register what he'd said, he was heading into the forest. "Hey!" she cried, "Wait! WAIT!"

The sound of branches breaking beneath his feet faded into the distance as he dove deeper and deeper into the blackness.

"Oh great!" sighed Prudence. She looked around at the dark forest that surrounded her, at the broken minivan, and at the stretch of moonlit road before her. She sighed again, slumping against the side of the van. "Now what?"

AJ wondered how it could be that Prudence didn't hear the music. As he jogged through the trees and fought through the forest, it got louder and clearer. A pagan rhythm, pounded out on taut animal hides, laid a foundation for ceremonial chanting. A group of female voices, low and sultry, uttered in unison words he'd never heard before. Soaring over the chanting was a heavenly female voice. How could Prudence not hear this? Parting some branches before him, he saw with his own eyes the source of the music.

"Wha...?"

There, before him was a coven of witches. They danced naked around a fire, writhing and throwing their hands into the air with abandon, in what appeared to be some kind of pagan ritual.

The fire wasn't red or yellow or orange—it was blue. It had an almost ghostlike or preternatural glow, as if imagined or magical or not there at all. It was then he realized no one was playing drums. The strains of music, the singing, it all seemed to be happening magically, as if beamed from another dimension. The whole scene was… unreal.

AJ closed his eyes hard and looked again. It was real enough. The bluish flames rose, fell, and danced, casting an otherworldly tint on the pale, nude bodies of the dancers. They were beautiful— their bodies lush and curvaceous, their skin supple and smooth. They twisted and swayed their bodies, serpentine, to the otherworldly music. The blue tongues of the bonfire seemed to lick and kiss their flesh. Then, the circle dance came to a halt and the witches knelt in place around the fire. They closed their eyes and leaned back, arching their spines in ecstasy. They began caressing their own bodies, rubbing hands along the inside of their thighs, then gliding them over their smooth, white bellies up toward their firm, voluminous breasts. Sighs of euphoria filled the circle as they pleasured themselves before the flame. Then, two witches came together, sandwiching a third between them. They each kissed her neck, then caressed and massaged her body from head to toe, fondling her breasts, sweeping their hands over her smooth, pale waist, gripping her full, round bottom.

"Now, that's what *I'm* talking about!" AJ whispered to himself as he licked his lips.

Back at the crash site, things were decidedly less entertaining. It was quiet—very, very quiet. Prudence paced back and forth, back and forth, rubbing her arms and waiting for AJ to return. Each time she walked the full length of the vehicle, spun on a heel and marched back, returning to the driver's side door. She stopped there and, with arms crossed, tapped her foot impatiently a few times before beginning another walk down the runway.

On her thirteenth trip down the length of the vehicle, something happened. She caught her reflection in the minivan window. It instantly grabbed her attention. Admittedly, glancing at herself in a mirror was far from unusual for Prudence, but this time was different. As she gazed at herself, she could not help but notice that, in the full moon light, at this angle, in this particular piece of glass, she was more beautiful than she had ever been in all of her life. Truly, something about this moment was different.

Any of her acquaintances, or anyone who'd spent *any* amount of time with her, would have said she was vain. Her insatiable need to admire herself in reflective surfaces, posing, pursing her lips—it all seemed like an obvious case of one in love with her own image, but *nothing* could have been further from the truth.

While the world would have described her as attractive, Prudence never truly saw it. Somehow, there was an ugliness about her that she couldn't put her finger on. It wasn't any one thing. It was myriad little things that added up to one giant ball of ugly.

In her opinion, her nose could have been a bit straighter and a bit smaller, her lips could have been a bit plumper and shapelier. Her face was a bit long and her chin a tad pointy for her taste. Her milky complexion, which most girls would have killed for, was not immune to the occasional blemish. Somehow, all of these little things, when added up, equaled an 'unbeautiful' person in the teenage girl's mind. It never lived up to *"the most beautiful girl in the world"*. How could it? In all of those countless hours she spent looking in mirrors, she hadn't been admiring herself; she had been scrutinizing herself, critiquing herself, and, yes, hating herself. Hating herself for not being *perfect*, not being pretty enough to make the only man who ever really mattered want to stay, want to love her, want to be… her Daddy.

She would never forgive herself for not being prettier. However, at that moment, as she gazed at her reflection in the minivan window, she was indeed undeniably gorgeous. She cocked her head from side to side to admire her countenance from different angles. As if by some kind of magic, her reflection was a glowing, extraordinary, idealized, and misty version of the face she'd known all of her life. She smiled in disbelief and was dazzled. Her smile could have lit the night sky with its radiance and beauty.

Crack! A sound in the forest broke the spell. Alarmed, she turned.

"AJ?" she called, "Is that you?"

There was no answer. She returned to her reflection and continued to gaze upon it in awe and disbelief. She was not alone. In the reflective window, Prudence noticed a small, pale, amorphous shape just to the right of her reflection. The blurry blob suddenly grew and undulated, taking up more and more of the minivan window. She turned.

Her mind could not immediately comprehend what was before her, except that it was hideous. She tried to yell, but the terror and disgust that surged into her throat seized her vocal chords. Before her stood a rotting crone. Its face was distorted by centuries of decay. Its skin was fetid and white, like the rotting flesh of a corpse dug out of a swamp after days of decomposition, covered in black boils and festering pus-filled sores. It was upon her. This hideous ghoul stared at Prudence with glassed-over gray eyes. It reached out to her and released a tortured, primal cry from its toothless maw. Globs of black, tarry goo splattered onto Prudence's dainty chin and neck. The terror exploded in her throat and she screamed a scream that could have shattered skulls. It cut through the darkness of the forest straight to AJ's ears.

"Prudence!" AJ called out, hearing his best friend's scream.

The ritual music stopped. The witches ceased undulating. When AJ turned to look back at the coven, the lot of them all stood in their nakedness, staring directly at him. Suddenly, the blue flame was extinguished, as if by the breath of some unseen giant, and the witches recoiled, contorting and crouching as if in pain. Their bodies cracked and snapped, as though being crushed by the hands of the same giant, and their skin wrinkled, sagged, and transformed into sheaths of cankers and putrescence. Where once there were firm bosoms and youthful pale flesh, now were all manner of sores, blemishes, and maggot-filled pustules.

There was silence. All traces of the bluish fire were gone. Darkness returned to the forest. The twisted and broken armada of ghoulish rotting crones stood mere feet from AJ, heads lowered from the evident pain of their transformation. He took one cautious step backward. Beneath his feet, a twig snapped so loudly he might as well have set off a firecracker. One of the ghoulish crones snapped her head up to see him. She was hideous, pale, and wrinkled, and had blackened, diseased holes where her eyes and mouth were meant to be. AJ gasped. She opened her gooey maw and out came the most deranged and rage-filled battle cry human ears have ever suffered.

"Oh, that is *not* what I'm talking about!"

He turned and ran for his life.

Prudence was shoved against the body of the minivan by the drooling old creature. Drooping, maggot-filled rolls of flesh pushed up against her and caressed her soft thighs, leaving patches of moist puss. She cringed, quivering in a state of unbearable disgust. Then, the rotting, filth-covered fingers of the fetid hag rose to examine the flesh on her pretty face. Prudence gagged from the smell! The smell! The bony fingers seemed dipped in rotting food and feces. The aroma charged into her nostrils and punched her in the back of her throat. In terror, she clamped her eyes shut and swatted at the sickly demon before her.

"Get off me!" she screamed, more out of disgust than fear. "Don't fuckin' touch me!"

Her clenched fists hit the beast again and again, and with every blow she retched with disgust as her hands sank into the decomposing, spongy flesh. Her efforts were in vain. Every blow just seemed to go through the monster's flesh like she was boxing against a hundred hanging pounds of pizza dough. The thing only pressed closer. And then, the ghastly, stinking hands slid down from her face onto her dainty throat. Prudence clenched every muscle in her neck, expecting to be choked. But the hands continued downward, sliding down her breasts towards her waist. Her eyes sprang open in confusion, and then she felt a feeling that dwarfed any horror she'd experienced so far. The rotting hag slid her ghastly, cold hands onto Prudence's thighs and pressed her firmly against the minivan.

"No!" she screamed and pushed with all of her might against the body of the crone, but it was no use. The hag lunged forward, pressing her cracked lips against Prudence's tender mouth. She filled her warm mouth with a black, wormy tongue. Next came a mouthful of yellow puss that muffled her cries into a train of gagging noises. A burst of brownish-green vomit comprised of salad and Diet Coke burst from the crack between their mouths, forcing out a cupful of the demon's throat puss in the process. It dribbled down both of their necks. Prudence retched again. A stomach full of puke shot up her throat, but this time it had nowhere to go. With the hag's lips pressed so tightly against her mouth, the vomit was forced back down her own throat, causing her to choke. Her head began to spin. This was it, and she knew it. Death suddenly seemed imminent. With a renewed vigor, she punched for her life. Prudence slammed the thing with her fists, pounding the sagging breasts of the beast as hard as she could, again and again. She grew more and more lightheaded. After a while, she could no longer tell if they were hitting anything at all.

She opened her eyes. She was alone. She turned from side to side, frantically looking for the horrible ghoul. It was nowhere to be seen. The forest was quiet again. She slumped against the minivan. Was she going mad? She wondered if she could have imagined such a thing—she *couldn't* have imagined such a thing! And then came the proof. She buckled over, and a last burst of vomit shot from her throat onto the pavement. It wasn't her own. The loud splat that hit the ground was a pint or two of the thick, yellowish puss the thing had jammed down her throat.

She shuddered at the sight of it and spat over and over again to clear her mouth. Suddenly, a strange sensation shivered over all her flesh. She felt an itch on her right hand. She scratched it. But the itch could not be relieved. It traveled up her arm. She scratched her arm. But again, that only exacerbated the feeling, which spread like a wildfire to her other arm and to her chest, shoulders, head, and all over her body. She furiously scratched herself. Something caught under a fingernail as she clawed at the pale underside of her right arm. She looked down at her forearm and dread seized her heart—boils were forming on her skin. She let out a desperate, little yelp. She looked at her other arm. Black boils bubbled up there, too. Her cries became more and more desperate. She touched her face, and her eyes shot wide open. All over her beautiful countenance, fluid-filled abscesses blossomed.

"*Nooo!*" she wailed.

She fell to her knees and cradled her head for comfort. But it only led to more dismay—her hair was falling out in large clumps. She looked at her hand, filled with strands of her beautiful, black locks, and cried. And then she made the mistake of looking up. There, in the hubcap, she saw her reflection again. Though distorted, the image in the oddly shaped piece of metal revealed her deepest fear. Her face was hideous. Her skin was pallid, wrinkled and sagging. Her beauty had been ripped from her. In its place was the face of the diseased crone who'd laid hands on her moments before.

AJ ran madly through the dark forest. Blindly hurling forward like a rocket, his speed barely gave him enough time to maneuver. He collided with a tall pine, and then another, ricocheting off like a pinball before continuing his mad dash toward the road. He clipped yet another trunk so hard that the bark tore through the clothing and flesh on his right shoulder. He grimaced and stumbled, spun around and lost his balance, before righting himself and running faster toward salvation. He could still hear the sickly moaning and uneven, wet cracking twigs behind him. But they were more distant now, quieter. He was putting space between himself and the abominations, but that would not cause him to slow down. He instead picked up the pace, sprinting through trees that were getting further apart. Between the trunks he could make out the boxy, white shape of the minivan. Like a cork out of a champagne bottle, he shot from the woods and landed on the asphalt several feet from the dilapidated vehicle.

He rolled on the road, realizing for the first time that he was hurt as he ground his lacerated shoulder into the asphalt a few times before coming to a stop. Despite the pain, his first thought was of Prudence. He sprang to his feet.

"Prudence!" He looked around. "Where the hell is she?" He yelled again, louder. "Prudence!"

He took a few steps toward the minivan and glanced inside, half expecting to see her curled up in the back seat. There was no sign of her.

A familiar sound was growing in the darkness—cracking twigs and shuffling leaves mixed with inhumanly horrible laments. AJ spun around to find the noise's source. It came from behind him. He turned to find it also came from in front of him. The ghouls were coming from *everywhere*.

He could see them now, blobs of sickly white weaving back and forth among the black trees. One of the monstrous things was emerging from the woods by the driver's side door. AJ darted behind the van for cover. From behind him gargled a guttural vociferation that sounded like a dozen toads sliding down a drainpipe. He spun around. A ghoul shambled from the forest behind him. He ran to the passenger side door and tugged at the handle. It was jammed. Looking over his shoulder, AJ saw monsters approaching from all sides, emerging from the darkness, stepping onto the moonlit road. He tugged again. Nothing. He put his boot on the side of the minivan and pulled with all his might. It burst open, nearly knocking him to the ground. The ghastly things were well onto the road as he scrambled into the vehicle as fast as he could.

Safely inside, he gently and quietly closed the door and locked it. At his feet was a tire iron. He grabbed it for protection. He crawled low through the minivan on his elbows. It stretched the wounded skin on his shoulder, but he mustered the strength to keep in the yelps. He shimmied, in pain, until he was in the back row, then dropped to the floor and kept as close to the ground as he could. He could hear those things all around, lumbering outside the vehicle, moaning and whining as if in agony. He shot a look at every window, in front, behind, making sure none of those things could see him.

He curled into the fetal position and shrank himself as small as possible. Using his feet like a flagellum, he squeezed himself as best he could under the back row seat. It was tight. The sharp, metal support that attached the seat to the floor dug into his scalp, but he pushed in harder, his pain far less intense than the fear of being discovered. Unable to wedge himself in any more, he ended up with most of his body squeezed under the seat and his head smashed against the cold steel seat leg. He lay there, motionless, hugging the tire iron, as anguished moaning bellowed all around him.

Something came closer. He could hear dead feet shuffling near his head, just on the other side of the minivan wall. He froze and terror rippled through him like an electric shock. The shuffling froze, too. Something was standing right there, inches from his face. His heart pounded a painful drumbeat in his throat. His breathing quickened, grew bigger, louder. He held his breath, but that made it worse. Seconds later, when he exhaled, his breathing rushed with three times the speed and intensity it had before. He desperately tried to breathe more slowly, less deeply, but it made his head spin. He held his breath again. The beating in his throat was now punching him in the larynx. The veins on the sides of his head throbbed.

The misshapen thing on the other side of the wall opened its putrid throat. It birthed from that canal the sound of a dozen leprous howler monkeys dropped into an acid bath. AJ let out every single last bit of air from his lungs. He breathed in and out with abandon, quickly, deeply, *loudly*. He gripped the tire iron for dear life. But then, the creature nearest to him did a wondrous thing—it recommenced its shuffling. AJ listened intently as the piles of rotten meat that comprised the feet of this wretched soul shuffled on, delivering the abomination away from him. The moaning, too, faded. All around him, it was growing quieter. And then there was the sound of branches breaking and twigs snapping as the monstrous things returned to the darkness of the woods.

AJ lay there for a while in silence, just to be sure. His heart rate slowed, his breathing eased.

His throat felt bruised and cramped, but was no longer throbbing. Relief washed over him.

"Man," he said to himself aloud, "I thought they heard me for sure!" He reached out a hand and placed his palm solemnly on the minivan wall. "Thank you, General Motors. I'm going to send you a fruit basket for Christmas."

He waited another moment to be sure. It was silent in the forest. Still, he proceeded cautiously. Slowly, he squeezed himself out from under the seat and rose to his knees. He inched his way up and peeked out the minivan window that stretched along the passenger side of the vehicle. That thing that had menaced him earlier was gone. He could see the trees on the periphery of the forest and only darkness beyond. He looked up toward the front. The view out the cracked windshield was clear. The forest, illuminated by the headlights, was clear of the offending things. He turned to the back. That was clear, too. Relieved, he took a deep breath, let it out and leaned against the long window that stretched along the driver's side of the minivan.

"Alright. It's time to get the fuck out of here, for real!"

He grabbed the tire iron and crawled through the minivan toward the driver's side door. He looked out the window to make certain it was clear. There was nothing but forest and road. Slowly, he opened the door. He emerged from the vehicle, lowering one foot gingerly to the ground. No sooner had his boot touched the asphalt than a ghastly white hand grabbed his ankle. AJ screamed. He jumped out of the van and tried to run, but this festering corpse had his ankle in a vise-like grip.

"Get off me!"

The ghoul looked up at him from a crouching position. It was truly disgusting—a naked, rotting female with white sagging flesh, covered in festering sores. Her stringy, black hair was too thin to hide the piercing blue eyes that glared desperately from within skeletal hollows.

"Damn!" He brought the tire iron down with a mighty blow to the monster's head. The creature recoiled but didn't let go. "I said get off me, you ugly bitch!" He slammed the tire iron again and again into the monster's skull until it cracked and caved in, black liquid oozing out onto the asphalt.

Finally, the monster let go and collapsed to the ground. AJ wasted no time. He hopped out of the creature's grip and ran down the road. He glanced over his shoulder once or twice to ensure that *thing* wasn't getting up and following him. Satisfied, he sprinted out of sight to get as far away as he could.

The rotting hag lay on the tarry asphalt. A stream of black goo oozed from the spider web designs on the side of her head. Gathering what little strength she had left, she raised her head just enough to see AJ run into the night. One arm rose, stretching out, desperately tried to seize his tiny, little, distant form in her hand. With her last human breath, she made one final, pained utterance:

"*Aaaay... Jaaaay!*"

Had he not been so far away, he could have recognized the voice of his best friend.

Chapter 11

Villy, Stuey, and Ari huddled by the fireplace.

"What are we going to do?" asked Stuey.

Villy cradled his head in his hands. "Hold on, I'm thinking."

Suddenly, a voice came from outside. "Hey guys! Open the door!"

Villy looked up and turned to Stuey and Ari. "I guess your friends didn't get very far." He rose to his feet and headed for the door.

"Uh…" Stuey swallowed. "That doesn't sound like AJ."

It was too late. Villy had already opened the door. Standing at the threshold was Aleister. He wore a huge smile and a sunny expression. His hands were firmly pressed against his ears as if he were trying not to hear something. "Um, hi!"

Villy, Stuey and Ari screamed in unison. Mid-scream, Villy slammed the door in Aleister's face.

"Oh my God! Oh my God! Oh my God!" chanted Stuey.

Aleister was undeterred. He walked down the length of the porch and peered in through one of the front windows of the cabin.

"Come on, guys! I wanna come in!"

"You're dead!" shouted Villy flatly.

"No, no man!" insisted Aleister. "I'm not… look, I'm sorry about all of that Dark Gods shit. It was totally stupid, I admit it. I just lost my head is all." He chuckled. "Okay, I lost my head… but then I found it!" He laughed heartily.

Stuey turned to Villy, whispering, "Maybe we should let him in. I mean, maybe we can help him."

"Hell no!" countered Villy. "He's fuckin' dead! I saw him get his head chopped off! There's no way he's coming in here."

Aleister disappeared and found his way to another window on the north side of the cabin, one that faced the trio head-on.

"Come on, guys," he pleaded. "Let me in."

There was silence.

"Guys?"

Villy, Stuey, and Ari turned toward the window and there stood Aleister, holding his head between his hands about a foot above his body in order to be able to peer in through the high window. Again they screamed in unison. Villy sprang from the couch, shot over to the window and closed the curtains as fast as he could.

"Oh, come on, guys!" cried Aleister.

Villy retreated to the center of the room and frantically looked around the cabin.

"What are you doing?" asked Stuey.

"I need a weapon," said Villy. "Look around! See if you can find a gun or a knife or a baseball bat or something."

Ari and Stuey rose and joined Villy's search, rifling through the cabin.

Aleister's voice could still be heard from outside. "Come on, fellas… let me in! It's cold out here."

Stuey turned to Villy. "What are you going to do?"

"We need to get him away from here," explained Villy, still searching, "somehow."

Villy found himself in front of an old wooden cabinet, and he yanked open the doors. It was completely filled with all manner of odd objects, so full that merely opening the doors caused a waterfall of books and other curios. Stuey picked up a large, odd-looking book.

"Whoa!" he marveled. "Look at this!" He displayed the book for all to see. It was enormous, and bound in a brown leather that resembled tanned human flesh. On the cover was the image of a contorted, tortured human face. "Maybe there's something useful in here?"

Villy glanced at it for only a second. "Don't be ridiculous." He went back to searching for a weapon.

"Wow, there's a lot of weird stuff in here! Candles… incense… and look at *these*!" He held out his hand, and in it was a small pile of metal trinkets. "What are these? Amulets?" Stuey's eyes widened. "The person who lives here must be a witch!"

Villy was less impressed. "Either that or they do all of their shopping at Spencer Gifts."

Having thoroughly investigated the shelves of the tall cabinet, Villy knelt down and began going through the bottom drawers. Stuey joined him, opening a drawer out from which bloomed a patch of frilly women's panties in an array of pastel colors. Stuey grimaced and stuck his hand into the drawer, feeling through the silky lingerie. His eyes shot open, revealing that his probing digits had encountered a hard object buried in the lacy unmentionables. He removed the item and held it before him—it was an unusually large dildo. Both he and Villy looked upon it with expressions of bemused disgust as the fleshy, silicone member flopped from side to side.

"Another satisfied customer?" offered Villy.

Outside, Aleister was growing impatient. "Come on, I'm getting pissed! Let me in! I'm going to find my way in eventually."

Villy accelerated his searching. "Shit!" he cried. "You'd think someone who was into this crap would have a sword or a dagger or something!"

Ari cut in. "What about this?"

Stuey and Villy turned to see her standing at the far corner of the cabin, holding a large spade. Villy marched over to her, taking it from her hand.

"It ain't an Uzi," he confessed, "but it'll have to do." He headed toward the front door. "Aleister!"

There was no reply.

"Aleister!"

The sound of creaking floorboards indicated he was making his way around to the front of the cabin. When he spoke, it was clear to all that he was standing directly behind the front door again. "Are you going to let me in, or what?"

Villy responded in as authoritative a voice as he could muster. "You need to get away from here!"

"What?" Aleister laughed.

"You need to go away and leave us alone!" demanded Villy.

"Come on," repeated Aleister. "Stop fuckin' around!"

"I have a weapon," announced Villy. He turned to Stuey and Ari, shrugging his shoulders. They knew it wasn't much of a weapon, but they were relying on the fact that Aleister didn't. "Don't make me use it."

That put Aleister right over the edge. Without another word, Aleister began violently kicking the door. Villy, Stuey and Ari jumped. They all looked at each other with growing concern on their faces. The kicking intensified. Soon, the wooden planks that comprised the door began to dance, moving in different directions. It was clear the door wouldn't hold on forever, and Villy knew he had to act. He began to unbolt the lock.

"What are you doing?" whimpered Stuey.

"I'm going to get rid of him," said Villy sharply, mostly to convince himself it was true. The kicking stopped. There was a long, pained creaking sound as Villy slowly opened the door with his foot. He held the spade in front of him with both hands and stepped out onto the porch. Aleister was not, as expected, standing in the doorway, and for a split second, Villy hoped the whole ordeal was over. Then, he turned. A mere yard away, just to the left of the door, stood Aleister, still holding his head onto his body. Villy turned to him, menacingly gripping the spade.

Aleister laughed. "*That's* your weapon?"

"Get away from the cabin," demanded Villy.

"No!" Aleister retorted defiantly. "I have just as much right to…"

"I'm warning you, get the fuck away from this cabin!"

"Or what?" scoffed Aleister. "You're going to hit me with your little shovel?"

"Yes! I'm going to hit you with this shovel."

Aleister cranked up the childish, mocking tone in his voice until he was practically singing. "Oooh," he bellowed, "and just whattaya think that's gonna d…"

He didn't get to finish the sentence. Mid-word, Villy slammed Aleister as hard as he could with a downward swing of the spade. The blow caused undead Aleister to emit a Chihuahua-like yelp as his

head came down, smack dab, at Villy's feet. Villy shrieked like a schoolgirl and, without thinking, instinctively kicked the head as hard as he could.

"Ow!" Aleister's fat and very-surprised-looking head went flying through the air, landing with a thud in the wet grass in front of the cabin.

His headless body remained standing. It turned to the left. It turned to the right. Then, with arms outstretched, it dove off the porch and ran toward where it thought its head might have landed. The look on poor Aleister's disembodied face turned to horror as he watched his sightless body lumber forward, miscalculate, and accidentally kick him with Beckham-like force straight across the clearing.

"Owwwwie!" The head crossed the clearing and landed somewhere in the darkness of the forest.

Loyal to the end, Aleister's clumsy, blind body ran after its head. Sightless as it was, the figure smashed directly into a tree with a dull, muted thud. The headless body quivered like an airborne Pike Place tuna before falling ass-ward to the ground. It twitched helplessly in the grass while its head yelled angrily from beyond the periphery of the woods. "Come on, man! Give me a hand! I can't see shit out here!"

Villy stood motionless on the porch, partly in an attempt to make it seem like this was the outcome he'd hoped for, partly out of pure shock. Stuey and Ari poked their heads out the front door.

Aleister's head continued screaming from the darkness. "You're an asshole, dude! A washed-up, fuckin', has-been asshole!"

Holding out one hand, Villy addressed Ari and Stuey. "Hand me that brick."

Ari reached down and picked up a brick from the small pile of them that sat on the top step of the porch. She inspected it for a moment, then handed it to Villy. Villy gazed into the forest, gauged the distance, wound up, and threw the brick as hard as he could in the direction of Aleister's head. Aleister yelled from the darkness.

"Hey!" There was silence for a moment, and then, "You missed me, fucktard!"

"Hand me another brick," said Villy. Again, he threw it as hard as he could into the dark woods. His second attempt seemed to land closer to its intended target.

"I swear to God, I'm going to kick your gay ass, you piece of shit!"

Stuey's eyes lit up. "Can I try that?"

Villy nodded and gestured to the bricks. "Be my guest."

Apparently, Aleister's head had overheard the exchange. "You better not, you fat retard!"

Stuey wound up and threw the brick into the darkness. He never had been very athletic, so the brick didn't make it all of the way to the forest. It did, however, come down with a good deal of force right onto the crotch of Aleister's twitching body. The body jerked violently.

"Oops." Stuey appeared sincerely guilty.

Villy thought it was hilarious. He laughed wholeheartedly, and Ari let out a little giggle despite herself. She, too, picked up a brick. Not to be outdone, Villy reached down and re-armed. Stuey followed suit. Before long, all three were chucking bricks into the darkness, hoping to get lucky and hit Aleister's obnoxious block.

From the darkness, there was a barrage of exclamations from the irritated head. "Hey! Whoa! You missed me! Stop it, you dicks! *Ow*!"

Villy turned to Stuey with a fatherly smile. "I think you hit him."

"Yeah, I think I did, too!"

And then from the darkness they heard, "Holy shit!" Villy, Stuey and Ari froze. They turned back to face the trees, baffled by the exclamation.

Villy put up a hand for silence. "What's Aleister on about now?"

They waited silently for more. Aleister's head spoke again.

"Oh shit! What the fuck is... um... guys?"

Their eyes were glued to the pitch black just beyond the trees; their ears strained for any sound. Stepping from the shadows into the clearing came a man. He was tall and spindly, his arms and hands unusually long and bony. He was mostly naked, save for some tattered and faded clothes that vaguely resembled those of a Pilgrim. He wore a tall black hat that covered his features. He raised his head and they could see his face. His sightless eyes were two pallid orbs sitting in black, hollowed-out wells. His cheeks, sharp with bones, practically cut through his parchment-like skin. Thin, veined lips barely covered his skull-like mouth. He raised a spidery arm and pointed with his bony hand directly at the cabin. The threesome gasped. Then the… for lack of a better word, man, threw his head back and his gaping, black maw issued forth a ghastly, dreadful roar like a hellish shofar calling forth the legions of Hell.

There was restlessness in the forest. A chorus of agonized voices rose in the darkness. Twigs snapped, branches broke, dry leaves crackled. The black spaces between the trees spewed forth amorphous, white blobs. Twisted and broken, they stumbled forward. As they entered the moonlit clearing, their decaying and diseased forms were revealed. "Oh shit!" yelled Villy. "Get inside! Get inside! Come on, go! Go! Go! Go!"

Stuey and Ari shot back into the cabin. Villy pushed his way in behind them. All three slammed the door shut. Ari instantly ran toward the fireplace and crumpled before it with a whimper. She buried her face in her forearms to block out the maddening cries. Stuey bee-lined to the stack of books and frantically, if hopelessly, began leafing through them. Villy stood in the center of the room with the spade gripped tightly in his hands. With a manic look in his eyes, he spun from left to right, as though anticipating a siege from all sides.

The anguished moaning grew louder as the ghouls approached. A terrible, telltale noise followed—the brittle creaking of the porch's floorboards announcing the arrival of the monsters. Villy and the kids jumped as a thud shook the entrance. Then, there was another. And another. And more. How many hands were beating on the front door they didn't know, but it was soon a maddening percussion of rotting meat, bone, and wood. The creaking fanned out around them as more hellish crones began walking the length of the porch, beating on the cabin walls. Soon, the pounding came from all sides, a dark jungle rhythm of necrotic flesh on aged planks. The creaking intensified as the rotting corpses shifted their weight from side to side, from one festering appendage to another. And still they howled, decaying crescendos through ragged throats.

"Make it stop!" cried Ari.

Villy looked at her desperately, helpless to end the cacophony. His gaze shot to Stuey, who was rummaging through the dusty, old tomes. "What are you doing?"

"Maybe there's something in these books," answered Stuey. "Something that can help us?"

"You don't know anything about the occult!" scolded Villy. "Do you?"

"No," replied Stuey dejectedly, lowering his eyes. A beat later, they widened and popped right back up. "But I know someone who does."

Villy was perplexed for a moment. "Wait! You don't mean… Aleister?"

Ari screamed at the top of her lungs. Villy and Stuey turned to her. She shook in place, gripped in terror. They turned toward the source of her horrified gaze. Pressed against the glass was a grotesque face. Its pale skin was bloated and festering like it were weeks dead and fished out of a bayou. Eyes like rotten eggs sitting in seeping, black sores fixed upon them.

Villy choked down a scream of his own, shoving it back into his throat like a shovelful of coal into a furnace. He leapt through the air toward the window, fueled by panic and, in one motion, yanked the drapes shut. His shoulders rose and dipped as his lungs struggled to remember how to keep air in them.

Crash! A sharp blast came from the back of the cabin. They all turned their heads at whiplash speed. Shards of glass flew toward them, followed by something far worse—the mangled arm of one of these hellish wenches. Like a blind worm smelling the air for carrion, it felt around, touching, searching.

Ari screamed again, so shrilly she nearly shattered the rest of the windows. Villy ran to the back of the cabin. Placing his hands on a large wooden armoire in the corner, he used all of his might to try to push it in front of the window. It was heavier than it looked.

"Stuey!" he yelled. "Give me a hand with this."

Stuey froze for a moment, locked in fear. His frightened eyes were fixed on the ghoulish, festering arm that was reaching inside the cabin.

"Stuey!"

The boy grabbed hold of his wits and hurried to his hero's side.

"Push!"

Together, they pressed their bodies into the massive armoire and heaved for their lives.

"Think about it…" said Stuey, straining.

"What?" Villy glared at him across the armoire.

"Think about it," continued the boy. "Maybe Aleister could help us. He seems to know about this kind of stuff."

"Are you crazy?" Villy sneered. "We just got rid of him. God knows what he was going to do to us! He might have been trying to eat us!"

They thrust their bodies against the massive armoire, but it wouldn't budge.

"But maybe if…" continued Stuey.

"Forget it! He can't be trusted. He's a fuckin' severed head!"

Villy and Stuey pushed the armoire with renewed vigor, but despite their efforts, it remained unmoved. Two and a half centuries of standing in the same spot would not be undone so easily.

"Come on!" rallied Villy. "On three!"

Stuey nodded in agreement.

"One… two… THREE!"

The two pulled back for an instant, then hit the stubborn hunk of ancient furniture with everything they had. The wooden giant creaked and jerked in defiance. Again, they hit it in unison, and again. After a few good blows, it slowly slid across the floor. As the hard-edged cabinet covered the window, the monster's arm moved with it until it was finally trapped between the edge of the cabinet and the window frame. Like a nightmarish doorstopper, the arm convulsed, keeping the cabinet from moving any further.

"Push harder!" yelled Villy.

"But, the arm's in the way!"

Villy shouted over the banging, the creaking, and the chorus of anguished moaning, "You want those things to come in here?"

Stuey looked at the front door practically getting pounded off of its hinges, and at the other windows about to succumb to the same fate as the one before them. He furrowed his brow and plunged his body weight into the cabinet again. Villy joined him. Their combined force jerked the cabinet forward. From just outside, the owner of the arm issued a tortured cry. The arm convulsed faster, slapping at the cabinet and the wall next to the window like a reeled-in fish sensing its impending death. *Slap! Slap!* They pushed harder. The arm clawed at the walls, peeling fingernails backward until the sinewy strands of meat that held them on snapped like licorice sticks. The shrieks from outside were like Hell's teapot about to blow.

"Push for your life!" screamed Villy.

The cabinet advanced again, followed by the sickly sound of brittle bones slowly breaking. Ari covered her ears and pressed her eyes shut with every muscle in her face. The guys pressed on and the cabinet slid across the floor one last time. There were no more sounds of breaking bones. This sound was a wet one. Black bile and pus-like fluids squirted from the severed arm. Finally, there was a dull thud as the putrid appendage hit the rug.

Stuey craned his neck around the cabinet and saw the arm twitching on the ground. "Oh man, that's so gross."

Bam! The pounding on the front door grew louder and lower, as if the ghouls were now slamming their entire body weight collectively against it.

"I don't know how long that door is going to hold out," Villy worried. He looked around for something to shore it up with. "The table! Come on, give me a hand!"

Stuey and Villy were only halfway across the room when suddenly there came a crash—another window had shattered. This time, not one but several rotting arms burst into the room.

Villy dropped his end of the table right where it stood. "Jesus!"

Blam! *Blam*! *Blam*!

The door was being pounded off of its hinges. The clamor on the walls also grew more and more violent. A framed picture fell to the ground across the room, shattering. With two windows broken, the howling of ghouls was louder, vibrating beyond their eardrums and into their bones. The lights flickered. Ari gasped. They flickered again. Each additional time, the period of darkness grew longer until suddenly, with a short crackle, the room went black. From the darkness of the cabin, Villy could see through the broken window, past the hardly human shapes of those malignant beings, and there, in the moonlight, hovering menacingly over the generator, was the Pilgrim man.

In the darkness, all of the terrible sounds they'd endured became more rich, more clear. The pounding on the walls resonated like many drums, each with its own timbre determined by the wood's condition and the drummers' hands' state of decay. The body-slams on the front door were low and menacing, like a timpani at times, and at others like an Afro-Cuban *tumbadora*. After each distressing boom, there was the faint sound of bones crackling, followed by a noise like viscous fluid sloshing in a fleshy sack. Villy noticed for the first time some higher-pitched rattling; chattering tea cups clanked against each other in a cupboard.

The most distressing sounds, however, came from the gullets of the ghastly abominations fighting all obstacles to reach the trio. Villy could now hear each individual voice; their sounds were less like menacing growls and more like tortured laments. There was an unendurable, maddening anguish in their cries. Villy had only heard hints of it before, in the howls of abandoned dogs and in the gut-wrenching laments of women who had lost their children.

In the midst of this calamitous symphony of horrors, Villy noticed a new sound. He turned to its source. Sitting in front of the fireplace, Ari was weeping. He rushed to her side.

"Are you okay?" He realized the futility of asking as the words were leaving his mouth.

"I'm scared," she cried.

"Me too," he confessed. "Me too."

He knew the door wouldn't hold much longer, and it wouldn't be long before all of the windows were broken. Eventually, those things would get in. There simply weren't enough tables to shore up every possible entrance, and he sure as hell couldn't fight them all off with just a spade.

He sat down next to Ari and put an arm around her, comforting her as best he could. Stuey joined them. The three huddled together as the siege continued. There was a low, rumbling and grinding. They looked toward the back of the cabin. From outside, something was pushing the cabinet away from the wall. The pounding on the front door grew slower but stronger, more methodical and determined. Another window shattered.

"Make it stop!" cried Ari.

Powerless, Villy held them closer. "I just want you guys to know," he said slowly, "I'm glad I came here. I mean, I'm glad I met you guys. I just want you to know that."

Stuey mustered a smile. "Well, I'm sure you already know, meeting you has been the highpoint of my whole life."

Villy meekly smiled and nodded.

Ari wiped the tears from her eyes and turned to Villy. "I'm glad I met you, too."

Villy smiled and held Ari close to him. "And thanks for the note," he said to her softly. "I really needed that."

Stuey perked up. "What did the note say?"

Villy fished through his pocket with his free hand. He extracted the crumpled piece of paper and handed it to Stuey. Stuey unfolded it, holding it between his fingers like a miniature scroll. He read aloud, incredulously. "'You're a douchebag'?"

Ari nodded. "Well, he *was* being kind of a douchebag."

Villy made no bones about it. "I was *totally* being a douchebag." He almost managed a light chuckle, but looking around cured him of that desire. "And any minute now, I'm going to be a *dead* douchebag."

"Come on!" urged Stuey, the eternal optimist. "You have to stay positive. You have to *think* positive!"

The ghouls were pushing their way in through two windows. The front door was on the verge of being smashed into splinters.

"Stay positive?" Villy shook his head, as if trying to rid himself of the annoying fly of such preposterousness. "Stuey, look around!"

Suddenly, there was silence.

The banging stopped. The moaning stopped. The lights came back on. The arms in the window receded, and there was no sign of the undead things. The three sat stiffly in silence.

"It stopped!" Stuey proudly donned the mantle of Captain Obvious.

He began to rise to his feet, but Villy reached up, grabbed him by his shirt and pulled him back down. "Hold on."

They sat in silence for a moment. Villy scanned the room, straining to hear any sign of the monsters. He could hear nothing, nothing at all, not even the sound of crickets or the wind in the trees. It was *so* quiet. It was *too* quiet.

His concerns were immediately justified. A sharp creaking could be heard from the back porch. They froze. All eyes fixed on the back door. They waited for more, but there was only silence. For what seemed like a long time, they waited, frozen, holding their breath. Nothing. Only the sound of three beating hearts could be heard. Still nothing else.

Just as they were ready to exhale, the floorboards creaked again. There was something out there. They froze. It froze. There was another period of silence, and then the creaking continued, louder now, brazen and sure of itself. They followed the sound with their eyes. Whatever was out there was walking along the length of the back porch away from them. And then they could hear it as it hopped off the porch and onto the wet grass. They followed the footsteps along the north wall of the cabin. Villy strained his eyes to see if he could make out what it was through the broken windows, but the curtains, though torn, were intact enough to obscure his view. Through the curtains he caught a glimpse, just a sliver of it. *Something* was out there, and it was headed toward the front of the cabin. All doubt about its presence, if there ever had been any, was erased as this thing mounted the creaking floorboards of the front porch. All eyes darted toward the front of the cabin. Again, they followed the sounds in terror, each footstep growing louder as they approached the front door.

Creeeak! *Creeeak*! *Creeeak*!

It stopped at the front door. The three huddled closer together, waiting for the worst. The doorknob moved, dryly creaking, to the right. It stopped, and was followed by a clicking sound as the door unlocked. There was a moment of silence, then the door burst wide open. Villy, Stuey, and Ari screamed together at the tops of their lungs.

"*AAAaaahhhhhhhh*!"

There in the doorway before them stood a pleasant-looking, forty-something-year-old woman.

Chapter 12

Villy leapt to his feet, staring at the woman in the doorway. "Who the hell are *you*?"

"Who am *I*?" She yelled back indignantly. "This is my house! Who the hell are *you*?"

Villy rushed forward, his demeanor totally changed. "Oh! You're Henry's aunt!" A smile washed over his face as hope of getting out of the Pine Barrens (not to mention, *not* being eaten by monstrous ghouls) presented itself.

The comely woman smirked and raised an eyebrow. "You know my jackass nephew?" She tucked her shoulder-length brown hair behind her ears.

"He booked me to play a show here," said Villy. "He said you gave him permission to use your cabin."

The woman rolled her eyes. "Typical!"

Villy pressed on, trying to get to the point. "It's a long story. Anyway, it doesn't matter. Do you have a cell phone? Did you drive here? We have to get away…"

"There's no time for that." The woman spoke bluntly, pushing her way past him. She walked to the big wooden table and plunked down a messenger bag she had slung around her shoulder. The abrupt action mussed her red flannel shirt, exposing a tight, white tank top underneath that bulged in all of the right places. She examined the denizens of the room as she hurriedly fixed her shirt. Her eyes met with Stuey's. He looked up and away awkwardly.

"You don't understand!" pressed Villy. "There are… *things* out there! Like, some kind of fucked up zombie-like people!"

Stuey rose to his feet. "Yeah, and we saw some kind of weird creature, like a… flying demon!"

"We think it was the Jersey Devil." Ari looked intently at the woman's expression, as if fully expecting she'd think them all crazy, but the woman's face didn't change at all.

She nonchalantly undid the ties on her bag and replied without looking up. Her tone of voice had only mellowed, if anything. "Long legs? Wings? Ugly head?"

Ari nodded.

"Highly likely. I've sent him back to Hell a dozen times. Keeps coming back."

Now, it was Villy, Ari, and Stuey who were looking at each other, expressions silently asking each other if this strange woman was the crazy one.

"Are you a witch, or something?" asked Villy.

"Yeah, you could say that." She flipped open the front flap of her bag and reached inside. "Does this belong to any of you?"

Like a rabbit out of a hat, she extricated the severed head of Aleister. Everyone gasped as she placed it on the wooden table. Aleister opened his eyes to see he was amongst friends.

"Hi guys!" He beamed jovially and flashed a cheesy grin.

Stuey was the first to own up. "That's our... *friend*. Aleister."

"Nice friend you have," scolded the woman. "He bit my ankle."

Aleister's eyes shot her a look of disdain. "Yeah, well, you nearly stepped on my head, you fat cow!"

"What can I tell you?" sang the lady. "Don't loiter on my porch."

"How did you get all of the way back to the porch?" Villy asked the disembodied head, his voice betraying how intrigued he was by this piece of information. Last the group had seen Aleister's head, it was past the clearing in the dark of the forest.

"I have my ways," grinned Aleister in a sleazy tone.

Villy tilted his head, raised both eyebrows, and showed Aleister the palms of his hands, indicating he was all ears.

"Well, after my... *friends*... and I use that term very loosely, were done throwing *bricks at my face*," he recounted, putting such emphasis on the word "friends" that it was safe to assume he would have been very busy making air-quotes, if he had had hands, "I found myself in the dark, all alone, face up in a muddy pile of wet leaves. And you'd think that being face up would be distinctly more pleasant than being face down in the muck. It was. That is, until some creepy hag monster sat her rotten, worm-filled, decomposing asshole right on my face, thank you very much. Oh, and by the way, now I know what hundred-year-old, festering, pus-covered pussy tastes like—and let me tell you, it ain't Depends! It tastes like hundred-year-old, festering—"

"Okay, okay! Get on with it!" spat Villy.

"Well," he continued, "when Little Miss Mucus-Puss finally got off her ass, *and my face*, I did what any self-respecting fellow in need of a ride would do. I bit down on that hanging slab o' rotten labia and hitched to the porch! Pretty clever, huh?"

Everyone groaned. Ari looked like she might puke.

"It wasn't all glitz and glamour, let me tell ya! These things pretty much fart with every step. And my nose was, like, *right there*! Anyway, when we finally got to the door, this stupid, festering sack of shit just stood there, pawing at it with her lifeless meat mittens. '*DOORKNOB,*' I said, best I could, but you know it's a little hard to *enunciate* while biting down on a maggot-covered puss-purse. So, the third time I tried to tell this useless shit-sack to use the fuckin' doorknob, I lost my grip and fell onto the porch. And that's when *this* fat cow nearly crushed my skull with her feminist man-boots."

The woman glared at Aleister, then looked back at the others. "If more guys were like your gem of a friend here, *all* women would be feminists." She shook her head. "I was able to clear the porch and run the rest of those things off. I probably should have just let them eat him. But no, I thought I'd be nice and pick him up. I had to go around the back to get the generator started. This idiot tried to bite me through my bag all the way there. What a prince!"

The woman grabbed Aleister by the hair. "*Owww!*" he cried. She carried him across the room and slammed him down on an end table by the front door, then wiped her hands with disgust on her tight blue jeans. With a spin, she continued toward the large cabinet of books.

Aleister forced his eyes as far over toward his friends as they'd go and whispered to them as loudly as he could, "We have to get *out* of here! This bitch is *crazy!*"

Villy and Stuey followed the woman to the cabinet. Ari lagged behind, regarding Aleister's head with a look of intrigued disgust.

"What are you lookin' at?" barked Aleister.

Ari jumped and hurried to join the others. Once she had moved out of Aleister's line of site, his eyes widened as they beheld a glorious image. Through a broken window, he could see his headless body stumbling about outside. He choked back a happy exclamation and quietly schemed with shifting eyes.

"Jeez, what a mess!" The woman threw her hands in the air.

The cabinet doors were open, and most of the books were in a giant pile on the floor, along with her candles, amulets and other occult paraphernalia. Figuring Villy and Stuey were the cause of this mess, she scowled at them before dropping to her knees. Item by item, she began picking up her things and returning them to their rightful places in the drawers and on the shelves. Stuey joined her on the floor, conscientiously pitching in. He handed her a trinket, then a book, then a small box of incense. His chubby hand reached down and grabbed what at first appeared to be a large candle. It was halfway to the woman's hand when he noticed that it was not a candle at all, but it was too late. The woman reached out to take it. Between them was her large, fleshy dildo, and they each had a hand on it.

"Oh, God." Stuey dropped his hand from the phallus like it was on fire.

The woman unabashedly held it in her hand as it flopped from side to side. The embarrassed looks on everyone's faces did not elude her.

"What?" She asked matter-of-factly. "It gets lonely up here." She placed the rubbery member into the panty drawer and continued straightening up. Villy tried to divert his gaze. Looking around, he accidentally met eyes with Ari.

"It's *so* big!" She whispered to him.

Villy mouthed the words, "Oh my God, I know!"

"Here!" declared the woman. "Help me with these things." She handed Stuey a couple of large candles, an amulet, and some heavy books. "Put them on the table."

Stuey handed them to Villy, rose, and helped the woman onto her feet.

Villy wasted no time. He placed the items on the thick wood and immediately turned to her. "Those… zombie things… what are they?"

"Sit down," she replied. She took a seat at the head of the table and lit the two candles. Villy, Stuey, and Ari joined her. The woman cracked open an old, dusty tome and leafed through it. "Those '*things,*' as you call them, are my ancestors… or their souls, anyway. Well, the ones that allowed themselves to get dragged into Hell."

Stuey, Ari, and Villy looked at each other with widening eyes.

"About four hundred years ago, the English colonists came to this place, many of them to escape religious persecution. Ironically, not long after arriving, they started persecuting everyone else, *anyone* around them who didn't share their beliefs. My great, great grandmother, as it happens, was one of those people."

She turned the book around for all to see. There on the page was an old woodcut print depicting a group of nude women dancing around a fire.

"Her name was Ursula Romani. She was a witch. She had a coven. They practiced white magic. She was a harm to no one. Unfortunately, people are afraid of what they don't understand." She flipped the page to a gruesome image of women being dragged into the town square by their long, flowing locks. "When word got out, well, the town didn't take too kindly to them. They started rounding them up and hauling them into court. They accused them of being in league with the Devil."

She flipped ahead a few pages, opening the book to a frightful woodcut worthy of Albrecht Dürer. In it, a group of condemned witches was assembled on a hill. They stood, hands tied, under a tree from which several nooses hung. Some of the women were crying. Some clasped their hands, begging for mercy from an unforgiving mob.

"That man!" Villy pointed at a grim figure in a corner of the image—a powerful man on a horse. He wore a tall black hat and was dressed like a Thanksgiving pilgrim. Like Death himself, his face was fierce and grim, constructed of harsh, hateful angles and unforgiving lines. He sat high and erect upon his black steed. His angular head was thrown back, his wide eyes glaring downward as he gesticulated menacingly at the condemned with a long, bony finger. "Who is he?"

"That's the Governor," said the woman flatly. "Governor Douglass."

"I think I saw him," whispered Villy, chewing his lip.

"I'm sure you did," said the woman. "Never has a more wretched and twisted soul walked the face of this Earth." She took a deep breath and continued. "This tale has been passed down from matriarch to matriarch in my family for four centuries, lest we forget it. As the story goes, it was he who started it all. He was married, he was a Christian, a leader of men, a '*pious*' man. But of course, none of these things stopped him from feeling lust. As it happens, he fancied a young girl, a beautiful redhead. He tried to seduce her, but she wasn't interested in a man three times her age. He wouldn't take no for an answer, so he followed her into the wood, to spy on her, to pleasure himself while watching her 'make water'. Little did he know that she was a witch, and even *less* did *she* realize she was leading the Governor straight to her coven—the coven of my great, great grandmother, Ursula Romani!

"He watched them as they danced in the wood, the pervert, his soul torn between the lust he felt for these beautiful, nude, unabashed women, at one with nature… and the horrible shame and guilt he felt for having betrayed his God and his wife and those he served. The next day, he hauled the innocent young girl into his chambers and tried to coerce her to satisfy his lascivious desires in exchange for silence. But she refused. That pig wrongly believed that '*witch*' is synonymous with '*whore*'." She turned her head and spat on the floor.

"He was wrong. Anyway, you know the rest. He accused the poor girl of being in league with Satan. She was tortured mercilessly until she gave up the names of other members of the coven. She never betrayed her high priestess though, never mentioned Ursula's name. So, my great, great grandmother watched in horror as her closest friends were tortured and executed for alleged devil worship. I guess that must have put the idea in her head because, shortly thereafter, she began practicing *black* magic. Got pretty good at it, too, by the looks of things. I guess she figured that, if the followers of God were trying to kill her, perhaps the Devil could help. Eventually, she was suspected. She was dragged off and burned at the stake."

Stuey perked up. "I read once that no witches were ever burned in America." She shot him a stern look and his resolve crumbled. "I mean, I heard that… in history class. They were hung, but not… you know… burned. Not that *hanging* is good…"

"You believe everything your government tells you?" Her face was a cold, blank slate.

"Um, no." He nervously chewed on a piece of cuticle. "I guess not."

"History, as they say, is written by the victors. And let me just say that there are things that have happened here in this country that would make your skin crawl and your blood boil. But they wouldn't make us look very civilized. They'd make us seem no better than the witch-burning place we came here to escape. So, those tales are buried. You know what I mean?"

"Yes, ma'am." The woman was turning her gaze away from Stuey, but he caught her. "I'm sorry about your… relative."

"It's okay." A wry, one-syllabled harrumph escaped her. "It seems she got the last laugh. Before they dragged her off, she managed to open a doorway to Hell. And as it happens, that doorway is right here."

"In New Jersey?" howled Stuey. "New Jersey is the gateway to Hell?"

Villy crossed his arms and leaned back in his chair. "Explains a lot, really, when you think about it."

The witch furrowed her brow. "Really. Like what?"

"Well," answered Villy, "like why Elizabeth, New Jersey, smells like devil farts, for starters."

She frowned and began gathering her occult paraphernalia.

"What makes the gateway open?" Ari asked the woman, clearly believing her.

"Well," the witch replied, "Hell is *made* of souls, and so it *needs* souls to exist and to grow. And believe me, it wants to grow! It would take up the whole universe if it could. So, it reaches out. It calls to us to join it, to help it expand. It feeds on people's weaknesses, tries to seduce them into willingly joining it. Some people will answer the call, some won't. But either way, when that gateway is open, even just entertaining the notion can be enough to get tricked or pulled in. As all of those tortured souls and demons enter our world, they can drag you back to Hell with them, whether you want to go or not. So it's important to keep your wits about you while it's open. I can close that door, but sooner or later, it will open again. This is a fulltime job."

"Wow," marveled Stuey, "that's a really hard job to have."

"Yeah!" agreed the witch emphatically. "And believe me, some people don't make it any easier. Some people actually *try* to open the gateway to Hell! There's a particularly powerful entity that's been *purposefully* opening the doorway from, believe it or not, the back of a Spencer Gifts store at the Maplecreek Mall."

Aleister's voice filled the room. "Oh my God! That's me! I knew I could do it! I told you guys!"

All eyes turned to the end table, but he wasn't there.

"Where the hell did he go?" asked Villy.

They scanned the room for the wayward head. Suddenly, the witch sprang up from her seat and stomped across the floor, reaching down and picking Aleister's head off of the carpet by his hair. He sadly glanced at his hapless body lumbering just outside the window.

"How'd you get over here?" she asked the bodiless rascal.

"I used my tongue." Aleister hissed, punctuating the phrase with a dozen or so lascivious flicks of his slimy red organ.

"You're disgusting," said the woman.

"You should let me move in here with you," he continued. "I bet you could *use* a little head!" Aleister laughed heartily as the witch marched him back to the cabinet. "Hey," he added, "help me get back together with my body and you'll *never* need to use that pathetic dil-dong ever again!"

The witch opened the cabinet with one hand, and removed from it a copper candleholder, a simple metal disc with a spike on which one could impale a fat candle. She marched back to the wooden table, slammed down the candle holder, and then slammed Aleister's head onto the spike, ramming it up through the meat of his severed neck.

"*Ooow!*" cried Aleister. "What the fuck's wrong with you? You've got some serious man-hating issues, you crazy whore! You know that?"

Villy shook his head, regarding the decapitated teen with a wrinkled nose. "What are we going to do with him?"

"Well," she said matter-of-factly, "I had planned to make a fire and toss him into it."

"Wait. What?" cried Aleister.

Bleeding-heart Stuey came to the rescue. "Is there any way we can save him?"

"Your friend's already dead," said the witch. "The only reason he seems alive is because the gateway is open. Once it closes, he'll be as dead as anyone else who's ever gotten their head chopped off."

"Uh, *hello*!" yelled Aleister. "I'm right here! I can hear you, you know."

"Could we at least attach him back onto his body?" offered Ari.

"YES!" Aleister grinned. "I knew I liked you! Put me back on my body!"

"No," said the witch, "he'd be far too dangerous reattached."

"Yeah," agreed Villy. "I'm pretty sure he'd get us all killed."

"The best we can do for him," suggested the witch, "is throw him into the gateway."

"What would *that* do?" asked Aleister's head.

Finally, someone addressed him directly. The witch stared him in the eye. "You'd live forever. In Hell."

Aleister was over the moon. "Oh my frickin' God, YES! Let's do that!"

"I don't know," said Villy. "I say we go with your original plan and chuck him in the fire. It's the safest bet."

"Dick!" yelled Aleister's head.

"Come on," said Stuey. "He's our friend."

"He's not *my* friend." Villy scowled.

"Ditto, asshole!" spat Aleister.

Ari turned to the witch. "He really couldn't hurt us if he was in Hell, right?"

"I really don't care either way," said the witch, "but if that's what you want to do, I'm not carrying him. One of you has to do that."

"I'll do it," offered Stuey.

"Dude, you are the best!" beamed Aleister's head. "You are totally not a fat retard! You are awesome. I mean that!"

The witch placed her hands on Aleister's face and turned him on the table to face her.

"If we're going to do this, you'd better be quiet and do exactly as I say!"

"I won't say a word, I swear!" insisted Aleister.

She grabbed him by his hair and slid his head off of the spike with a *slush*. Aleister winced but didn't dare complain. The witch swung open her bag and placed the head inside of it.

"I won't say a word, I swear! I'll be quiet as a…"

And then she closed the bag.

Whatever magic she'd used to stop the awful siege before was fading. A chorus of ghouls shuffling and moaning could be heard outside. They were returning.

"We're running out of time," said the witch. "We need to get going if we're going to close the gateway. I'm usually stuck doing this alone. It will be nice to have some help this time." She smiled at her new helpers.

"This is crazy!" bawled Villy. "What can *we* do? We don't know anything about this stuff! Seriously!" He danced around moronically, imitating Rick Moranis. "It's all like, 'I'm the key master of Gozer, I'm looking for the gatekeeper!'"

The witch fixed on Villy with a laser-beam stare. "Hey! I didn't ask for this! A member of my family opened this doorway. And I come from a long line of witches who frown mightily on that fact. For every generation, one of us is chosen to keep this shit in check and, lucky me, this is my century. Believe me when I say, it's no picnic." She turned to Ari. "Take a wild guess what I was doing on prom night. Or halfway through my first date." She looked into Stuey's eyes. "I can't have children, can't start a family. Can you imagine? Me, with a baby—here?"

Stuey squirmed and gazed at his shoes. She turned her attention back to Villy.

"I can't have a career. I can't have goals, dreams."

An introspective look washed over his face. These were words that resonated with him.

"Do you think that, when I wake up some days with really bad menstrual cramps, I really want to get up and come down here and…"

"Whoa!" yelled Aleister's head from inside the bag. "Okay, okay, we get the picture!"

She swatted the bag and continued. "Anyway," said the witch to Villy, "if I could do this when I was eight years old, you can, too. Besides, if you've grown accustomed to breathing, you'd be wise to give me a hand."

She picked up the big book of spells and turned to Ari.

"What's your name, sweetie?"

"Ari."

"Alright, Ari, you take this book," she said. "Don't let it out of your sight. It's very important."

She handed the book to Ari, who examined it with great curiosity. The witch then turned her attention to Villy. "And what would *your* name be?"

Stuey jumped in, babbling effusively. "Oh my God, that's Villy Bats! From the band, Raised By Bats!"

The witch stared blankly at Villy, who looked more embarrassed than anything else.

"Just Villy is fine," said the Gothrocker.

The witch nodded and simply announced her name. "Caroline."

"And I'm Stuey!"

"Great," said Caroline.

"I'm Aleister!" said a muffled voice from inside of the messenger bag.

"I told you to shut up," growled the witch.

"Okay, sorry," replied the muffled voice.

Caroline turned to Stuey. "Hand me that amulet on the table." As he did so, she passed him the canvas bag containing Aleister's head. "Here, I'll trade ya."

Stuey took the bag from her. His lips and eyebrows moved towards each other in a mix of disgust and apprehension.

"Come here, all of you," said Caroline. She led them all to the front door of the cabin, grabbed the spade that was leaning in the corner, and handed it to Villy. "You're a big fella, Villy. Take this."

He looked at her apprehensively. "What's this for?"

Her reply wasn't to his question. "We are going to walk out this door and calmly walk across the clearing and through the woods to the site of the disturbance. Once there, I'm going to close the gateway to Hell with this book."

Again, Villy motioned to the shovel. "And this?"

Still no reply.

"This amulet," said Caroline as she placed it around her neck, "will protect me and, with any luck, the person who is closest to me, preferably behind me. The rest of you are on your own. Those things are largely blind, but you need to be *very* quiet."

She began to turn toward the door, but stopped and looked at Villy. "Oh yeah, and if anything tries to eat you, hit it with the spade."

"Great," deadpanned Villy.

"Hey! Wait!" yelled Stuey. "*I* want a weapon!"

Villy rolled his eyes, shook his head, and handed the boy his spade. He looked around for a replacement, finally settling for an umbrella.

The sickly moaning of ghouls could be heard from outside of the door. Caroline placed her hand on the doorknob and looked over her shoulder at the gang.

"Everybody ready?"

"No," said Villy sullenly.

"Okay, then," announced Caroline. "Let's go!" She paused and turned to Ari. "I want you to stay close to me, sweetie. Okay?"

Ari nodded in agreement, but her entire face quivered.

Caroline gripped the doorknob in her hand. Slowly, she turned it to the right. It creaked like an old curmudgeon. Villy shook his head from side to side. Everything about going out there felt wrong. The doorknob turned a little more, and a metal clicking sound was heard. The door unlocked. Stuey licked the sweat off his upper lip. Caroline inched the door forward. It swung open to reveal a nightmarish panorama of pale, twisted corpses shambling aimlessly about in the clearing before them.

They were *everywhere*.

Chapter 13

Caroline stepped out onto the porch. Villy and the kids stuck so closely behind her that they seemed attached, like one living organism. With each step, the floorboards yelped and squeaked. As if telepathically linked, all members of the party shared the same thought—floorboards have never screamed so loudly before in all of human existence. They looked up at the nightmarish panorama before them. Brittle bones, baked in the furnaces of Hell and draped in white, fetid flesh, lumbered aimlessly. A dozen or so shambled about the clearing and beyond; in the darkness of the trees, they could see amorphous, pale blobs lurking. Somehow, they had to cross this ghoul-spotted clearing without being noticed.

They advanced onto the first step of the porch. The old, splintered wood protested so loudly it made the cries of the floorboards sound like gentle whispers. They froze. Eight eyes scanned the clearing for any sign the ghouls had detected them. There was none. The dead continued, unaware in their moribund meanderings. The group took another step, then another. A silent sigh of relief was shared as their feet landed on the far quieter sugar sand.

Caroline turned to address the others. "One last thing before we enter the clearing. Hell will call to you." She raised a finger in warning. "Don't answer."

No one seemed entirely sure what that meant, but Stuey responded anyway. "Don't answer calls from Hell. Got it!"

They proceeded forward, tiptoeing into the moist, cool night. Caroline led the way, holding the amulet out in front of her. Ari cowered behind her, gripping the book in one hand and the fabric of Caroline's flannel shirt for dear life in the other. Villy and Stuey pulled up the rear, eyes revealing that they secretly wished they, too, could hide in Caroline's shadow. Stuey clasped his shovel for comfort, Villy his umbrella. Within seconds, their feet sloshed from sugar sand to the wet grass of the clearing. Their odyssey across this green sea of monsters had officially begun.

Under the moonlight, they crossed the clearing. The hellish ghouls seemed not to notice them as they advanced into the heart of the grassy field. Close up, the group could get a really good look at these abominations—not that anyone *wanted* to. The creatures' skin was white from a distance, but now revealed itself to be speckled with mold and lesions, covered in all manner of contusions and sores. This mottled membrane hung like rotting pizza dough over their bones so that it gathered in rolls at their midsections and swung to and fro from their outstretched arms. Their mouths, in almost all cases, hung open and were completely rotten inside. Some had teeth, brown and broken. Other mouths were merely decomposing holes from which dribbled tarry bile. Some had eyes, the healthiest of which had gray irises barely visible under milky cataracts. On others, the eyeballs were entirely a translucent greenish black, like hardboiled eggs buried for a century in the soil. Still others had no eyes at all, just gaping holes full of muck and maggots. What they had in common was that, luckily, they *all* seemed devoid of vision.

The witch, Villy, and the kids drove cautiously forward through the crowd of creatures, careful to go unnoticed, minding every movement, measuring every step. About a third of the way through the clearing, the concentration of ghouls increased, meaning there was less space between them and these fiends. Before long, they were passing ghouls only a yard or so away from them. The chorus of moans had become an arsenal of personal laments from each unholy being, delivered directly into their ears.

Ari kept her head down, buried in Caroline's back, but eventually her peripheral vision got the best of her. She could see, just to her left, a gargantuan, rotting hag, not a yard away from them. Hanging from the boney sternum of this foul shrew were long, wrinkled breasts. Ari's face contorted at the site of them. Dangling like shriveled, rancid fruit, they were oblong, pale, and covered in veins and contusions. Most distressing were the necrotic areolas and nipples, pitch black as if charred in an open flame. Ari began to turn her head away from the horror when suddenly, something grabbed her attention. The left breast—it seemed to… *move*. She could have sworn that she'd seen it twitch and vibrate, as if with a life of its own.

She closed her eyes and opened them again, refocusing her vision on the pestiferous udder. It jumped! She saw it for sure that time. It jerked again, and the flesh rippled in a way no breast could—or should—be able to. At least… not one that was controlled by its owner. Ari's eyes widened as the sickly, black areola swelled and then the nipple swelled as well, as though the diseased pustule was about to pop. A greenish amber liquid, like evil honey, leaked from the tip of the swelling black nipple. A most alien shape emerged from the end of the stygian teat—a twig-like protrusion, about two inches long, black and shiny with tiny barbs along the length of it.

Ari's eyes ached from opening so wide, unable to close. Then, another shape just like the first emerged, and then another. These strange black sticks then bent themselves around the end of the sickly tit and pushed against it, helping out another form. A long, black wormy appendage birthed from the diseased breast. It was followed by a thorax, a head, and finally… Ari's very breath pained her as she identified the shape emerging from the necrotic nipple. It was a dragonfly.

A pang of nausea rushed from her gut. She retched in her mouth, but more peripheral movement lassoed her gaze again. The right breast was moving, now. The whole damn thing started to percolate, then the left one rejoined it in a accursed rumba. The revelation was too much to bear: both breasts were rotting sacks full of feeding insects. Ari gasped out loud.

Caroline abruptly stopped and shot up her hand to signal the others. They all froze. She looked around. They had remained unnoticed by the ghouls. They were safe for the moment. Glancing at the crone to her left, she identified the cause of Ari's vociferation.

"It's terrible, I know." She whispered over her shoulder. "But you have to reel it in. It only gets worse."

Ari nodded in agreement, still covering her mouth.

Caroline motioned for them to continue. She hadn't taken half a step before she was shocked by what loomed directly before her. Her hand shot up again, as fast as she could move it, but it was too sudden. Ari banged into her, Stuey crashed into Ari, Villy knocked into Stuey, and Aleister's head was mashed in the melee, as evidenced by some muffled curse from within the bag. Barely ten feet in front of her stood one of those undead crone ghouls. Caroline stood motionless, wondering if it were aware of their presence. The blind thing craned its decomposing head toward the sky and sniffed the air as if sensing someone was near. Caroline held her ground, left arm outstretched with the amulet before her, right arm out to her side to keep the others behind her. The beast sniffed to the right, sniffed to the left… then seemed to lose interest, turning toward the forest.

Caroline signaled that it was okay to continue forward. Slowly and cautiously they proceeded past the loathsome creature. One wary step forward, then another. Like molasses, they crept across the field.

They had just about passed the thing that had nearly discovered them before when—

"*BEEEP! BEEEP! BEEEP! BEEEP!*"

Everyone jumped.

"Oh my God! My phone! Oh my God! Oh my God!" gasped Stuey as he fumbled through his pockets.

"*BEEEP! BEEEP! BEEEP! BEEEP!*"

Ghouls all around them were immediately aroused. They fondled the air with outstretched arms.

"*BEEEP! BEEEP! BEEEP! BEEEP!*"

Villy lashed out in angry surprise. "Your phone *works*?" he yelled at Stuey.

The boy haplessly shrugged.

"Turn that damn thing off!" yelled Caroline.

"*BEEEP! BEEEP! BEEEP! BEEEP!*"

Ghouls were turning toward them.

"Give me the fuckin' phone!" demanded Villy.

In a manic panic to retrieve his phone, Stuey crammed his chubby hand deeper into his pocket.

"*BEEEP! BEEEP! BEEEP! BEEEP!*"

Stuey looked up to see the undead Pilgrim man emerge from the darkness of the trees into the moonlit clearing. He raised his skeletal arm and pointed with his bony finger at the source of the commotion.

"*BEEEP! BEEEP! BEEEP! BEEEP!*"

"Give me the phone!" screamed Villy.

"I can't," whined Stuey. "My hand's stuck!"

"Jesus!" Villy wrapped his hands around Stuey's arm to dislodge the plump extremity.

"*BEEEP! BEEEP! BEEEP! BEEEP!*"

The Pilgrim man, throwing back his skull-like head, opened his black maw and released a bone-shaking battle cry. The ghouls turned toward Caroline and the gang.

"We have to run!" she cried.

Villy yanked one last time and jerked the boy's arm so hard his plump appendage finally burst from his pants. But the force was too great. The phone blasted out of his sweaty grip and flew through the air toward the cabin behind them. It landed in the moist grass about thirty feet away.

"Come on!" yelled Caroline. "We have to go!"

Villy ignored her, running, instead, toward the hurled cell phone.

"Villy!"

She turned to Stuey and motioned for him to join her, but Stuey's loyalty to Villy was too great. He shook his head and ran after his hero. Caroline threw her right arm around Ari, and the two women sped across the clearing, weaving through the ghouls.

Stuey found Villy kneeling in the grass, frantically pushing buttons on the cell phone.

"Why didn't you tell me your phone worked?" demanded Villy.

"It doesn't," insisted Stuey. "That was my alarm!"

"What the hell are you setting an alarm for?"

Stuey shrugged his shoulders, taking the phone from Villy and sliding it into his back pocket. "It was from yesterday."

A terrible sound rang out across the clearing. They looked up, and there, at the edge of the trees, back by the cabin, was the Pilgrim man. He was pointing directly at them, howling louder than before.

"It's the Governor!" yelped Stuey.

"Come on, let's get out of here!" said Villy.

They turned and ran straight into the chest of another hellish ghoul. The Gothrocker and teen stumbled backward from the blow. This particular *thing* was bigger than the other creatures, towering

over Villy. Its head and limbs were less human, more beast-like than the others, as if centuries in Hell had contorted it beyond recognition. They stood frozen for a moment, in awe of the monster's hideousness. Then, the creature cranked its head to the side, wrenched its contorted jaws open and roared at the dazed men.

Without thinking, instinct kicked in and Villy lunged forward, spearing the beast in the gut with the metal tip of his umbrella. The abomination recoiled in agony, throwing its head skyward and yowling into the night.

"Villy, watch out!" yelled Stuey.

Villy spun around to find two ghouls hobbling toward him, their filthy, necrotic fingertips reaching for his face. He flipped the umbrella, holding it by the lower portion like a baseball bat, and with a mighty swing he bashed the heavy, wooden handle into one ghoul's skull. There was a loud *crack,* and black ooze spurted from the pasty, white cranium like a fountain of squid ink. He spun the umbrella again, until he held it like a rifle, left hand cradling the body, right hand firmly gripping the handle.

He lunged toward the other ghoul and, in midflight, shot the sharp, glistening metal tip of the umbrella deep into the horrified creature's chest. Taking one big step backward, he retreated, sliding the umbrella out of the monster's chest and leaving it to wail desperately into the night.

Stuey stood in awe. If he hadn't already worshipped this man, this moment would have sent him completely over the moon. It was one thing for Villy to be a rock star, but now he was a savior, samurai, ninja, and swordsman as well. The events of this night had been nothing short of a nightmare and yet, somehow, the fact that he was experiencing them side by side with his idol made them all worth while.

"Wow!"

Villy turned to him. "Stuey, behind you!"

Stuey spun around, and there, shambling toward him, was a being so putrid, ancient, and decayed that it was impossible to discern its sex. Stuey froze again in horror.

"Hit him with the spade!" yelled Villy.

Stuey didn't budge. The creature continued to spasm toward him on broken legs, reaching out, moaning desperately.

"Whack him with the spade!"

Villy gripped his umbrella like an axe and was prepared to jump to Stuey's defense when a disconcerting groan wormed its way into his ear. He glanced over his shoulder to find Ari's horrifying, rotten hag with the bug-filled breasts approaching rapidly.

"Stuey!" He screamed at the boy again before turning to deal with the trouble at hand.

Stuey finally snapped out of his trance without a second to spare. The wiry beast was practically on top of him. He gripped the spade with two hands and smacked the ghoul in the face with it, but the monster was too close for the blow to do any harm. Besides making a reverberating *ping*, the attack only enraged the thing further. The monstrosity took a step back, stretched its drooling mouth into an impossible chasm and projected such a ferocious shriek that it covered Stuey's whole face with rancid bile. Stuey let go of the spade and dropped to his knees.

The monster lunged forward, but its talons found no victim. Stuey knelt on the ground, rubbing his burning eyes as the beast scanned the air before him, wondering where his prey had disappeared to.

"What going on out there?" demanded Aleister's head from within the bag.

The emaciated corpse heard him, but couldn't figure out where the voice was coming from. It spun around and around with arms outstretched, looking everywhere but at its feet, where they actually were.

"What's happening?" called Aleister. "I wanna see!"

"Shut up, you idiot!" whispered Stuey.

He rubbed most of the stinging demon goo from his eyes and looked for the monster that had nearly killed him. It had wandered a yard or so away and was still blindly and futilely searching for him. Satisfied for now, he checked over his shoulder for Villy.

Villy was engaged in a dance macabre with the obese, bug-filled hag. Fighting this porcine, undead crone was more challenging than the rest. There was more of her, for starters, and he found it difficult to cause a fatal, or at least damaging, injury. Thus far, he'd stabbed her twice in the belly and, other than calling forth small streams of black ooze, it seemed to have little to no effect. She was also harder to get around, so that every time she lunged forward he had really no recourse but to move backward. Her body consisted of heaping masses of fetid flesh on her frame, collected mostly in putrid rolls around her midsection, legs, and upper arms. There was only *one* area where the hanging meat was stretched so thin it was downright bony. And that was the area around her sternum.

That's when it dawned on him—one strike to the heart should do it. He danced to get in the right position. He took one step to the left, but so did she. This caused him to take a step to the right, and annoyingly, she followed suit. They carried on in this ballroom dance of bedlam for longer than seemed reasonable. Then, he heard again, that low, guttural howl like a cursed clarion call.

Villy turned. The Governor was marching across the field toward them, ghouls in tow. As he walked, more ghouls joined their numbers as if drawn to him.

"Oh, fuck it!" spat Villy, thrusting his umbrella in the general direction of the hag's heart.

He missed. The metal tip of his weapon pierced the bulbous center of her left breast, plunging into her ribcage. The anguished howl she emitted was an ear-piercing shriek: shrill, sharp, and unbearable, like a bouquet of glass shards run along a mile of chalkboard. He tried to pull his umbrella from her chest, but it wouldn't budge. She stumbled backward, pulling him toward her. The fear of falling on top of her was sobering, so Villy struggled to regain his balance. He tugged again on the umbrella, but it was stubbornly lodged between her ribs. There was, however, strange movement all around the point of entry. Villy's eyes narrowed as he focused on the weird phenomenon. Her breast seemed to be disintegrating, but it wasn't. It was being torn from the inside out.

All of a sudden, a small black bug emerged and ran up the length of the umbrella. He let go in a panic and swatted it to the ground. Another emerged, and then another. They ran along the length of the umbrella, covering it faster than a colony of termites overtaking a rotting log. Her breast erupted, and a swarm of black arthropods burst from the tarry, black wound, running in all directions over her pale flesh. She screeched and floundered, waving her arms, and weaving from side to side, until finally, she came crashing down on her back with a tremendous, resounding *thud*.

The impact must have startled the insects because they took to the air, and suddenly, Villy's head was in the midst of a swarm. He swatted the space around him helplessly. "Jesus Christ!"

"What the hell's going on out there?" demanded Aleister's head from inside the bag.

"I told you to be quiet!" scolded Stuey in a loud whisper. He wrapped his arms around the messenger bag to muffle Aleister's voice. "You're going to get us all killed!"

"Hey!" yelled Aleister. "What are you doing, shit-for-brains? You're going to smother me!"

"I said 'shut up'!" commanded Stuey, putting his chest and belly on top of the bag to drown out the cries as best as he could.

It was too late. The emaciated corpse zeroed in on their voices. It was behind them, only six feet away, and now knew exactly where they were.

There was a loud rustling in the trees. As the swarm around his head dissipated, Villy saw more pasty ghouls emerging from the forest not far from their position, joining the ranks behind the advancing Governor. They were getting closer.

"Stuey!" Villy called out.

He turned to see Stuey lying on the ground facing away from him. Between them was the skeletal ghoul, its murderous hands inches from Stuey's neck. Villy sprang through the air with two big leaps and pushed the creature as hard as he could. The monster tripped over Stuey's stocky frame and crashed to the ground in front of the boy. Stuey was speechless as it wriggled on its back, like an overturned tortoise, unable to right itself. Villy picked up the spade from the grass. He stepped over Stuey and positioned himself over the ghoul's body. The creature seemed to stare up pathetically with giant black eyes as Villy placed the edge of the metal spade on its pale throat, his boot on the back edge. The monster swallowed a mouthful of bile. Villy could feel the spade rise and dip below his foot. His disgust urged him on.

He tightened his grip and rammed it downward, simultaneously stomping on the spade with all of his body weight. There was a sickly crunching, and a voluminous spurt of black goo, as the hideous head was severed. Stuey jumped to his feet as the head rolled in a big circle on the grass, headed right for him. The messenger bag, no longer smothered by the boy's belly, fell over, and out flopped Aleister's head. The circular path being traveled by the ghoul's severed head came to a sudden stop, halted by none other than Aleister's face. The two heads lay nose to nose in the grass.

Aleister looked into the sightless, black eyes of the monster. "I feel ya, bro."

"Jesus Christ!" exclaimed Villy. He yanked Aleister's head off the grass by his greasy black hair and shoved him back into the messenger bag.

"Hey!" protested Aleister.

Whatever he said next was drowned out by the inhuman groans of the approaching Governor. Villy looked up at the advancing contingent of the broken dead.

"We have to get out of here." Villy handed Stuey the messenger bag. "Come on!"

Stuey threw the bag over his shoulder and turned to retrieve the spade. It stuck out of the ground like a cactus growing from the corpse's throat. The teen danced tentatively over the ghoul's body, trying to get his footing. He placed his hands on the handle of the spade and gave it a tug. It didn't move, firmly stuck in the cold soil. The left hand of the ghoul twitched, causing Stuey to jerk back, throwing his hands off of the spade's handle. Villy's eyes darted around them at the oncoming horde undead. "Just leave it!"

Together, they turned and ran across the field. They sprinted as fast as they could across the grassy expanse, weaving around the occasional ghoul. There seemed to be fewer of them now. Villy glanced over his shoulder and saw why— the Governor was surrounded by them. These monstrous, and otherwise mindless, beings, seemed attracted to him, seemed to have purpose around him, as if they telepathically knew what he wanted. He had amassed a troop of them, about two dozen strong, and they were steadily approaching Villy and Stuey.

Turning and looking ahead, Villy's eyes fell upon a decidedly more pleasant, if unexpected, sight. Caroline and Ari were waiting for them at the end of the clearing. He thought he had lost them to the darkness of the forest. Villy and Stuey reached the women and came to a sudden stop. Clouds fumed from their mouths as they furiously breathed in and out, trying to catch their breath. Finally, Villy found the air to speak.

"We thought we'd…"

"*Shhh*." Caroline raised a finger to her lips. "Listen."

They all trained their ears on the darkness around them, but Villy and Stuey could hear nothing more than their own labored breathing.

Stuey took a deep breath, let it out, then began, "I don't hear…"

"Listen." Caroline pointed to the sky.

They all tilted their heads, directing their ears skyward. That was when they heard it. From the distance came the sound of great, leathery wings flapping. "You know what *that* is?" she asked the group.

"I have a pretty good idea." Villy frowned, turning his eyes upward.

Caroline took a few steps closer to the edge of the trees and listened intently for any telltale sounds of the flying devil, or other undead menaces, approaching. Ari joined her. With the shock starting to dissipate, it was only then that Stuey truly realized just how close he'd come to dying.

"Thanks," he said sheepishly, "I mean, about…"

He gestured like a hitchhiker over his shoulder to the site of the skirmish. Villy placed a hand on the boys shoulder and nodded. "That was *crazy*."

In a flash, Stuey's face lit up again as he rewitnessed Villy's heroics in his mind. "You were amazing back there! Where'd you learn those moves, man? You were all, like…" He karate-chopped the air around him. "*Kya! Whooo! Ka! Ho!*"

"*Shhh!*" demanded Caroline from the edge of the forest.

Stuey lowered his voice. He brought his hands together as if in prayer, and bowed while continuing in a faux-Chinese accent, "Yo zombie ass no match fo mai umbrella style!"

Villy smiled.

Stuey was beaming. This was possibly the most exciting moment of his entire life, and the fact that he'd shared it with his idol made him want to explode. He tried to relive it all again in his mind, trying to recall every detail—Villy lunging with his umbrella, the way he spun it in his hand like a master Jedi, the way he decapitated the monster with that spade. The spade… something didn't sit right inside of Stuey when he thought of the spade. His mind reached further back, and he saw himself standing there, holding the spade in front of him. He was frozen in fear, and a wave of shame washed through him. The smile melted from his face. He looked up at Villy.

"I'm sorry about, you know, the way I…"

Villy looked at him with a confused expression.

"The monster… I wanted to hit him, but…"

Villy raised a hand to stop him but was interrupted.

"Hey! Come on, let me out," yelled a voice from within Stuey's bag. "I can't breathe in here!"

Stuey pulled Aleister's head out of the bag.

"Come on, man. I agreed to help you," explained Stuey, "but you have to keep quiet."

Aleister's features contorted as he obnoxiously sang, "Well, *excuse* me!"

Just then, the severed head saw something noteworthy across the clearing—his headless body lumbering. The sightless corpse was facing away, feeling the trees at the periphery of the clearing.

"Hey!" Aleister's head screamed. "Over here! Turn around, dummy!" He narrowed his eyes. "Jeez, why didn't anyone tell me my ass was so fat?"

Villy shot Aleister's head a fiery glare. "Do you ever shut the fuck up?"

Caroline spun around angrily. "Keep it down! What's wrong with you guys?"

Ari's eyes were fixed on the sky. The sound of flapping was getting louder. Aleister paid no mind to them. He clearly had bigger fish to fry.

"Follow the sound of my voice, you moron!" He yelled as loudly as he could at his wayward body. "Relish your master's voice!"

Ari spun in place, frantically trying to find the source of the flapping sounds. So did Caroline. It was louder than ever, really close, but they could not zero in on its source.

"Come on, neck-face!" screamed Aleister. "Over here!"

The sound of flapping wings changed. It was now the *swoosh* of rushing air, like a jet soaring, or a waterfall. Aleister looked up. "Oh shit."

Everyone turned toward him, but it was too late. In a blur, the airborne thing swept down before their eyes and yanked Stuey from the ground and into the darkness of the sky. They all cried out.

"Stuey!" Ari called desperately.

"Oh my God, Stuey!" Villy yelled into the night sky.

Villy, Ari, and Caroline spun with their heads thrown back, searching the starless sky for their friend. There was a loud *cracking*, like a sack of bones being crushed by a garbage truck, and they barely had time to cringe as a shower of blood rained down on their faces. They howled in dismay. A second later, Stuey's body tumbled from the sky and hit the ground with a resounding thud. They wiped the blood from their eyes and ran to their friend. Villy knelt before his broken body and carefully took Stuey's hand in his.

Thop!

Startled, they turned to the left. A few feet away, Aleister's head had hit the ground, and now bounced twice before coming to a stop in the grass. "*Ow*! That's going to leave a mark."

No one paid him any mind.

Villy looked down at the teen before him. "Stuey," said Villy earnestly. "Can you hear me?"

He held the boy's hand with both of his. His heart sank. Stuey's hand was cold and heavy, and as gently as he held it, he could feel through the flesh the rasping vibrations of broken bones rubbing against broken bones. It sent a sickening tingle through his intestines. Villy gingerly lowered the hand to Stuey's chest and softly placed his palms on the boy's heart.

"Stuey." He whispered.

The boy stirred. Villy and Ari and Caroline perked up. He turned his head laboriously toward his hero. Stuey wheezed through his broken body. "I'm sorry."

Villy's eyebrows wrinkled.

"I'm sorry... I wasn't more... brave for you."

Villy shook his head from side to side once, twice, and then again and again, more and more violently. "No! No, no, no! Don't say that!"

Villy's eyes welled up with tears. He desperately tried to gather his thoughts, to find the words to tell this young man how much he admired him, how much he liked him, how his brilliance and optimism had helped Villy overcome his own cynicism, his own failings and, more importantly, despite all of the madness, how he had truly enjoyed meeting him, truly enjoyed sharing the boy's company. He never got to. All the life dissipated from Stuey's face. His head collapsed to the ground, falling away from Villy's gaze with a dull thud.

"Bummer," said Aleister's head. "Oh well, another one down, only three to go."

That was *it*. Villy could bear no more. He leapt to his feet, marched over to Aleister's head, and snatched it up.

"Whoa! What are you doing?" cried Aleister. "Don't be rash, now!"

All of the hate and hurt and anguish that Villy had ever felt in his whole life rushed like a red-hot serpent of blood inside of him. He gripped the noxious head in his fists so hard he was pulling the hair out by its roots. Pure venom shot out of Villy as he growled through clenched teeth. "I hate you so fuckin' much."

"Hey! Hey! Wait!" blubbered Aleister.

Villy let go of the head and drop-kicked the fleshy block as hard and as far as he could. It soared, yelling all the way into the blackness of the forest. Villy felt only minor relief. He stood there, head down, fuming, marinating in his anger. Then, a growl called to him. He turned to see the army of pasty ghouls, black tarry mouths agape, reaching with hungry fingers. The Governor, in their midst, held out a skeletal digit, seemingly pointing right at Villy.

"Come on!" shouted Caroline. "We have to go!"

Villy stood his ground. At that moment, so much rage coursed through him that he thought he could tear every one of those monsters to shreds.

"Villy!" yelled Caroline.

Caroline put her arm around Ari and the two started to back away. Villy knew he had to join them. Begrudgingly, he turned his back on the advancing Governor and his battalion of abominations. Villy, Caroline, and Ari managed one step of retreat.

Blam!

Directly in front of them, the Jersey Devil landed with a rumbling crash. They gasped. It flapped its leathery wings and stepped from side to side, shifting its weight, examining them with glimmering black eyes. It seemed so much bigger now than when they'd seen it atop the cabin. Bony shoulders taller than their heads, it had to lean over to bare its rows of razor-sharp teeth—each long enough to skewer a human skull.

Caroline, Villy, and Ari crept a step backward. The anguished moans of the ghoul army behind them were getting louder, seeming less like laments and more like deranged cries of hunger. They took half a step forward. Before them, the winged devil reared its horn-covered head and, with its snake-like neck, whipped forward. It *screeched* the most berserk cry ever issued by any beast in Heaven or Hell.

The three were surrounded.

"Into the woods!" Caroline led the way.

Chapter 14

With the Jersey Devil in front of them, and an undead Governor leading an army of flesh-starved ghouls behind them, there was little left for Caroline, Villy, and Ari to do but run. At Caroline's command, they bolted for the trees.

A mighty wind pushed them onward as the Jersey Devil flapped its wings. The ground trembled as he leapt into the air after them. He wasn't the only one angered by their sudden departure—a loud, unearthly howl echoed through the clearing as the Governor opened up his throat and released an enraged call to arms.

Flap. Flap. Flap.

Heavy wings carried the Jersey Devil higher and higher. Caroline, Villy, and Ari ran, faster than they thought possible. There was a sickening silence as the monster turned in the air and pointed earthbound.

They ran faster. As before, the next sound was the howling of wind as the beast nose-dived toward the three running morsels. The trees were right before them. Jumping over brush and clawing through scratching branches, they leapt into safety, crossing the border of the clearing into the haven of the woods.

The flying demon wailed like an immolated banshee. A hurricane-force wind swept through the forest, blowing sand and twigs and thick clouds of leaves as the Jersey Devil stopped short of the trees. Frustrated by the narrow spaces between the pines, it hovered for a moment, flapping and shrieking in rage, before bursting into the sky once again. As Caroline, Villy, and Ari caught their breath in the safety of the woods, they could hear the thing flying over the treetops, screeching.

"He can't get us in here," said Villy. "He's too big."

"That may be true," countered Caroline, "but *they* aren't." She pointed toward the ghouls in the clearing.

Ari took a step toward the edge of the forest and using a tree for cover, peeked at the throngs of undead souls. "They're not following us!"

Caroline joined her by the tree and took a look for herself. "You're right. They're not."

The pallid monsters were hobbling and slithering out of the clearing. They fanned out, each disappearing at a different spot into the woods, away from the big oval of grassy expanse.

Caroline narrowed her eyes. "But I think I know what they're up to."

Villy finally caught his breath. "And that is?"

"They are going to try to beat us to the barn."

"What barn?"

"The gateway to Hell... it's in a barn."

Villy rolled his eyes.

She knew that it all sounded a bit strange. "Witchcraft, especially hundreds of years ago, has never been something you could perform out in the open, at least not without getting ostracized, at best, or burned at the stake, like my ancestor. She had a barn where she practiced her black magic, and it was there that she opened this damned gateway to Hell. You know the rest. Every so often, the gateway opens, and I have to schlep down there and see that it gets closed before all Hell breaks loose."

"Why don't you just burn down the barn?" asked Villy.

"Because that would only serve to burn down the structure itself. The gateway would remain untouched. Besides, it's much easier to spot a building than a tiny fissure in space. A giant, red barn is a damn good landmark. Better than coming down here with a sextant and a compass, you know what I mean? Although, truth be told, this amulet..."

She reached for the bauble around her neck. Her hand came up empty.

"Goddamn it, I dropped the amulet!"

She scanned the ground around her. She knew she wouldn't find it at her feet. She had felt an uneasy feeling while running across the clearing. She didn't know what it was then, perhaps because she was busy running for her life and trying not to be eaten by a winged devil. But she knew now—and that's where she would find her amulet.

"I'll be right back," she told Villy.

He opened his mouth to protest, but never got a chance.

Caroline pointed to Ari, who was sitting on a log a few yards away. "Keep an eye on her," she whispered sternly. "Don't take your eyes off of her."

"Okay. Okay," answered Villy.

Caroline spun around, and with a couple of hops, she was through the trees and out of the forest.

Villy looked to his right. Ari sat on the log with her head bowed, all of her fingers pressed gently to her lips. She was deep in thought, distraught. He considered joining her, consoling her. But he knew that wouldn't help. He'd never quite learned how to express sympathy for others. Maybe he *had* none. He wasn't sure, but he knew he wasn't good at it. He never *could* find the right words to offer condolences that didn't sound phony, hackneyed or preconceived to him. Thus, in cases like this, he usually opted to say nothing. He assumed she was thinking about Stuey. He was, too. He didn't even know the boy, but still he was in shock, in disbelief that Stuey was dead. It all seemed so unreal. And his last words... It tore him up inside knowing that the boy died apologizing to *him*, feeling unfit, unworthy. If only he had had another chance, just another day or hour or even minute to tell Stuey... to reassure him... of what? As Villy stood there, he couldn't even find the words to formulate what he could have said to Stuey, and he wondered if he ever would, even in a multitude of eternities. "You're worthy of me"? "Of all of my fans, you are the greatest"? It all sounded completely preposterous to him. Maybe because, somewhere deep inside, Villy had accepted that he didn't *have* any fans—maybe he didn't deserve to.

He looked into the woods and tried to imagine which way it was to the barn. He looked back at Ari. She seemed okay by herself on the log. He looked to the left. It seemed the trees got thinner up the hill, and there appeared to be a reddish glow in the sky. *That must be the way*, he thought. He took a few steps up the hill for a better look. The ground was sandy and covered in wet leaves, twigs, and branches. Taking another step, his foot came down on a thick, rotten branch that gave beneath his boot. He placed his hand on a thick pine for support. His pale hand shone brightly in a puddle of moonlight that fell on the sappy bark.

In the moonbeam, he noticed the blood—Stuey's blood. His white hand was caked in it. He found it most upsetting to have not just any blood on his hands, but Stuey's blood, the blood of someone he had just seen die. He wiped his hands on his shirt, but the blood was dry. He held his hands out before him to try and catch a pool of moonlight, the better to see it in. Finding a patch, he rotated his hands and rubbed each with the thumb of the other as if washing them in liquid light. The blood would not come off. He scrubbed them on his black pants, then threw his hands back into the light. There was no change. Once more, he rubbed them violently on his legs, trying to keep his balance on the moist, uneven ground. No change. The leaves squishing moistly underfoot gave him an idea—he'd wash his hands with fallen rain and mud. He bent to grab some wet leaves off the ground.

"What are you looking at, asswipe?" snarled a pale, dead face in the muck. It was Aleister's head.

"Oh my God, really? Are you fuckin' kidding me?" Villy was startled. The shock made him embarrassed, and the embarrassment fueled his rage. "Why won't you die already?"

"I'm already dead, dickweed. And you're going to die, too. It's so obvious. Why don't you just embrace it? Think about it; you could live forever in Hell. You could rule there and be famous and have millions of hot devil-chick fans!"

"That's bullshit!" It didn't stop Villy from listening to Aleister's pitch.

"What's so great about being alive anyway?" asked the pale, severed head. "What are you living for? To *maybe* play a Goth festival for five mallrats in the woods of New Jersey?" He laughed heartily. "It's fuckin' pathetic."

"Shut up!" snarled Villy.

Aleister smirked. "You're going to Hell one way or the other, buddy." He stopped smiling. "The washed-up, has-been circle of Hell. How do you like that? Huh?"

Villy had enough. He looked around and set his eyes on the biggest rock he could find in the muck. With both hands, he dislodged it from the soil and held it over Aleister's disembodied head. Aleister's eyes widened.

"Don't you fuckin' dar…"

Villy smashed the heavy boulder down onto Aleister's head. There was a loud crunching. Then, silence. Villy stood and brushed off his hands.

"Who's a has-been now, asshole?"

Ari sat on the log, deep in thought. She thought about her friend, Stuey. He had texted her to come on this crazy misadventure. If she hadn't agreed, he'd still be alive. Her having access to a car was the only way they had all reached the Pine Barrens. The more she thought about it, the more she realized that it was her fault that he was dead—not just him, but AJ and Prudence and, well, Aleister, too.

What made it even worse was *why* she'd agreed to take them. It had little to do with wanting to see her friend. The second anniversary of her father's death was a week away, and if this year was going to be anything like the last, she simply didn't think she could handle it. Her mother hadn't been the same since his death, and while most of the time the two got along, the anniversary of her father's death seemed to take things back to how they were right after he died. That meant lots of arguments, disagreements, punishments, yelling, screaming, name-calling, and hatefulness. However much her mother claimed it had nothing to do with her father's death, Ari knew otherwise. The simple fact was, her mother had never forgiven her for missing her father's dying words, and some part of her would forever hate her daughter for it.

As of a week earlier, the arguments had begun. It started with little things like, "Clean up your room. It's filthy!" and, "It was extremely inconsiderate of you to eat the *last* slice of pie!" In the last few days, however, it had escalated to, "When do you think you might get your own place?" and, "You are an irresponsible and selfish human being!" and most recently, "No man will ever love you!" But by far, the worst agony she had endured was what remained unsaid. Just one day earlier, while having breakfast, Ari had suddenly noticed a heavy silence in the room. She'd felt a fiery stare burning into the back of her neck. Upon turning around, she'd seen her mother in the doorway—just looking at her. The look on her face had not been the look a mother has for a daughter; it had been the look a mother has for her daughter's rapist or her daughter's killer. It had taken a moment before her mother had even realized that Ari was staring back at her. Then, she had just shaken her head and stormed off. She hadn't even tried to explain it or cover it up.

Ari's heart was so heavy with sorrow; it felt like it might fall to the ground and burst. She knew that, once the month passed, things would gradually go back to the more or less quiet monotony that she'd grown accustomed to. This week, however, Ari had been feeling particularly fragile, and she simply couldn't endure another moment of being loathed, or even slightly resented, by her own mother. When she received that fated text from Stuey, she felt freed from a prison. She suddenly had a reason to get out of the house, to get away from the hateful glares of her own mother. She communicated to her mother that a friend's car had broken down, stranding them, and they had needed a ride home. Under normal circumstances, her mother might have been skeptical, might have wanted more information. But she didn't, because, in truth, Ari knew her mother wanted Ari gone as much as she wanted to leave. Ari knew it, and it crushed her heart.

Ari went on to imagining what her father's last words might have been, as she had done nearly every day for the past two years. "Tell your mother I love her," or, "Please don't cry, I've had a wonderful life," or, "The money is hidden under the floorboards."

Just then, her daydreams were interrupted by a sound in the forest. It sounded like a voice. Ari rose from the log. She stared into the darkness between the trees. There was nothing there, nothing she could see. About ready to sit back down, she heard the noise again. It *was* indeed a voice—but she couldn't make out what it was saying.

She looked around her. Villy stood off to her left, up the hill a ways. It didn't seem to be coming from him. Straining her eyes and ears, Ari leaned forward, as if doing so would help penetrate the darkness of the forest. She heard it again, and this time she could make out what it said—the voice whispered *her name*.

A shiver rattled through her body from her scalp, down her neck, down the backs of her arms—where goose pimples formed and hairs stood on end—all of the way down to her knees. She looked over her shoulder again at Villy to make sure it wasn't him. He was staring off into the red sky. The voice came again.

"*Aaarrriii*," it cried, like a distant whisper.

"Who's there?" she asked.

There was no reply.

"Who's there?"

Out of the darkness, the voice came again. "*Aaarrriii.*" It sighed with a tremendous longing, as though the voice were calling to her from far away, desperate to reach her.

"Who is it?" she called out.

She looked again at Villy. He was motionless, as if in a trance. She heard a crackling in the woods. She turned again to face the darkness.

"Who's there?" she demanded.

From the opaque blackness, a shape appeared. It was pale and white, ghostlike and hard to grasp. She squinted her eyes and tried to pry the image out of the darkness.

"*Aaarrriii,*" it called.

"Who are you?" Her voice sounded more and more desperate.

Finally, the figure stumbled from the darkness. It was a tallish man. His arms and legs were bare, his face not unappealing. He had slick, black hair combed to one side, and he wore thick, black horn-rimmed glasses. He stood about ten feet away, clad in a ghostly hospital gown.

"Papa!" called Ari, half-crying.

He spoke faintly, his words weaving in and out of reality so that only some were completely audible. "Ari, there is… much I… tell you…" His translucent image faded in and out with the words.

"I can't hear you!" Ari felt tears catching her voice.

"That day… hospital, when… I… your mother… *whriyyynrrr… gaaahhhh…*"

His words droned and deformed, becoming more garbled and impossible to understand. At times, his mouth moved, but no words could be heard at all.

"Papa, I can't hear you."

Ari wanted to run into his arms, but trepidation kept her stuck where she stood.

"*Cooome cloooserrr.*" He offered his arms in a loving embrace. "*ThereiissSomethiiingIeeeWishhh-ToooTelllYouu…*"

Ari took a tentative step forward.

"*Cooommme clooossserrr,*" he beckoned.

Villy stared off into the red sky, stewing in his own juices. He hated Aleister with a passion, but somewhere deep inside, he knew the hatred was born of something else. All of the insults uttered by that wretched creature were things he'd heard before. Not from another human being—no one had ever dared be that bold… or honest. They were things he'd heard in his own head, things his subconscious whispered to him in his most vulnerable moments. He hated Aleister because he feared he was right. But Aleister was dead now—really dead—and knowing he'd never hear that voice again awarded Villy a surprising sense of calm.

He took a deep breath and let it out, filling the chill air in front of him with wispy, white clouds. They dissipated, revealing the crimson sky beyond. He gazed into the distance and wondered what lay beyond the trees and over the hill. His eyes had seen things that night he could never have imagined existed. From what Caroline suggested, this was just the tip of the iceberg. What maddening horrors resided just beyond his sight? What monstrosities would he witness in that barn that housed the gateway to Hell? He tried to imagine the worst of what awaited him by digging through his worst memories, conjuring up the most horrible concepts his imagination could birth. It wasn't out of morbid curiosity; it was out of fear and self-preservation. Somewhere inside, he feared he would not be able to bear much more. He feared he was close to buckling and that, at any moment, he might lose his resolve. He might just cut and run. If he could catch at least a glance of what awaited him, maybe he'd be able to prime himself, to be strong for Ari and for Caroline.

His ears were suddenly invaded by the crunching of branches underfoot.

"Got it!" Caroline declared as she returned.

She victoriously held before her the gleaming amulet. Villy reassured her *and himself* with a nod of his head. Caroline glanced off to her right, and instantly the hopeful expression on her face gave way to a look of anger. The log upon which Ari had been sitting was vacant.

"Where's Ari?" she snarled. "What did I tell you?"

Villy and Caroline scanned the woods.

"Relax," sighed Villy. "She's right there." He pointed to a dark clearing just beyond the trees to their right.

There, in the darkness, stood Ari, stoically, stiffly, staring into the black void.

Where Villy and Caroline saw only darkness, Ari saw something else.

"*Cooommme cloooserrr,*" begged Ari's father.

His face was friendly and inviting. He held his pale arms out to greet her. Still, she moved tentatively, inching ever so slowly forward. Then, he melted her apprehension.

"*My little babushka,*" he sighed.

It *was* him—now she knew it for sure. She'd heard him say it thousands of times throughout her childhood. She'd hardly noticed the absence of those words from her life, but now, hearing them again after so long, it was like a rush of cool water through a dried river bed, the first rain after a long, agonizing drought.

Suddenly, a hand came down on her shoulder. Villy spoke, "Come on, we have to get going."

Ari spun around, startled. "No, I have to go…" Even as the words were coming out of her mouth, she realized they didn't convey exactly what she meant. "Look!" She pointed just ahead of her. A smile stretched across her face. "It's my father! He's calling me."

Villy looked in the direction in which she pointed. "There's no one there." His grip tightened on her shoulder.

"I have to go! Let go of me!" she cried.

"*Babuuushkaaa…*" Ari's father called.

Ari broke free of Villy's grasp. She spun around and leapt through the air, throwing herself into her father's arms. Tears poured down her face as she felt his strong and gentle arms cradling her, the softness of his warm chest surrounding her face.

"I missed you so much, Papa!" she cried.

Caroline stormed up the wet, leafy hill with a purpose. Villy turned to her. He opened his mouth but never got to speak.

"Ari!" screamed Caroline.

Villy turned back towards Ari to find the girl engulfed in the grip of a monstrous ghoul with long, pale arms and tattered clothes. A tall, black hat sat upon its gaunt, skeletal head. As if from thin air, the Governor had appeared, and he had the young girl in his rigor mortis grip.

"Villy, grab her!" belted Caroline.

The Governor turned to Villy, opened his black maw, and let out a sickening growl. Black, tarry goo drooled down his chin and onto Ari's pale cheek. The girl was oblivious. She smiled contently, nestling her head in the rotten, bony chest, blissfully unaware that what she clung so desperately to was the leader of the undead ghouls.

In one only semi-conscious motion, Villy grabbed the girl and, as hard as he could, yanked her from the grip of the demon. The undead Pilgrim threw his head back and, squalid tongue quivering, howled with rage into the treetops.

"This way!" yelled Caroline.

The two adults ran through the forest, jumping over rotten logs and weaving through the trees, dragging the near-unconscious Ari behind them. The Governor lumbered after them, as did other pasty ghouls who appeared from the darkness. Villy dragged Ari by her wrist. Her head bobbed from side to side as if she were drugged. She was practically a dead weight behind him, barely moving her legs, stumbling from one step to another. He looked over his shoulder at her.

"You have to pick up the pace!"

Her eyes rolled into the back of her head as he yanked her forward, up and up, toward the top of the densely wooded hill. When they crested the hill, they could see the reddish glow that bled into the sky. The barn was not far away. They could hear the moaning of ghouls in the trees, but there was another sound now. It was a windy howl, like a vacuum cleaner tube being whirled through the air.

Caroline knew time was running out, and there was still a forest of trees and a battalion of monsters ahead of them. She turned to Ari.

"Ari," she said, "are you okay?"

She placed her hands lovingly, but firmly, on the girl's face. Ari's cheeks were clammy and cold. Her eyes were still rolled back into her head.

"Ari!" Caroline gently patted Ari's face. The girl's eyes rolled back down like two balls in a roulette wheel, finally finding their pockets. She was coming around.

"I'm okay." The trance seemed to be fading as her head ceased rocking and rolled to a stop. Then, as if she could finally understand what she had just seen, a wave of emotion filled her eyes. Tears welled and her voice cracked. "I'm okay." She was crying.

"There's a trail just down the way," said Caroline. "Follow me."

Villy and Ari followed Caroline down the other side of the hill. They slipped and slid on wet leaves as they worked their way downward through the trees. Relief soon came in the form of a sandy path through the woods. She motioned to them with her hand, and they followed her down the moonlit trail. "Follow me, and stay really quiet."

The two nodded, and all three proceeded down the dark forest trail, careful not to attract any ghoul's attention.

The path wound through the trees. At times, Villy swore they were trekking down the side of a mountain. At others, the path seemed to level out. More than once, he was convinced they had doubled back and headed in the direction from whence they came. Regardless of his lack of orientation, he trusted Caroline's focus, determination, and confidence.

They were walking along a long, quiet stretch when, suddenly, Caroline's hand shot up. Villy and Ari halted. She turned to them and brought her forefinger to her lips. Her eyes were wide and crazy. She had every ounce of Villy and Ari's attention as, slowly, she turned toward the darkness of the forest and swept out her arm to point into the murk. Villy and Ari's eyes followed. At first they saw nothing, but then their eyes landed on the pale blobs. Caroline gestured for them to step toward her. Clearing the trees, they got a better vantage point—now they could clearly see.

Just a few yards ahead of them, just inside of the dense woods on the other side of the sandy road, three pasty ghouls knelt on the ground voraciously feeding on something. As they tried to sneak by, Caroline, Villy, and Ari watched, trying not to breath. One of the abominations stirred, and the three stiffened. The monster got onto its haunches, scuttled a couple of feet to its left, and went back to eating. Apparently, it had simply finished the part on which it was feeding and was moving toward fresher flesh. That was when the party saw what was being feasted upon.

Henry Burger, Caroline's nephew.

Villy's hand shot to his mouth just in time to trap the gasp that tried to escape from his lips. He looked at Caroline, expecting to find her sobbing, but instead she was shaking her head solemnly. Her brow furrowed, and she wore the pained expression of someone who would have been deeply hurt if not tempered by decades of exposure to this kind of horror. She signaled for them to continue down the path.

A few steps onward, they saw Henry's duffle bag in the trees, just off the sandy path. No one dared speak, but all moved in for a look. One of the straps had been ripped; one of the things must have grabbed him by it. The zipper was open, and the contents were few but clearly visible. Rope, duct tape, plastic zip ties, and a box of Oreos spilled out from the abandoned bag. Barely visible, tucked behind the Oreos, were a box of rubber gloves and a jar of Vaseline petroleum jelly. Without saying a word, the group moved on.

They walked in a painful silence for what seemed like an eternity. Eventually, they came to a fork in the sandy path. Caroline stopped and faced the others.

"It's down this way. We should be able to follow this trail, then cut through the woods to the field where the barn is. Once I get that doorway closed, we'll be safe. Okay?"

Villy and Ari said, "Okay," practically in unison.

They were about to turn when Villy placed a hand on Caroline's shoulder. "I'm sorry about your nephew."

Caroline closed her eyes and pointed her head toward the heavens. She took a deep breath and let it out. Then, she opened her eyes and fixed them on Villy.

"He kind of had it coming," she said flatly. "He was sort of an asshole."

Villy and Ari were taken aback. They looked at each other uncomfortably. Villy, however, realized, the more he thought about it, "He was *totally* an asshole!"

Caroline wryly smiled.

"Vaseline petroleum jelly?" queried Ari with a raised eyebrow.

"Yeah, and rubber gloves?" added Villy. "And duct tape? Seriously, what the fuck was he planning?"

Chased by flying demons and monstrous ghouls, watching loved ones die before their very eyes, their emotions were a jumble of delicate wooden pieces precariously placed in a leaning tower of Jenga.

Caroline cracked a smile, then a giggle escaped from her lips. Villy couldn't help himself. He burst into laughter, and Ari, too, couldn't control the urge. The three of them laughed out loud at the absurdity of it all. It felt good. It felt *so* good. The laughter massaged lungs, bellies, and insides that had been so rigid, so tense, and so cramped for so long. Villy brought his hands to his face, covered his eyes, and howled with laughter. His ears reverberated with the rising and falling pitches of his own voice, Ari's sweet, little giggles, and Caroline's husky guffaws as well.

Then there was less of Caroline's laugh, and then still less, until there was none at all.

Villy opened his eyes. Caroline stood before him, motionless. She wasn't even smiling. Her face was frozen, mouth slightly ajar.

"Run," she said softly.

"What?" chuckled Villy.

"Run!" cried Caroline.

He whipped his head around to see what held her gaze captive. The Governor stood before them, just off the path. He was steadying himself between two trees with his giant, bony hands, grasping their coarse trunks. He was breathing heavily, in and out, in and out. It was not the kind of panting that comes from being out of breath. It was the furious heaving of rage.

"Run!" Caroline screamed at the top of her lungs.

Villy and Ari and Caroline ran as fast as they could down the sandy trail. The Governor had amassed his horde, and like sickly, white blobs, they were bleeding out of the dark trees onto the path. They came from all directions. They were behind them, next to them and, to the threesome's horror, gathered on the path directly before them, too. There was little time to think. Caroline cut to the left. Villy cut to the right, grabbing Ari's hand and dragging her as they sprang from the sandy path into unbroken forest.

Getting separated from Caroline was not reassuring, but Villy knew it was unavoidable. The least he could do now was stick with Ari.

"Come on! Hurry!" He dragged the girl behind him by the wrist.

"I can't run any faster!" hollered Ari.

That didn't slow Villy down any. If anything, he picked up the pace. Branches swiped at him and Ari, scratching their arms and faces as they ran, desperate to escape the unrelenting undead mob. He leapt vigorously through the brush. His stride, being twice that of Ari's, meant the poor girl's feet hardly touched the ground. It was run or die, and though he had no idea where he was going, he knew he had to put as much space between them and those *things* as he could.

Caroline exploded from the woods onto the moonlit sugar sand road. She was on her feet in the center of it for a mere second before she began her search.

"Ari! Villy!" She turned in place, throwing her voice to all corners of the forest. "Ari! Villy!"

The sky was red. The wind howled in a most unearthly way. Then, a new rustling came. She turned to face the trees. The rustling grew closer, and then the blackness spat out one Villy Bats and a teenaged girl named Ari. Villy was out of breath. Ari was out of pretty much everything.

Caroline rushed forward and put a hand on each of them. "I thought I'd lost you two." Exhausted, the three heaved like an orchestra of bellows, sometimes in unison, sometimes in an accidental and syncopated rhythm. As Ari struggled to catch her breath, her voice creaked and wavered. "Why are they doing this? What do they want?"

Caroline answered as best she could through her labored breathing. "Hell is full of tortured souls. Hate, despair, all of the worst sides of humanity—when that door opens, it spills out into our world. All of that anger, all of that anguish. It wants us. It wants us to join them."

"Misery loves company?" Villy managed a wry smirk.

"Something like that," said Caroline.

"Couldn't Heaven want us instead?" Ari only half-joked.

"I'm sure it does, sweetie," insisted Caroline.

"Yeah," sighed Villy, "it's just not as eager to show it."

Noises in the forest heralded the coming of more monsters.

"Oh, no." Caroline spun around to see the ghouls approaching from behind her. "This way!" she demanded, turning back towards the road. There, across the narrow sandy path, ghouls were emerging from the trees on the other side. They poured from the forest onto the road, instantly surrounding the threesome. Beside her, Ari looked as if she could take no more. Her delicate hands formed fists and her face twisted to a mask of rage.

"Leave us alone!" She screamed at the top of her lungs. "Leave us alone!"

"Get behind me!" cried Caroline. "Come on, right now. Get behind me!"

Ari dashed behind the witch. The ghouls inched closer. Caroline saw Villy look for a weapon and settle for a thick tree branch, large and fat enough to serve as a battering ram. He held it menacingly over his head.

"Get away!" he growled.

The fiends inched closer. Caroline removed the amulet from her neck. Closing her eyes, she held it up in the air and out in front of her with one hand. The other hand reached behind her to find Ari, cradling her to keep her safe.

"*Restless souls*!" called out the witch. "*This passage is closed*! *I hold the lock*! *See the obstruction before you. See this impassible barrier*! *There is nothing beyond it. Go back to your place of resting. Go back and find peace. This passage is blocked. This passage is closed.*"

The festering beasts before Caroline halted. They swayed from side to side, shifting their weight from rotting foot to rotting foot as they took in this curious new development.

Villy was not so lucky. Monsters spilled out from between the trees to his left and, unfettered by the amulet, approached him hungrily. He jabbed at them with the heavy, thick branch, but no sooner had they taken a step back than would they take two more steps toward him. Again he jabbed. There was one in front of him, one to his left, and more emerging from the tress before him. He swung wildly. But it was clear, he couldn't hold them off much longer with this *weapon*. It was no spiked umbrella or metal spade. The blows dealt only briefly stunned the reeking hulks. Again and again they pressed forward, and in greater numbers. Villy screamed and yelled. He threw out his chest and swung that hunk of tree like a wild man, trying to seem as big and as bad an adversary as possible. It was *almost* working, but it certainly wasn't going to work forever.

Villy was howling. Just a few feet away from him, Caroline was spellcasting at the top of her lungs. This cacophony drowned out the loud crunching in the trees behind them. Then, without warning, six diseased arms reached out from behind them, seeking one prize. They grabbed Ari, ripping her from Caroline's grasp and dragged her screaming into the darkness.

Villy turned to see Ari disappear.

"Oh, hell no!" he shouted.

He dropped the bough and dove into the pitch black after her.

Caroline was left with an army of the rotting dead flanking her from three sides. She was desperate to run into the darkness after the young girl as well, but she knew she wouldn't make it far. Two steps, and the angry gang of rotting corpses would seize her and tear her to shreds. Instead, she stayed put, continuing the incantation as her heart ached for Ari and Villy. She tried to console herself, convince herself that, in keeping the monsters at bay, she was giving Ari and Villy a fighting chance.

"*Mournful spirits!*" She projected as loudly as she could. "*This passage is closed!*"

She sidestepped to her right to try to herd the horde in front of her.

"*See the obstruction before you!*"

She took another step and turned fifteen degrees. Now, she faced the road head-on, and the monsters were a ghastly mob before her, transfixed by the amulet.

"*See this impassible barrier! There is nothing beyond it. Go back to your place of resting. Go back and find peace.*"

From the forest, she heard a struggle. There was a loud, low gasp, as if uttered by a man succumbing to a fatal blow. She feared the worst. She held the amulet higher above her head, and it began to glow. The light of the moon shone into the facets of the amulet's crystal and burst forward like through a magical prism. Crimson, turquoise and amber lights shone forth from the crystal like a flickering, celestial rainbow. The ghouls groaned in unison and lumbered awkwardly backward. From the blackness beyond the trees came a bloodcurdling scream. It was Ari's voice. Caroline shuddered. There was nothing she could do, save finish the job at hand.

"*Go back!*" She yelled to the monsters before her. "*Go back and find peace!*"

The light shone brightly, like a multi-colored star fallen in the center of the black forest. The creatures retreated.

"*Go back!*"

They continued to back away from Caroline, away from the light. They turned, and solemnly returned to the dark womb of the woods.

Caroline stood alone in the center of the sandy road. There was silence all around her. She yearned to hear something that would give her an indication of Ari and Villy's whereabouts and wellbeing. Rustling, crying, a shriek—anything! But her wish went unanswered. Like so many times before, the mouth of Hell had opened, devouring everyone she cared for.

Chapter 13

Caroline took a deep breath. The image of her nephew's body being devoured by ghouls was starting to sink in. Granted, he had been something of a thorn in her side. He had been strangely immature for his age, boastful and ambitious.

If Caroline had learned anything from a life spent in New Jersey, it was that arrogance and stupidity made for very bad bedfellows. She saw it again and again in some of the men that surrounded her. Her nephew had shared those very traits. He had been constantly coming up with big, unrealistic plans beyond his abilities, and directing more attention to himself than was reasonable. When people are both arrogant and stupid, they inadvertently shine a light on what gargantuan morons they are. And Henry did just that—often. Nevertheless, he had been her last remaining living relative and that hit home. Her mind soared back to the time his parents met their untimely demise.

Henry's parents, Caroline's sister, Lucy, and her husband Mel, a balding accountant from Metuchen, had died only three years earlier when last the gateway opened its vile mouth. Lucy was Caroline's only living female relative, and her death weighed heavily on the witch. The family was sitting in the cabin, watching an episode of The Golden Girls *on Mel's laptop, when suddenly the Jersey Devil appeared and made a meal of Lucy and Mel. When Caroline finally arrived at the scene, she found the carnage—and Henry, then a high school senior. He was hiding under the couch with three days of feces in his pants. She knew she was on her own when she asked him to help her close the fissure to Hell, but he instead insisted on staying under the sofa. He had two more days' worth of filth in his pants when she returned—only three hours later.*

As for Ari and Villy… Caroline didn't make friends often. It wasn't, in short, convenient. Truth be told, she'd seen everyone she'd ever really cared about killed, mauled, eaten, or seduced into entering Hell. When she was a child, her grandmother, her mentor and the matriarch of her family, had brought her to the Pine Barrens to show her how a woman of her lineage was to deal with demons. Her intention had been to demonstrate to the young Caroline how to close the gateway to Hell. Instead, the poor girl had watched as the person she loved most was beheaded by the sharp talons of the Jersey Devil. From the time Caroline was a small girl, the weight of this burden had fallen upon her shoulders; she had been in charge of the family curse ever since.

Caroline had seen something of herself in Ari. Ari reminded Caroline of when she was a young girl, soft and fragile, but with a burning passion inside that could hurl demons back into the abyss. With no female descendants left in her family, who would stop the tide of evil from entering this world after she was gone? She had for a moment thought that maybe, just maybe, she could teach Ari the ways—but now Ari was gone.

Caroline took a deep breath and let it out slowly. She looked down and saw the book at her feet. Ari must have dropped it when she was taken. The witch remained calm on the outside. She bent down slowly, took the book in her hands and rose. Her palm swept across its leathery cover, wiping it clean of pine needles and sand. Every fiber of her being struggled to turn the anguish and rage that was boiling up inside of her into some sort of gentle gesture.

There was a rustling in the forest. Caroline spun to face the trees that stood behind her. She glared into the darkness with fire in her eyes. Whatever wretched creature emerged from that murk was going to pay. It would be the sole recipient of forty-some-odd years of rage and sorrow built up within her. The rustling grew louder. Caroline tightened her grip, the fingers of her right hand squeezing the amulet, the left ones digging into the old tome.

"Come on," she beckoned under her breath.

Twigs snapped. Branches were breaking clean off the trees. She took a deep breath. A figure formed in the darkness before her, coming at her in a full sprint. It burst from the trees and landed on the sandy road. It was Villy. He was carrying Ari on his back.

"I'm going to kill you!" growled Caroline.

"What did *I* do?" Villy sang as he let Ari down to stand on her own beside him.

"Never mind." Caroline looked at the two and shook her head.

Ari turned to Villy, her eyes still wide, her face still wearing a stunned expression. "Thank you."

Villy meekly smiled and nodded. He turned to Caroline. "Can we please finish this and get the hell out of here?"

"This way!" Caroline turned to head down the sandy path. Ari and Villy scuttled after the witch, who now jogged among the trees. Hastening through the forest, they wove past trees and leaped over fallen branches, occasionally stopping to sneak past lingering ghouls. The sky was getting brighter the farther they advanced, until eventually, there was a fiendish red glow over everything. The trunks of trees and edges of leaves were lined with bright red rims of light, like neon, that traced their bodies and branches, separating them from each other in a most surreal way. The moaning of ghouls hung in the air like a malevolent, ceremonial chant. Growing in volume was a maddening, constant noise, like the sound of turbines powered by cries of misery and human despair.

They were coming to the edge of the forest. Caroline placed a hand on a tree that towered above her. She looked over her shoulder and gazed upon Villy and Ari with an expression carved in pale marble.

"This is it." She stepped between the pines into a grassy field.

Villy and Ari crossed the threshold of the trees to stand at either side of their guide. Before them was a field of unkempt wild grasses, washed in an eerie red glow. At the end of this crimson, grassy Styx was a towering old barn. At first glance, the structure appeared to be engulfed in flames. A second glance revealed that the glowing red lights that burst forth from every crack, every opening, every splinter, of the ancient wooden edifice came from no ordinary fire. The throbbing, ethereal light that burst forth from the Hellbarn seemed otherworldly, as if coming from an alien ship that hovered within the structure, or as if Mephistopheles himself had opened the world's biggest nightclub in the Pine Barrens of New Jersey.

With a ghastly, low groan, the doors slowly slid ajar, as if a sigh from Hell were pushing them open. Inside, silhouettes shambled against the flickering light. Ghouls, monsters, abominations, creatures that defied all manner of reasonable explanation, waited impatiently in the beams that cut through a smoky mist. A horde of ghouls had amassed at this gate.

"It's worse than I thought." Caroline's voice croaked. "We have to hurry."

"What do we do?" Villy looked at her. She could tell he was trying to conceal his own panic.

"I will read an incantation from the book. It's a closing spell." Caroline explained, trying to look calm and collected. "But we have to get closer."

Villy's eyebrows contorted and his throat tightened. He wondered if she heard him gulp.

"Don't worry," she said, "the amulet will protect us. Just stay directly behind me at all times."

Her words only partially soothed the pained look on the Gothrocker's face. He looked at Ari, half for reassurance, half to see how she was taking all of this. She stared at Caroline, taking in her every word with an intense concentration. That didn't make Villy feel any better about himself.

"Let's go," commanded Caroline.

Leading the way, Caroline leapt like a gazelle through the grass until she was about thirty yards from the barn's façade. She knelt before the glowing edifice and placed the book on the ground in front of her. The infernal winds blew it open and rattled its pages. Villy and Ari scampered after, conscious to stay directly behind her in the protective path of the amulet. Ari crouched so close to Caroline it gave away her fear. Villy hunched down and placed a hand on Ari's shoulder, more for his own sake than hers.

From that position, they could see everything more clearly. Pasty white ghouls leaked from the forest and lingered by the sides of the Hellbarn— loitering, waiting. The giant wooden doors of the barn were creeping open. Between them, tortured souls stood, waiting to escape. Some resembled the things that had plagued them already—sickly, white, rotting corpses. Some had less skin on their bones, some none at all. Living skeletons swayed from side to side in this army of the undead.

Caroline turned her head just slightly, keeping one eye on the Hellbarn and the other on her companions.

"Listen," she started, "This wind is stronger than ever before. I'm going to need both of my hands to hold this book, so I want you to take this." She removed the amulet from her neck and passed it back to Ari, placing it in the girl's soft palm. "Hold it directly in front of me like this." She directed the girl's hand to a spot just over and in front of her own head. "Do you understand?"

"Yes." Ari followed her instructions.

"As long as the amulet is directly in front of us they won't be able to see us. They won't be able to hurt us."

"What should *I* do?" asked Villy.

"You need to watch the rear," answered Caroline without turning. "We can't afford to have them sneak up on us from behind again. This is it. This is the only chance we'll get."

There was a sickly and all too familiar roar, a low, rumbling bellow like that of a malignant horn. They looked up to see the Governor. Like an infantry commander, he had found his place before the Hellbarn, his enslaved battalion of ghoulish crones gathering obediently behind him.

"You'd better hurry!" Villy pointed at the nightmarish gathering.

"Right." Caroline picked up the old tome between her calloused hands.

Almost instantly, the rank winds burst with greater force from the barn, as if Hell could feel her presence, feel the presence of the offending manuscript. The doors creaked open at a decidedly more worrisome pace. The demon army howled impatiently, waiting to be released from their torments. Caroline's eyes were glued on the phantasmagorical spectacle. She didn't dare admit to the others that she'd never seen the doors opened this far, never witnessed so many monsters ready to burst forth.

The book! Her eyes shot down, and she tore through the text with frenzied fingers for the pages of the closing spell. With a gust, the same winds that sought to obstruct their progress ironically flipped the pages open to the very spot she searched for.

"*Spirits of evil,*" she bellowed into the winds. "*Unfriendly beings, unwanted guests, be gone! Leave us! Leave this place, leave this circle, that the Goddess and the God may enter. Go, or be cast into the outer darkness! Hear me, demons of the abyss. This world rejects you! This world casts you back from whence you came! Mighty are the four winds of this realm…*"

As though on cue, the winds picked up force. They were not the ones she'd hoped for. The smell of rot, filth, and disease that battered their faces revealed their origin. They were blowing directly from the abyss of Hell. The doors crept open. Inside the barn, the ruddy light intensified, pulsating like an enflamed heart. The fissure was getting bigger. The gateway was widening.

"It's not working!" Ari panicked.

"Yeah, you'd better hurry it up!" urged Villy.

Caroline tossed him a small dagger of a look, then focused on the task at hand.

"*Go, or be drowned in the watery abyss! Go, or be burned in the flames! Go, or be torn by the whirlwind! Mighty is the Earth that pushes up mountains. Mighty are the oceans that consume all in their path. Mighty is our will against thine. Mighty is our lo—*"

The words were ripped from her lips as a monstrous wind plowed into her mouth and eyes. It tore the book from her hands and spread the text's pages like a bird, flapping over their heads, soaring hopelessly away. The barn doors swung wider. The ghoul army of monsters, reanimated skeletons, and winged demons eagerly awaited the call. It came.

The Governor cranked open his putrid jaw, and released a bone-crumbling battle cry steeped in four centuries of hatred.

Every manner of rotting, festering, and grotesque thing that had stood at the doorstep of Hell screamed out in a chorus of madness. Agony, hatred, euphoria, delirium, insanity—all tones and colors burst forth in an unbearable symphony. Then, they charged. Forward they ran, lunging, hobbling, slithering from the barn doors like an explosion of snakes and spiders and bats from a cave. Caroline's eyes widened, then Ari's, then Villy's.

"Get behind me!" screamed Caroline. "The amulet will protect us!"

The threesome lowered their heads and crouched behind the bauble as Ari held it as high as she could over Caroline's head. They could feel the ground shake as the ghoul horde charged toward them, groaning and grunting.

"Oh my God." Villy whimpered, his confidence in their surviving this onslaught shriveling.

Soon enough, the creatures were upon them, running along both sides of their terrified bodies. They held each other tightly as heavy footfalls vibrated around them, some from rotting feet, some from stumps, others from the bony appendages of screaming skeletons. Ari had appeared to have learned her lesson not to give into temptation and sneak a peek. She buried her nose deep into the crevice between Caroline's arm and her back, seeming to trust in the amulet.

Villy, however, was sure these things would see them, notice them there in the grass, and kill them on the spot. He cautiously turned his head and opened one eye, certain that it would meet the gaze of a ghoul staring right back at him. He was relieved when his sight found only a blur of rotting bodies passing them by. As hard as it was for him to believe, the amulet was working.

In time, the deranged cries of the monsters lessened, faded. Their worrisome footfalls grew less frequent and further apart. Villy glanced over his shoulder. The demons disappeared behind them into the darkness of the forest like wan intestines winding their way down a slaughterhouse drain.

As though she sensed the macabre charge was behind them, Caroline raised her head. She scanned the wild grasses until her eyes landed on her treasure. "The book!"

As fast as she could, she jumped up, ran to a spot of crumpled grass a few yards behind and to her left, and retrieved the sacred tome. In a flash, she had plunked back down before Villy and Ari.

"Are they gone?" asked Ari. She rose only slightly and looked behind her. Villy followed her gaze. Beyond the trees and the darkness of the forest, pale, amorphous forms wormed into the murkiness. Their distant howls still filled the air, but all in all the nightmarish battalion seemed to have been fooled by the amulet.

"What happened?" asked Villy. "Did we fail?"

"No," answered Caroline, "this is just the beginning."

Those words did not reassure Villy, whose face seemed to slide down as if every muscle in it had gone limp. Caroline leafed through the book to the closing spell and began anew.

"Hear me, Hell!"

A mighty wind roared in defiance, nearly knocking them off of their knees. Caroline dug her fingers into the book to keep from losing it again.

The hole to Hell was growing, throbbing, glowing. Terrible things, nightmares, collected again at the opening of the barn. The structure seemed to be filling with smoke as the brimstone fires burned nearer to this world. In those sulfurous clouds, ghouls appeared, crawling from the fissure. Worse, soaring over the barn, flying beasts and winged monsters flitted in and out of the billowing vapors.

"*By the Goddess!*" Caroline commanded with all of her might. "*By the forces of the Earth, we defy thee. We cast thee back. Begone from this realm!*"

A loud shriek pierced the night, echoing, as the Jersey Devil soared from the barn and aimed straight for them. They collapsed, recoiling in terror as the beast *swished* over their heads. They barely had time to right themselves before further crazed screeching heralded even more beasts. Three winged creatures flew from the barn, grotesque and monstrous, though smaller than their predecessor. Caroline, Villy, and Ari braced themselves, but these demons seemed too elated with freedom to pay mind to the three of them. They shot into the dark sky, weaving and bobbing like bats out of Hell, emitting high-pitched chirps and screeches that sounded almost like laughter. Then, they were gone.

Taking a deep breath, Caroline raised the book to her face. "*By the power of the Mother, we banish you! We banish you!*"

That last line seemed to get someone's attention. A low rumbling shook the ground. The glowing red smoke of the barn swirled and danced as if something were swimming through the fissure into this world. From the depths, a massive form appeared; giant, black tentacles writhed in the noxious gasses, silhouetted by the glowing fires.

The Beast had arisen.

Chapter 16

The trio froze in awe. The doors of the barn parted wider, revealing an infernal vista. Festering ghouls shambled from the portal, as did reanimated skeletons. Above them, winged things darted and swooped through the mist. In the center of this fiery landscape, a giant, black, tentacled beast was rising. It wriggled and writhed and lashed tendrils through the smoky atmosphere inside of the barn, its vastness defying the very laws of physics. When it let out its first blistering groan, it was like an armada of steamboats blowing their cyclopean horns in unison.

Caroline, Villy, and Ari unintentionally and uncontrollably cried out at once, in the kind of primal scream no one ever wants to or intends to emit. They shook, mouths agape, eyes glued to this Brobdingnagian behemoth.

A monstrous projectile broke their trance. Screaming like an escaped bedlamite, a soaring bat-winged fiend exploded from the sulfurous vapors and careened directly toward their heads. They all ducked as quickly as their wits allowed. The creature screeched just inches over their scalps. Villy turned around to see it fly off, if just to verify the unbelievable notion he held in his mind. His assessment, however quickly made, had been correct. As it screamed and rose toward the dark sky beyond the tree tops, he could see that it was little more than a skull with leathery wings and a tail that resembled a barbed trail of intestines.

"Jesus Christ," he hissed.

At that moment, something else in the woods caught his eye. Between the trees, a ghoul lingered. It was pale and naked, like many of the monsters they'd suffered that night, but different somehow. He strained his eyes to try and pick it out of the darkness, like a fossilized trilobite from a block of obsidian, but the thing slinked behind a tree, eluding his probing eyes. He waited a moment—there it was again. This time, as it passed between two trees in the near darkness at the edge of the forest, he could make out more of its form. It was a woman but, unlike the other crones they'd encountered throughout this ordeal, it was slender and less deformed. Its skin seemed smoother, not fetid or blemished. He tried to grasp it with his gaze, but again it disappeared behind a tree.

"Damn it!" He cursed under his breath.

He quickly stole a glance behind him to stay abreast of the trouble at hand. Ari and Caroline were still frozen, staring ahead at the Lovecraftian spectacle before their eyes. Surely, he had a moment to investigate further, and so again his gaze dove into the dark spaces between the trees, searching for this unusual abomination. He saw just a pallid sliver as it lurked behind a pine, leaning against its bark.

"Come on," he urged in a tight whisper.

As if the thing had heard him, it stepped from behind the pine, and he could see it clearly now— he could see *her*. She was pale and svelte, her body smooth, white, and pristine, completely free of any blemish. This deathly beauty slowly and gracefully walked from behind the tree. Her long black hair, shining in the moonlight, swept the contours of her form. It caressed her firm, young breasts and fell slowly in a gentle wind over her shoulder, coming to rest at the curved small of her back. It beckoned Villy to stare at her round, smooth bottom, to savor it with his eyes.

Again he looked over his shoulder, guiltily. Ari and Caroline were still, almost like statues, their eyes locked on the Hellbarn. The giant, tentacled Beast writhed on, more sluggish than before. Its tentacles waved through the smoke like loving hands through warm waters, undulating in slow motion.

Villy languidly spun again toward the trees. Now, the girl was moving through the woods, gliding, floating like an angel in all of her naked, youthful beauty. Her delicate feet barely touched the ground. Her face was smooth and white, like that of a porcelain doll, her lips pale, shapely, and luscious. He swore he had seen those lips before. She brought a dainty finger to her shapely ear and swept a lock of her raven-black hair behind it. She turned to Villy and smiled. Was it…Prudence?!

Villy tried to spin around quickly to Ari and Caroline, but his body inched through the air like molasses. When his gaze finally fell on the women, he found them sitting in the grass motionless, locked in some sort of stasis, the monsters before them barely moving, barely advancing from the mouth of the barn. The grasses waved in slow motion, like a field of sea anemones. Leaves tumbled sluggishly through the air on a languid, liquid breeze. And then, there was the sound of sweet laughing. He turned back toward the trees, and Prudence was smiling, hugging the tree trunk before her. She giggled and pushed off like a swimmer in a pool, drifting gracefully backward until she lightly bounced off another tree like a pinball in slow motion. She glided playfully toward another pine. Putting her hands out in front of her, she stopped herself on the tree's surface. She stood there for a moment, looking back at Villy coyly, and then again she pushed off and drifted backward into the darkness.

"Prudence!" Villy called out.

The only reply was her sultry laughter echoing through the blackness of the wood. Again she appeared for a moment, barely stepping into a pool of moonlight. Sweeping over her body, it lit only her face, her nipples, the softness of her belly, and the smooth mound between her thighs. Villy's heart leapt. He gasped. A wetness came to his mouth. A gypsy violin called from somewhere deep in the forest. Prudence bent her spine in ecstasy, slowly throwing her head back and her slender, pale arms into the air. Swooning from side to side, she was intoxicated by the sensual strains of the violin that snaked through the woods. She began dancing, waving her arms toward herself as if washing her face in the waves of music. The soft, pale toes of her left foot crept backward and landed on the moist ground behind her. Then, the ones on her right foot followed suit. She was backing away into the darkness, and the waving gestures of her arms were a clear message, a beckoning. Seemingly drunk and hungry for Villy to follow her into the madness of the trees, she took another step back and then another. The darkness was swallowing her pale flesh.

"Prudence, wait!"

She took another step back. Then, she was gone.

Heart pounding, Villy checked over his shoulder again. Ari and Caroline were fine, he thought. They weren't moving. The monsters weren't moving either, and anyway, they had the amulet and book to protect them. They wouldn't miss him. He'd only be gone for an instant, only long enough to grab Prudence—to save her, he told himself.

He took a tentative step toward the woods, careful to stay in the path of the amulet. The gypsy melody of the violin was fading. He took another step foreword. Prudence's lilting laughter was dwindling.

"Aw, fuck it." Shaking his head, he ran as fast as he could into the black depths.

In a moment, he too vanished into the blackness of the woods. As he crossed into the trees, he could have sworn he'd peripherally seen the Governor lurking by a nearby pine. In the residual image it left on the back of his left retina, he'd swear the monster's toothy deformed mouth was twisted into a rigor mortis grin

Villy found himself in pure blackness. He threw his hands in front of him to help feel his way, but even his pale hands were imperceptible in the darkness. He stumbled forward, following the fading laughter of the beautiful Prudence. Spinning from side to side, he tried desperately to locate its source, but it was hopeless. Eventually, there was as little noise as there was light. He had found himself in a place of silence. He took a step forward. The crunching twigs beneath his feet gave him small comfort. He took another step, and then another. Certainly, he thought, his palms would eventually fall upon the raspy bark of a tree. He took another step and then two more. How could it be, he wondered? The trees had seemed so densely packed before.

The tender skin on his fingers found a form in the darkness. It was soft and warm, and in an instant his heart beat faster, thinking he'd found Prudence's soft, naked flesh in the void. But no—it was too flat and fuzzy, and it went on in every direction. When he ran his hands along the surface, it gave way like a velvet sheet hanging in the darkness. He followed it with his fingers, taking a few steps to his right. The barrier had weight. It was thick and had folds that ran vertically for as high as he could feel. And then, he found a seam. He tested it with a finger and when he did a soft light shone through it. This was an exit of some sort. He put his palms together as if in prayer, slid them in and followed through their wedge, plunging forward.

Villy emerged from the red velvet curtains of the Dante Theatre to rapturous applause. He stood on the pristine wooden stage, practically blinded by the stage lights as the crowd bathed him in cheers of "Bravo!" and "Encore!" The house lights were on, and he could see the entire hall was packed, even the whole of the balcony. There wasn't an empty seat in the majestic theatre, and the euphoric patrons were rising to their feet, clapping, screaming compliments like triumphant savages, hurling roses at him. Disoriented, he did the only thing he could think of doing. He bowed.

Holy Hell, that made the crowd go completely mad. Any remaining restraint vanished. Women violently clutched their pearls and tore at their cleavage beneath their gowns as they howled like she-wolves in heat. Tuxedoed men clasped their heads as if the art they'd just experienced had caused doorways to open to other dimensions in their brains, and they cried and caterwauled in elated appreciation. There was a veritable hailstorm of roses falling at Villy's feet. They were landing closer and closer to him. He took a step back, and then another. He felt the heavy velvet curtain behind him. He ran a palm along its surface behind his back. His fingers danced along the folds until they found the part. He bowed slightly again to the audience. The mob of delirious gentry burst anew into a steady, communal scream. In one motion, Villy slid his foot between the curtains and disappeared from the stage.

He half-expected to find himself back in the darkness of the forest but, no. He was merely behind the thick, luxurious curtains of the Dante Theatre, surrounded by catwalks and rigging. He expected, also, to find himself unnerved and perhaps frightened or worried, but he was none of these things. This was evidenced by the small smile that, despite his efforts, crept its way onto his lips. He found himself feeling, for lack of a better word, *happy*. It was the first time he could remember feeling that way in what seemed like years. The audience went on roaring hysterically. In the cacophony, there were still traces of recognizable "Bravo" and "Encore" pleas. Villy could hardly contain the giggle that bubbled up from his gut.

"Well?" said the woman behind him.

Villy snapped to attention. He turned, red-faced and embarrassed to be caught with his ear pressed to the curtain, drinking in the adoration of the audience. There, before him, was a woman, smartly dressed in a charcoal gray blazer, matching pencil skirt, and pressed white blouse. She held a clipboard firmly in her hands. Her face was pale and pretty, eyes piercing blue gems behind Prada glasses. Long, raven-black hair framed her exquisite countenance.

"How long are you going to make these nice people wait?"

As he watched her lips form the words, he recognized her. It was Prudence—but like in a dream where several truths exist at once and intertwine with neither rhyme nor reason, he also knew she was his manager and his lover.

"Come on," she urged, "what are you waiting for?"

Villy was getting his footing in this new reality.

"Wow, so this is what it's like to have made it." He giggled again softly. "I'd never thought I'd see this day."

Prudence placed a hand warmly and firmly on his arm.

"You deserve this, Villy. You've worked hard for this. Now, come on, don't torture these poor souls any longer. Give them what they came for."

She smiled broadly, and her smile was infectious. Villy's mouth stretched to mirror hers. She leaned in for a kiss, placing her sumptuous lips on his. They were soft and cool against his mouth. When they parted and her tongue danced seductively around his, it was hot, wet, and passionate. His soul felt as if it had dived into a warm pool of sin and abandon. It felt *amazing*.

He opened his eyes mid-kiss and glanced down. Her blouse was open, and her firm round breasts seem to throb with desire. He knew they'd be making love after the performance, as he strangely remembered they had always done. She pulled away, smiled, and handed him his guitar, seemingly out of nowhere.

"Come on," she said, "business before pleasure."

Villy grinned widely, took the guitar from his lover, and turned back toward the curtains. Taking a deep breath, he composed himself, and then, with one huge, confident stride, he burst through the curtains onto the stage. The crowd went wild. He hardly noticed, nor did he care, that this was no longer the Dante Theatre. He was now at the Limelight in New York City, and the crowd of screaming fans was no longer filled with elegantly dressed gentry, but a sea of black-clad Goths, Punks, Deathrockers, and the like.

"This one's for the spooky kids!" he proclaimed to the dark congregation of ecstatic fans.

Like a giant, thousand-armed organism, they roared in unison and threw their appendages into the air. The curtains swung open behind him, and where previously only rigging and catwalks had existed, there were drums, amplifiers, and guitars. And playing them were the members of Raised by Bats. The band blasted into song.

"This one's called, 'Never!'" shouted Villy.

The crowd erupted in cheers. Drums pounded like cannon fire, an organ poured out an ominous wave of notes, and electric guitars rhythmically chopped out crunching power chords. The smoke machines kicked in, and waves of mist billowed around the band, engulfing them. As Villy stepped from the mist to sing the first line of the song, the smoke swirled around him. It rose and contorted like dancing demons, drifting upwards toward the tour banner that hung from the cathedral ceiling. It was a massive red thing, and in the center was the image of a giant, black, tentacled beast.

Caroline was dealing with a giant, black, tentacled beast of her own. It was rising higher and higher in the Hellbarn as it ascended into this world. She knew she could not allow that to happen. She brought the book to her face again and continued where she'd left off:

"*By the power of the Mother, we banish you! We banish you! Get thee back to Hell!*"

Obediently, Ari held the amulet above Caroline's head. She tried to keep it steady, despite the muscles in her arm starting to cramp. She didn't know how much longer she could hold it in the air like that. With every minute that went by, it became heavier, harder to keep up.

"*We banish you!*" yelled Caroline again. She straightened her back, took a deep breath, and, with all of her strength, again belted out the last line of the incantation.

"*Get... thee... back... to... Hell!*"

Nothing happened.

Caroline threw the book to the ground.

"What's wrong?" cried Ari.

"The book," Caroline panted, "it's not enough. We got here too late. I've never seen it like this, never seen the doorway so open, the fissure so... wide." With a heavy heart, she surveyed the shambling ghouls, the walking skeletons, and the winged monsters that soared in and out of the structure. "I've never seen so many of those things, and I've never seen *that* thing before... *ever!*" She pointed at the tentacled behemoth that had grown to take up most of the Hellbarn. Caroline sighed. "It's no use. I've done all I can."

At that moment a light shone through Ari's hand—the amulet started to glow. Beams of multicolored light radiated in a magical spectrum.

Music began to emanate between her fingers, as if the bauble were humming. The noise resonated like a voice, perfectly intoning a note, then two, then a handful in perfect harmony.

"The amulet!" cried Caroline. "Maybe... if I..."

Ari placed the glowing gem in Caroline's hand.

The celestial light shone on the women's faces. "I have to get it into the doorway. Maybe then..."

"Throw it!" Ari tried to speak over the hellish winds.

Caroline glanced at the barn.

"It's too far. I could never reach it." As though her own body doubted her words, she rose slowly to her feet. Ari stood as well, until they were side by side, illuminated by both the glowing wonder in Caroline's hands and the flames of Hell.

"We have to get closer!" yelled Ari over the din.

Caroline shook her head. Ghouls lurched out of the doorway—too many of them—and the giant tentacles of the Beast reached far out of the opening.

"It's too dangerous!" Caroline shook her head in defeat. And then, an idea popped into her mind. "Maybe, if we stick together..."

She glanced over her shoulder and, only at that moment, noticed that Villy was no longer with them. Spinning around, she found him standing at the periphery of the forest, staring, as if hypnotized, into the darkness of the trees.

"Villy!" she shouted. "Villy!"

He didn't budge.

Louder she screamed over the hellish winds, the moaning of ghouls, and the low, rumbling bellows of the Beast.

"Villy!"

Villy grasped the mic stand and leaned seductively toward his hungry audience at the Limelight. He swayed as he sang in a sultry croon.

"Don't touch me tonight. I might lash out in fright. Lie on my bed, but don't you move, dear. I know you know not with whom we sleep tonight."

"Villy!"

His concentration was broken. Somewhere behind him, behind the band, behind a heavy black velvet curtain that hung against the back wall of the stage, someone was screaming. "Villy!" The voice was feminine, motherly and familiar. He glanced over his shoulder, missing the first beat of the next verse. The band looked at him apprehensively. He jumped back in as quickly as he could.

"Don't touch me tonight while I'm sleeping. I may lose my head and hit the ceiling. I know you know not with whom we sleep tonight. Never! Never!"

"Villy!" The screaming female voice came again, from somewhere behind the stage.

Villy glanced over his shoulder. Standing stiffly behind the drum kit, his lover and manager, Prudence, nervously dug her fingernails into her clipboard. As the chorus kicked in, the audience burst into cheers and Villy's attention was drawn again to the front of the house.

"I never cried, I never cried, I let it eat me up alive. Under the light, I told a lie. I kept this secret safe inside. No devil hides beneath my bed. He slept with me tonight! He slept with me tonight!"

"Villy!" The unseen woman screamed again. He resisted the urge to look over his shoulder. He pointed dramatically into the crowd and belted out the last line of the chorus.

"He'll take this child's snow-white innocence... never! Never!"

The band kicked into the instrumental break. As the guitar solo wailed, Villy charged past the bassist and the drummer, toward the heavy, black curtain at the back wall of the stage. Prudence blocked his way.

"Where do you think you're going?" She tried her best to muster an authoritative tone.

"You don't hear that?" He yelled over the din. "That screaming?"

"No, I don't." Prudence was completely unconvincing. To make matters worse, an ear-piercing scream came from behind that curtain. But this time it wasn't the familiar, motherly voice. It was... much younger.

Caroline was staring into the forest trying her best to get Villy's attention when the shrill cry keened in her ears. She whipped around to see Ari shrieking in terror, her face pointing skyward. A burst of wind from directly above blasted into Caroline's face, and with a resounding crash, the Jersey Devil pounded into the ground, almost knocking the girl off her feet. Facing Ari, it sprang up, righted itself and stretched its bony wings. Snarling, it took a languid step toward the girl.

"Hey!" Caroline threatened the monster. Her voice rasped and burned in her throat. "I'm over here!" The thing whipped around, lashing its barbed tail and baring its shiny wet teeth at the witch. Her tone was defiant, taunting. "Come on! What are you waiting for?"

It hulked forward, pounding the ground so hard the vibrations tickled the soles of Caroline's feet in a strangely nauseating way. The beast stopped a mere yard from her and examined Caroline carefully. She looked up at it and saw her reflection in glistening, black eyes. She looked so… small. The devil's lips stretched, exposing more of its foot-long teeth. Viscous, clear saliva swayed like a pendulum in a rubbery stream from speckled gums. The thing seemed to almost… smile. Caroline looked frantically for the book. She spotted it over her shoulder, a good six feet away in the moist grass. She slyly slinked to her left, her eyes darting back between the book and the beast. It lurched forward and barked in her face, spraying her with steamy goo. She froze. Her plan wasn't going to work. She inched to the right, but the thing matched her movements exactly. It craned its skeletal head forward on its snake-like neck, nearly pressing its face against hers. The devil's nostrils widened as it sniffed the air around her. She looked up into those shiny black orbs and saw them widen. In the countenance of this misshapen horror, she saw something familiar. She saw an expression of recognition.

The monster jerked back. It huffed. It huffed again. It shifted weight from cloven hoof to cloven hoof. He barked and snorted, rocking back and forth like a hound when it threatens an inanimate dog toy. She could see it was enraged by something in particular. She knew in her heart it had recognized her as the one who had sent it back to Hell all of those decades ago when she was only eight years old… and a dozen times since.

"Caroline!" Ari screamed as loudly as she could over the roaring winds. "The barn!"

Caroline looked past the devil before her. The barn doors were open all the way. A multitude of undead souls were crawling, shambling from its mouth. The tentacled beast was rising higher. She glanced again over her left shoulder at the book. She knew she'd never survive a lunge for it, not with this raging villain before her. She thrust the amulet forward in her outstretched arm toward the demon's snarling countenance and began the incantation from memory.

"Spirits of evil, unfriendly beings, unwanted guests, be gone! Leave us! Leave this place, leave this circle, that the Goddess and the God may enter."

The Jersey Devil reared back and froze in place. It cocked its head as if stunned by her audacity.

"Go, or be cast into the outer darkness!"

"Caroline!" Ari wailed at the top of her lungs.

Villy pressed into Prudence. "Did you hear that? Did you?" Prudence didn't answer. He pushed past her and tore the heavy, black curtains apart. He was stunned by what he saw. There was no back wall. Instead, he was looking out into a grassy field on a chilly, moonlit night. Fifty feet away, Caroline stood, holding out an amulet toward the menacing creature, over twice her size. Behind the roaring devil, Ari trembled as a shambling army of pale ghouls spilled from a glowing barn toward her. His mouth went slack as he took it all in.

"So…" Prudence slinked over to give him room. "There you have it. You see what's happening now. So, what are you going to do?" She was completely expressionless.

He stared into the infernal diorama. "I have to help them." He could hear Caroline incanting in the distance.

"*Leave this place, leave this circle, that the Goddess and the God may enter. Go, or be cast into the outer darkness!*"

"Caroline!" screamed Ari again as the ghouls grew nearer.

Prudence pressed the clipboard to her breast and placed her free hand on a hip. "Really," she deadpanned. "And how are you going to do that? Do you slay demons now? You know how to do that?"

Villy said nothing.

She looked over her shoulder at the fiendish panorama behind her. "Look at her. Do you think she *needs* your help? Huh?" She lowered her head and raised her eyebrows.

Villy gazed at the witch in the distance, amulet in hand, keeping a demon at bay. The amulet was beginning to glow. "Well, no, but…"

Caroline stood her ground. *"Go, or be drowned in the watery abyss!"* The Jersey Devil's eyes narrowed as the light shining from the bauble grew brighter.

Villy gazed with sad eyes at the scene before him. He thought of Stuey and, for a moment, believed maybe he could prevent Caroline and Ari from meeting the same fate. It only took a split second to remember he had been helpless to save the boy. How could he possibly save these women from the same horrible beast that had killed Stuey? Still, he tried to convince himself. "They need me…"

Prudence's icy veneer cracked. "They need you? *They* need you?" Prudence dropped the clipboard to her side. "What about me? Don't I need you?" Her eyes began to glisten. "Villy." She pressed her body against his. "I *love* you. Don't you love *me*?"

He looked down at her, then back at the demented scene in the distance.

"Don't you?" She pressed, her voice becoming more fragile. "You can't leave me. You can't ever leave me." She dropped the clipboard to the ground and threw her arms around him. "Don't you *want* to be here with me?"

"Of course I do." He answered, never taking his eyes off of Caroline and Ari and the monster between them.

Prudence glanced over her shoulder. "That lady's a demon slayer. That's what she does. That's what she's *always* done. She'll be fine without your help." The band pounded out the last few chords of the song in a mighty crescendo. The audience erupted, screaming hysterically, as if pure madness had taken them over. She glanced over his shoulder. "This…" She pointed toward the crowd with her slender nose. "This is what *you* do."

The screams of the audience unified into chants of, "Encore! Encore! Encore!" Villy glanced over his shoulder.

Prudence slid a cool hand behind Villy's neck and pulled him close. "All I ever ask is that you do what you *love*…" She pulled him closer. "And that you never… ever leave me." She pressed her soft lips against his. Villy fell into the kiss, closing his eyes and swooning. Slowly, Prudence slid the curtains closed behind her.

The audience chanted with unbridled vigor. "Villy! Villy! Villy!"

His eyes shot open. Villy slowly pulled away from the passionate kiss.

Prudence sucked his lower lip, finally letting go as they parted. "Go." She raised her dainty chin towards the crowd. "Do what you do best. Feed the beast."

Villy opened his mouth, an apologetic look on his face as if to offer an excuse or a rationale, but no words came out. The part of him that felt shame was bullied into silence by his ego, stoked into a raging inferno by the roar of the crowd.

"Villy! Villy! Villy! Villy!" The audience chanted in unison.

He leaned in and pecked Prudence again on the lips and smiled. Then, in one motion, he gently pushed off from her, turned, and hurried toward the front of the stage. He bowed deeply in front of his raving fans, occasionally glancing offstage. Prudence stood motionless. She watched him bow again and again. A mischievous grin stretched across her face.

"Go, or be burned in the flames!" Caroline held the amulet as far up and out as the length of her arm would allow. The light that shone from it grew brighter. Like a prism, it split into beams of color that danced in an almost circular pattern. The Jersey Devil reared back. The thing shrieked and brought its long arms up toward its squinting eyes.

"Caroline!" screamed Ari, ghouls nearly on her.

Caroline held her ground. Just a few more words to go. *"Go, or be torn by the whirlwind!"* The light was now practically yelling, emitting a sound that could shatter glass. It was rivaled by the sound that came next.

Ari cried out with every fiber of her soul. The necrotic fingers of the ghoul army were now probing her body, their leaking mouths leaning towards her delicate neck. Caroline's arm dropped. The Jersey Devil shot around toward the girl.

"Ari!" Caroline struggled to see past the winged devil. Hunched over, the creature shook its head and rubbed its eyes with clawed hands the size of hedge clippers. It whipped its head toward the source of the scream, and there was the young, sweet morsel. It lunged, mouth cranked open, dozens of razor-sharp teeth set to snap on their target like a bear trap mounted to the front of a motorcycle.

The abominations caressed Ari with their rotting fingers. "No!" She yelped and fell backwards, rolling between the legs of the charging Jersey Devil. She narrowly escaped the venomous barb as the devil's tail *swished* past her face. Still dazed from the blinding light of the gem, the devil scooped into its jaws whatever stood before it. There was a loud crunching, followed by an explosion of thick, black liquid as massive jaws cracked a ghoul in half, splattering it over the cold grass.

Ari found herself on the ground near Caroline, looking at the back end of the feasting beast that would have been her undoing. She wasted no time. Finally on the right side of the fight, she darted for the book of spells. Sliding into the wet grass on her knees, she snatched the tome from the ground. In a flash she was up, racing to Caroline's side.

There was no time for words. Caroline looked down at Ari and simply smiled in approval. Standing side by side, they both turned their heads toward the Jersey Devil. The four-hundred-year-old ghouls must have tasted really foul, for the devil had turned around shaking its head wildly. It spat and grunted, trying to do everything possible to rid its mouth of the tarry, black innards of its previous meal.

Caroline gave Ari a conspiratorial nod. "Are you ready?" Ari nodded and leafed through the book. "The closing spell!" Caroline looked over her shoulder as the girl frantically turned the pages of the book. "There! That one!" Ari steadied the book before the two of them. "Say it with me." Caroline raised the amulet.

"Hear me, Hell!" They intoned in unison.

The beast whipped around to face the women, the Hellbarn in full demonic bloom behind its form. It spat one last time and slithered its serpentine neck, throwing its face toward the starry sky. A roar rumbled in its rib cage and shook through the snake-like neck, erupting like a volcano of sound from its quivering jaws. The women steadied themselves. Then, with a purpose, the devil's bony head came rushing down and fixed the women in a stony stare.

For a split second, it seemed as if time stood still. And then it charged!

"*Spirits of evil, unfriendly beings, unwanted guests, be gone! Leave us!*" Caroline and Ari read faster than before.

The thing lumbered forward, beating its full body weight into the Earth with each leap.

"*Leave this place, leave this circle, that the Goddess and the God may enter.*"

The amulet hummed, glowing at the end of Caroline's outstretched arm.

"*Go, or be cast into the outer darkness!*"

A shambling ghoul stumbled into the devil's path and was sent soaring through the air with a brutal swing of its bony arm.

"*Go, or be drowned in the watery abyss!*"

It was one leap away from the women who bravely held their ground.

"*Go, or be burned in the flames!*"

A burning light burst forth from the amulet, blinding the charging monstrosity. It stumbled, crashing to a knee before quickly righting itself. It threw its talons up to block the offending light from the amulet, which screeched like a celestial steam whistle.

"*Go, or be torn by the whirlwind!*"

The devil hobbled from hoof to hoof, rearing back from the burning light. Its serpentine tail lashed wildly as it stepped back with its left leg, then with its right, then again with the left, desperate to put space between it and the blinding orb. It flapped its enormous wings with such great force that each burst of wind punched the women in their faces. Another shambling ghoul happened into the path of the retreating beast and was trampled under its cloven hooves with a *crunch* and a *splat*.

Caroline threw out her chest. With the help of Ari, the creature before her was subdued. But it wasn't yet defeated, nor was it their only problem. Ghouls were everywhere. Just mere inches behind the winged devil, and on either side of the women, they shambled forward, moaning with arms outstretched.

"By the power of the Mother, we banish you!"

The amulet beamed like a miniature sun. The Jersey Devil screamed so loudly it seemed like it might burst. It writhed in pain, closing its eyes, shielding them with its shiny, black claws. It hopped to its left, eluding the beam. Caroline and Ari stepped to their left, edging along the circumference of an invisible circle, trying to keep the abomination directly in the path of the light. The writing demon hopped again to the left. The women did the same, fixing it with the beam. Flapping its wings, it hopped into the air, bouncing down several feet to the left. The women took several steps to match its position. Trying to keep the blazing light on her target, Caroline brought her other hand up to steady the amulet. With both hands, she directed the bauble from side to side, trying to zero in on her elusive adversary.

"We banish you!"

The Jersey Devil jumped again, and so did the women. They were locked in a dance, keeping at opposite points in a wide circle. Caroline glanced over her shoulder, and her eyebrows wrinkled as she realized their unenviable position. The Hellbarn, the ghoul army, and the giant tentacled beast were all... directly behind her and Ari. They were flanked, stuck between Hell and the Jersey Devil. Caroline pointed to a line on the page.

"Be gone, foul beast!" The two women read aloud in booming voices.

Ghouls approached from the rear. A putrid old soul gripped Ari by her hair and tugged her toward his yawning gob. The girl screamed.

Caroline jerked around. "Ari!"

"I've got this!" yelled the girl being yanked backwards. "Don't stop!"

Ari turned on a heel to face the ancient creature, and kicked him with all her might in his right shin. It snapped like a twig, breaking the bone and folding his leg back mid-shin. She slammed the book shut and thrashed his pale head with it so violently that it crushed part of his skull. The desiccated old corpse crumpled to the ground, shivering pathetically at her feet.

Caroline steadied the amulet, moving her hands like the sights of a gun to direct the light. The beam bounced around, following the moving target, until finally it landed right in its eyes. The black orbs on the sides of its head turned a fiery orange, filled with a burning fire. The monster recoiled in pain, throwing up its hands to shield itself.

"*Get... thee...*" Caroline spoke alone now. She felt Ari's movement behind her and heard the percussions of battle. The hordes must be upon them! There was no time! "*Back... to...*" The devil before Caroline took a big step backwards. It dropped its massive claws, which swung like pendulums at its side. Caroline took a deep breath to belt out the final word of the incantation. "*Heh...*"

The horned devil interrupted her with a pained, primordial birth cry. It was like no sound she'd ever heard the creature make before. It arrested the final word of the incantation right in her gaping mouth. The cry was tortured and mournful, and so loud it tingled in her eardrums. The beast collapsed to one knee and threw its left claw down to the ground to support its weight. The bony fingers of its right hand curled like a giant spider around its moaning face. Caroline watched in stunned surprise. The monster craned its misshapen head to the heavens and wailed on and on in an endless cry that brought to mind the unendurable anguish of a mother who's lost a child…

Or of a small child, who's lost its mother.

Caroline stood before the pathetic creature, holding the amulet before her. This was not the fearsome devil she'd fought all of these years, the harbinger of the Hellgate's opening. The first to escape from its mouth, born of this world, often the last to be cast back.

She recalled the stories she'd heard about this creature. They all started before it was even born. Back then, the creature was just a baby in its mother's womb, an innocent soul waiting to be born, waiting to feel a mother's love. She pictured Mother Leeds caressing her pregnant belly during happier times. Certainly, there must have been a moment of pride, a moment where she longed to see the child within her, to hold it and to love it. Then, she saw in her mind the screaming children, twelve other young ones crying in hunger, Mother Leeds' desperation turning to frustration and then to anger. She saw her punch her engorged belly, cursing the innocent baby within. "I hope this child comes out a demon!" In a moment of anger, those strange words spewed from her twisted, wrinkled mouth. In this place, so close to this gateway to Hell, they were more than just words.

And then the birth. Caroline saw it as if she were right there, witnessing it herself, unsure if the vision was a product of her imagination or something sent into her mind from beyond. She saw Mother Leeds sprawled on a table by the fire, and the innocent child emerging only to discover something was desperately wrong. The child was born a mutant, cursed with cruel—and by the sounds of its woeful bleating—painful deformities. It righted itself as best it could, its little body twisted into a wretched, unnatural form. As the newborn stood for the first time in this world, amongst its family, Caroline could see the expressions it was met with. Siblings cowered in a corner, huddled together, terror on their faces. And when the child turned to its mother, what it saw there was horror and disgust. The pitiful creature did the only thing it could. It tore out of the cabin and escaped into the darkness of the forest.

Ari stood back to back with Caroline, wielding the book of spells as a weapon. She thrust it into the chest of an approaching corpse. It crushed the putrid ribs with a *crackle* and left a sizeable dent in the thing's chest. It recoiled and moved off to her right, but there was another one right behind it and another coming from the left and another from the right again. She kicked a mummified corpse to her left, crumbling part of its thigh and sending it crashing to the ground. She waved the book in both hands like a wide, fat sword, trying to keep space between her and the approaching abominations. She looked over her shoulder. Caroline stood motionless, still holding the amulet in the air before her. She was no longer reciting the incantation. "Caroline!"

Caroline looked upon the wailing creature before her, still focusing the light of the amulet on it. She thought about the life it had led after that fateful night in the cabin—hiding in the shadows of the forest, hated and hunted for decades. Turned into a villain by those who feared it merely for the way it looked, this pathetic creature, a victim of its own mother's curse.

Yet, it had killed her mentor, her loving grandmother, thirty-five years ago. There wasn't a day that went by that she didn't think about that night, when the only person she'd ever truly looked up to was taken away from her—that fateful night when her life was changed forever.

But now, looking upon the killer, wailing like an unloved and abandoned child, some part of her softened. She could not help but feel sorry for the tortured wretch. She'd heard the call of the Jersey Devil, and it wasn't one of rage… it was one of unendurable, unending suffering.

Ari swung the book wildly, creating a buffer that was no more than the length of her arms and outstretched book between her and the ghouls. It was a ghastly high tide. With each swing of the book, the waves of rotting souls came closer and closer. She glanced over her shoulder at Caroline, and to her shock, she saw the light of the amulet descending toward the ground. Caroline was slowly dropping her arm, letting the light of the amulet fall from the face of the devil. It traveled off of its face, down its chest, down to its hooves, then along the grass closer to Caroline's feet. "What are you doing?" screamed Ari. Caroline didn't answer.

A loud rumbling shook from the barn, causing the ghouls to turn their attention to the fiery, creature filled orifice. The wooden planks of the structure trembled, as if a volcano was ready to burst forth from within. The ghouls gazed into the light, entranced. Ari seized the moment. She dropped the book and spun fully around, pressing her chest against Caroline's back. "Caroline!" She grabbed the woman's upper arms and shook her. Caroline did not respond. Instead, the witch dropped her arm to her side. The bright beam from the amulet diminished as it pointed at the grass by her right foot. Ari looked past Caroline at the Jersey Devil. It crouched in the unkempt grasses, clouds filling the chilled air with each anguished howl. Pained noises slowed into meek whimpers until they were silent. The creature kneeled in the grass, breathing heavily with its horned head bowed.

Ari looked at the pathetic creature. It seemed… defeated. She turned to Caroline and gave her a gentle shake. "Caroline! Caroline!" The woman gazed up into the black, starry sky, her face locked in a mask of sadness. "Caroline!"

And then she spoke in a voice barely more than a whisper. "I can't do this anymore."

"What?"

"I can't... I can't do this anymore."

Ari looked over her shoulder at the army of ghouls behind them. They were approaching at an alarming rate. Ari shook the witch, more out of desperation than a desire to rouse her. "We have to finish! We have to close the gateway."

"I'm... tired. I'm so... tired of this." Caroline lowered her head slowly until she was looking upon the Jersey Devil. "And so's he." Her eyebrows crinkled in sympathy.

She could see Ari looking at the devil, now, too. His heaving had slowed. He appeared almost motionless as he crouched in the grass. And then, he moved. Slowly, he began to raise his cumbersome, horn-filled head. Black eyes glistened, picking up the refection of the full moon. Finally, he looked right at them. His lips began to stretch and slowly part. A stream of shining saliva dribbled from his jaws.

"Caroline!" Ari nudged the witch.

A low grumbling was now coming from the monster. It revved into a steady growl, like an engine. The beast bore down on his front claws, pushing its body weight into the Earth. The muscles in his legs tightened.

"It's coming!" Ari yelled, and jerked Caroline's right wrist.

The demon kicked the Earth with all his might and shot up like a winged missile, aimed directly for the women. He screeched as he soared toward them. Caroline's eyes shot open. Her right hand thrust into the air.

"Get thee back to Hell!" she screamed, Ari joining in on the second half of the phrase.

A blinding beam of yellowish-orange light burst from the amulet. It pounded the monster directly in the chest and sent him flying backwards. The shrieking creature tumbled to the ground, rolling twice before collapsing. Caroline and Ari stood motionless, startled eyes fixed on the devil. He twitched once. Then he twitched again. The women were frozen in place, eyes locked on the thing as if burning him with their gaze, willing him to be dead. One of his spindly arms rose from his body like a snake. The talons on the end of the appendage opened like an evil flower. The claw came crashing down toward the Earth; when it did, it lifted the bony chest off of the wet grass. The snake-like neck followed, curling upward and whipping up the massive head. He met the gaze of the women and roared. In a flash, he was back on his cloven hooves. Ari and Caroline both took a startled step backwards into a group of festering ghouls.

Caroline spun frantically, still clutching the amulet, and she pushed away the undead who approached from all sides. The gem radiated a meek, amber light that caused the ghouls to shield their faces. She glanced over her shoulder at the Jersey Devil. He was flapping his leathery dragon wings, regaining his strength. "I'm not sure I know what else I can do." She looked over at Ari, who had picked up the book at her feet and was swinging it wildly at the monsters around her.

Ari turned to see the Jersey Devil, and the expression on her face alerted Caroline that things were about to get worse.

The creature roared furiously, curled his talons and sprang off the ground into a sprint toward the women. Caroline and Ari barely had time to react before—

BLAST!

An eruption shook the forest and nearly knocked the women off of their feet. Many of the frailer ghouls were sent tumbling to the ground. The Jersey Devil stopped dead in his tracks. The women spun around to see giant, black tentacles bursting from the roof of the Hellbarn, throwing shattered planks of wood into the night sky. The beast had emerged into our world. Everyone froze. Then, another tentacle, the size of a submarine, crashed through the roof, raining splinters down upon all the surrounding beings. The Jersey Devil screeched in fear. Caroline turned to see him flap his massive wings, turn, and shoot into the sky. He disappeared with a frightful wailing into the darkness of the forest.

She turned back toward the Hellbarn and then to Ari. "We have to get out of here."

"What do you mean? We have to close the gateway…" Ari's face was a picture of disbelief.

"There's no way. It's impossible."

"But the amulet… you said if we got it into the barn…"

"It can't be done. It's too dangerous. It just can't be…" Caroline lowered her head and closed her eyes in defeat.

Suddenly, her hands were slapped by an unknown force and, before she could react, the amulet was snatched from her grasp. She yelped and turned to see what monster had robbed her of the world's only hope. It was Ari, and to Caroline's great dismay, the girl was running as fast as she could toward the mouth of Hell.

"*No!*" cried Caroline. "*Ari, no!*"

Ari ran and ran with all the strength her lungs and legs would lend her. She wove and bobbed around the horrors that reached out for her with necrotic fingers. Ghouls, with gaping black maws, roared in her tiny face. Skeletons lunged with bony fingers toward her small frame. She leapt to the left and to the right as the escaped atrocities of Hell all shambled toward her. In her haste, the front of her shoe found a hard object in the grass—a rock? a skull? something worse?—and the girl went soaring through the air like a ragdoll. She crashed, collecting a mouthful of grass and dirt as she hit ground, and looked up. Directly before her, a ghoul hunkered in the grass. It was female; Ari could tell from the wispy, long black hair and the drooping, wrinkled breasts. The monstrous hag looked down and glared at Ari. The girl feared the worst, but apparently this hellish crone held something that was of greater interest to the abomination than Ari or even the amulet. The hag opened her ghastly, black mouth, drooling. She was eating, and the thing on which her rotting gob fed was a baby.

Ari gasped. The pale, squirming child yelped pitifully, and as the monster brought it to her lips, Ari could see the umbilical cord. They were attached, the undead mother and child. She was devouring her own offspring.

Vomit bubbled into Ari's mouth and tears welled in her eyes. She used that terror and disgust as fuel; like a rocket, she shot back to her legs and commenced her sprint to Hell.

In the distance, Ari saw Caroline clasp her head between her two hands as her face filled with anguish, but the girl didn't stop, not even when she heard Caroline call, "*Aaarrriii*! Come back!"

Ari ran until she reached the opening of the Hellbarn. There, she was stopped dead in her tracks by the spectacle of it all. The fissure was bright and huge. As it expanded inside of the barn, it defied the very laws of physics. An impossibly huge otherworld existed within the meager frame of the dilapidated, wooden structure. Ari was gazing straight into the very heart of Hell, with its monumental towers of volcanic rock, plasma skies, and seas of burning fire. It was... beautiful.

Her admiration of the vista was interrupted by the thing she realized was looming above her. It was the largest creature she'd ever set eyes on. The Beast seemed to tower miles over her head. It was gigantic, with its black tentacles reaching from the barn, slithering all around her. Ari noticed that a ring of ghouls had also converged around her. She was surrounded. Then, somewhere high on the scaly, black beast, there was movement. A ball on its slimy body, like a black, leathery pimple, began to wriggle, and then it opened. There on the monster, born from the black pustule, was a yellow eye. It looked down and fixed Ari in its gaze.

The monsters around her stopped, as if informed by the Beast to halt their attack. She clutched the amulet in her hand, and its glowing light brightened. The yellow eye of the Beast grew wide. The tentacles came to life, whipping around violently as the Beast writhed, undulated, and let out a thundering bellow that nearly knocked Ari off her feet.

The ghouls recommenced their approach, closing their circle around her. Ari held the amulet over her head, and from it burst a shining, multicolored light. The monsters gasped, covering their faces with their rotted stumps and putrid appendages. And then she saw the black skin around the eye of the Beast contort into a frown, and it let out a harrowing cry that nearly split her head in two. Its tentacles tensed, then curled, and she knew she was out of time. She held the amulet as high as she could over her head. The beams of light radiated like a magical sun. The mammoth, black tentacles all came whipping toward her.

"*Go to Hell!*" Ari threw the amulet into the gateway.

Everything stopped. The tentacles froze in place. The ghouls and skeletons went rigid like statues.

For a fraction of a second Ari held her breath, wondering if she'd succeeded...

BLAST!

The whole of Hell was rocked by an explosion, crumbling chasms and splitting mountains and sending demons flying in all directions. The Beast screeched like a spider on fire, and whipped its tentacles in all directions. Beneath, the ground was crumbling. It started falling through the fissure, away from our world. The blast shot from the Hellbarn's mouth, blasting Ari from her feet and sending her flying through the air. The same monstrous gust of wind, light, and smoke shattered all the skeletons in the doorway and beyond, reducing their bones to dust. It tore the ghouls' rotting flesh into unrecognizably small shreds and scattered them like a rain of gore across the field.

Ari landed yards away from the barn, her body crashing into the moist grass. Light burst from every door and window and crevice of the old barn, as if Hell were going to explode—but then a sucking sound was heard. The Hellish winds stopped and changed direction. The fissure to Hell began imploding, and it was taking all that was foul and rank back to where it belonged. The winds picked up, stronger and stronger, until flying demons were being yanked backward through the sky and into the abyss. Any ghouls not destroyed by the blast were lifted by their rotting stumps and pulled into the inferno.

A flying skull emerged from the trees and tumbled through the air, narrowly missing Caroline's head, before being pulled into the fissure. Ari saw Caroline drop to her knees and clasp her fists as tightly as she could around two clumps of grass while tornados of leaves blew toward the barn, and the trees, themselves, curved toward the cursed structure.

Ari felt herself being dragged toward the barn doors by the massive, sucking wind. She dug her fingers as deeply as she could into the ground. The sounds around her were deafening, like a million turbines in a cyclone. She longed to cover her ears, but didn't dare release her hold on Mother Earth.

A familiar screech blasted through the air. Ari and Caroline looked to the sky. Careening toward the barn through the night, leathery wings fully extended, tail lashing like a whip behind him, was the Jersey Devil. And he wasn't alone.

"So long, suckers!" someone cried from overhead. Gripped in one of the creature's talons was a badly beaten severed head. It was Aleister's. "See you in Hell!" He chortled gleefully as they soared toward the barn. As they disappeared into the fissure to Hell, Aleister howled, like a demonic cowboy, "*Whooo hooo!*"

And then they were gone.

The winds died down. The roars of the Beast were fading into a distant otherworld and, for the first time that night, the air was deliciously absent of the vociferations of ghouls.

"Ari!" came Caroline's cry.

Ari realized the woman must have seen her fly through the air. She heard the approaching footsteps pounding at a run and felt Caroline collapse to the ground beside her.

Ari lifted her head, smirked, and looked up at Caroline, still obviously in pain. "Not bad, huh?"

Laughter bubbled up from Caroline. "You did it! You did it, Ari. You closed the gateway! I'm so proud of you."

Ari shook her head as best she could, but she was afraid to move for fear she'd discover she had broken every bone in her body.

"Are you okay?" Caroline's mirth turned to concern.

"I'm not sure. My arm hurts."

"Let's see if we can get you up," said Caroline tenderly.

She gently helped the girl to sit. In the process, Ari's eyes fell upon the forest and stayed there, glued, searching.

"What is it?" asked Caroline.

"Where's Villy?"

Caroline now peered into the trees' darkness along with Ari. A creaking of old wood diverted their attention to the barn. The doors were closing. As the fissure shriveled, the light inside of the barn dulled to a reddish glow, fading quickly. The gap between the doors was only about a yard or so wide, but in that gap, silhouetted by the red glow, there was a black shape, a shape the two women knew well by that point. Villy Bats.

Slowly and willfully, their friend was walking into the mouth of Hell. They would have yelled his name if they thought it would do any good, but the doors were closing behind him and he was fading into the dim red glow.

He had some help. As Villy disappeared into the fissure, another shape emerged in the doorway. A long, bony arm reached for the handle inside of the door. It was followed by a lanky figure stepping forward between the two doors, and another bony arm reaching for the other handle. The appendages' owner raised his hideous, skeletal head, and beneath his tall, black hat, the Governor was smiling a dreadful, sardonic smile. A crusty, mucosal laugh gurgled from his rotten gob as he pulled the barn doors shut. With that, the lights were gone. There was silence. The barn, once again, was nothing more than an old barn.

The gateway to Hell had been closed.

Caroline and Ari held each other tightly, quietly grieving the loss of their friend.

Chapter 17

Caroline had always regarded the Beagle Rock Diner as a fine place to enjoy a meal—that is, as far as greasy spoons *in the heart of the Pine Barrens* are "fine" places. Frankly, she knew it was the *only* place to have a meal that deep in the forest, but to its credit there was hot coffee at all times and the presence of large insects in the food was infrequent enough.

The place had a sort of anachronistic, if run-down, charm which she found not unappealing. Fifties style, largely chrome-covered, she figured it had been built decades earlier to serve the dwindling iron mining community or the growing throngs of cranberry bog workers. Of course, the chrome didn't shine as it once must have, and the forest seemed to have taken its toll on the façade, giving the once-shiny metal edifice a look of brushed aluminum. Rust flourished in places, especially on the old sign above the front door, causing it to creak, moan, and complain, much like the one-person staff.

The owner, cook, and waiter, a wiry, old man named Vern, was pleasant enough for a lonely curmudgeon. He often commented that the diner was his wife and that she was "the only wife he needed, and a sexy one at that". That comment had always caused Caroline to look at the mayonnaise in a funny way.

As Vern lovingly massaged the Formica countertop with a warm, damp rag, Caroline fought back the urge to picture him giving his "wife" a sponge bath. She turned her attention to the tea she was sipping and the business at hand.

The witch sat at her favorite booth. Ari sat beside her on the same, sparkly, red banquette. Fanned across the table was a collection of drawings, maps, and prints, as well as a small stack of books. Ari eagerly combed through them. One weathered piece of paper in particular seemed to catch her eye. On it was a rendering of a monstrous, furry beast. She held it up. "Wow, who's *this* guy?"

Caroline craned her neck over to see the illustration. "Oh… Big Red Eye. He's a mean one."

"A demon?"

"No. He's more like a Sasquatch," said Caroline matter-of-factly. "You know, like Bigfoot. Big, hairy." She curled her hands into claws and held them at mouth level as she bared her teeth. "And always *huuungrrry*."

"Have you ever seen him?"

"Have I?" howled Caroline. She pulled up the cuffed sleeve of her shirt revealing two thick, white scars on her shoulder.

"Wow." As an embarrassed flush rose up her neck and face, Ari went back to admiring the image with newfound knowledge and fear. "Do you think Bigfoot is real?"

"I reckon."

"You ever think about looking for him? You know, going in search of Bigfoot or stuff like that?"

"Are you kidding me?" yelped Caroline. "Go to the Pacific Northwest? Leave here?" Some part of her loved the idea, but she had always felt tied to the Pine Barrens. Grounded, trapped. "Nah, this fissure to Hell keeps me pretty busy. What would happen if it opened up and I was somewhere else?"

"Well…" Ari chose her words tentatively. "Didn't you say it takes a while for the gateway to open again, once you've closed it?"

"Yeah. I suppose," conceded Caroline. "A few months at least… two or three years, sometimes."

"I think we closed it pretty good."

"Yeah." Caroline grinned in return. "I think we did, too."

"So, maybe now's the time for you to get away for a little while, use your knowledge to help people in other places." She glanced sideways at Caroline as if checking to see if she had taken the bait. "You could look for Bigfoot, or… the Loch Ness monster…"

"Or Mothman?" Caroline gave a gentle, teasing laugh.

"Sure! Or…"

Ari slid a newspaper across the table, gliding it directly below Caroline's gaze. The old witch read the headline aloud.

"'Chupacabra Blamed for Goat Massacre in Mexico'?"

"Yeah! Chupacabra!" Ari leaned closer, adding intrigue and drama to her pitch. "They say it's an alien, you know, from outer space. This is no demon like you're used to. This is all new territory."

Caroline laughed. "Someone's got a bit of wanderlust, huh?"

Ari couldn't hide it. Smiling more, she buried her face in her shoulder. "Maybe."

The sound of tinkling bells filled the air of the rusty chrome diner. AJ came through the front door, holding a stack of books. Spotting Caroline and Ari at the penultimate booth from the back, he bee-lined for them, stopping only to place an order.

"A coffee, please," he told Vern behind the counter before taking a seat on the shiny, vinyl banquette across from the girls. He placed the books on the Formica tabletop, sliding them over to Caroline. "Here are the books you asked for."

"Thanks." Caroline inspected the books: two old, dusty tomes—*The Alchemist's Bible* and *Spells for All Occasions*—and a newer, smaller paperback with an illustration of a raging werewolf on the cover, titled

The Sticks, by Andy Deane. "Yep, these are the ones. Thanks for swinging by the cabin for them. I was a little out of it today, as you might imagine."

"Yeah, it's no biggie," said AJ.

Caroline took a sip of her chamomile tea and leafed through the first book. AJ eyed her curiously.

"You got something big planned?" he asked the witch.

"Yeah." She grinned. "Ari, why don't you show him?"

Ari handed him the newspaper.

"Chupacabra?" he spat. "Are you ladies for real?"

"Have you ever been to Mexico?" Ari leaned in, eyes sparkling like Roman candles.

"Um, no. But I'm down. I like tacos, and you know…" He shook his head. "Alien goat-suckers and shit."

Caroline took a sip from her tea and placed the cup down gently, but with a good deal of purpose, on the saucer. She pushed them away, along with the books. Folding her hands, she brought them down to fill that empty space and fixed AJ with a thoughtful look. "You know, in all of the madness and craziness and exhaustion of the last twenty-four hours, you never did get around to telling us what happened to you. How you, uh, got out alive, as it were."

"Yeah," added Ari. She raised her eyebrows, and her mouth stretched into a wide, awkward smile. "We kind of assumed you were dead."

AJ took a deep breath. He straightened in his seat. He raised a cocky eyebrow and pursed his lips. "You see, ladies, it's like this. I'm a Deathrocker, and Lord knows I love to see some spooky shit. But first and foremost, I'm a black man."

Ari and Caroline looked at each other, blinking their eyes in surprise.

"What does *that* mean?" Ari furrowed her brows.

Caroline deadpanned, "Um, yeah, that sounds kind of racist."

AJ continued, undeterred. "It means that, unlike all of y'all who were all too eager to sit around pontificating on the nature of otherworldly occurrences, I did what any self-respecting black man would do when shit gets stupid."

Ari and Caroline stared at AJ for what seemed like an eternity, mouths agape, waiting for the rest of his statement. He didn't seem to be in a hurry to elaborate, so Ari broke the silence.

She bit back a grin as she tentatively echoed his words from the cabin. "You ran 'like a motherfucker'?"

AJ paused, as if letting Ari's question roll around in his head like the steel balls in a puzzle game. Then, planting the palms of his hands on the table before him, he rose from his seat, fixed the ladies with a fiery glare, and yelled at the top of his lungs.

"Damn straight, I ran like a motherfucker!"

Epilogue

Villy could swear he was standing in the very hottest corner of the place—which was saying quite a lot in a setting universally renowned for its heat. As he stepped onto the cliff, a rocky outcropping of dried lava, skulls, and bones that served as a stage, he wondered for a moment if the heat that blasted his face was coming from stage lights. A little giggle rippled through him as he realized there *were* no stage lights at the edge of the abyss. Who needed lights when blazing fires the size of mountains raged eternally in every direction and the sky itself is made of swirling plasma?

Villy grabbed the microphone. With the exception of the twisting spinal cord and other gore spiraling up the wrought-iron stand, it resembled an old mic from the twenties or thirties. A sudden realization that it was likely from that period eased a smile across his lips. He wondered what sad soul had been the first to use it on this infernal stage. Maybe it was someone famous, someone he'd heard of. Maybe one of his many heroes had crooned a tune for the Lord of Darkness, right here on this very stage. He spent a moment compiling a mental list of expired stars he would love to run into in a corner of this inferno.

For a moment, he almost forgot how excruciatingly hot his skin felt. A bead of sweat sizzled down his left temple. It evaporated into mist before reaching his chin. It was hot, *unbelievably* hot, and he was about as uncomfortable as he'd ever been in his life—but the master demanded entertainment, and some part of Villy was proud, almost tickled, to be the one providing it.

There was a low, bellowing roar. Villy teetered on the thin, rocky cliff gazing into the endless abyss below. A giant, black, tentacled Beast rose from the cavernous pit before him. It fixed on him with one eager, yellow eye. From miles above the behemoth, Villy appeared tiny, and yet strangely close to this Beast of incomprehensible size. The Beast roared again, and it echoed through all of Hell's corners, chasms, and torture-filled crannies. It was time.

To ensure Villy had not missed his cue, two towering red demons on either side of him took a step closer and gestured with their sharpened pitch forks toward the edge of the rocky crag. Villy stepped forward, all but perching on the sharp triangle that jutted out countless harrowing miles above the fiery, monster-filled pit.

"Hellooo Hell!" Villy belted out with all of the smarmy flash of a Vegas lounge singer. "Thanks so much for being here tonight! It's truly a pleasure to be here, devils, demons…" He snapped his fingers and pointed at his Hellish host. "And tentacled behemoths!" He sighed dramatically. "I'm glad to be here, too. I was originally booked to perform in Heaven today, but I couldn't get in. Apparently I had a couple of unpaid parking tickets. Who knew?" He laughed a phony laugh. "But seriously folks, this is definitely more my kind of place, if you know what I mean. I mean really, just look around at the ladies here tonight! Wow! They are nothing if not *HOT!*"

He turned to his left. Prudence, now a red-skinned devil girl with a barbed tail and horns, winked and wriggled seductively from side-stage. He turned to his right, where an adulteress was set ablaze, impaled on a vertical spit, screaming hysterically. As her demon executioner, a fat, tusked creature, cranked a rusty handle, the woman rotated like a shrieking, immolated carousel.

"Whoa! That's hard core!" joked Villy. He tossed the demon executioner a raised eyebrow and conspiratorial smirk. "Yo, pal, don't over do it, I said, 'medium rare!' *'MEDIUM RARE!'*" Villy burst into forced laughter again.

The tentacled Beast let out a roar that shook the mountains of Hell. Villy snapped to attention.

"Right! Right! Moving on." His tone changed and quieted into one of mock sincerity. "This little ditty is one of my favorites, and I hope it's one of yours, too. You might find it familiar; it's a little tune I like to call, 'Witchcraft!'" Villy turned his head and looked over his left shoulder. "Alright, boys!"

From behind a group of sharp, craggy rocks emerged a forty-piece orchestra of devils, demons, and imps, each carrying a musical instrument fashioned from the corpses of tortured souls. There was a ribcage xylophone and a drum kit made of skulls and flayed human flesh. The brass section was composed of tibia trumpets and femur flutes, each bone curved and deformed so severely as to force the mind to envision the terrible tortures these souls had endured. Yards of intestines stretched across shoulder-blade violins and pelvic-bone cellos. The Beelzebub Philharmonic Orchestra had assembled.

"Hit it!" yelled Villy.

The band kicked into an infernal version of "Witchcraft", with each monstrous instrument sounding every bit as terrifying as it looked. Villy pulled the grotesque microphone to his lips and burst into song.

"That ancient book of doom, those incantations too, that amulet you threw… it's witchcraft!"

He spun on a heel.

"And Hell's got no defense for it, the gateway's closed and bent by it. What good would ghoul laments for it dooo?"

He subtly reached down and picked up a prop, concealing it behind his back.

"It's witchcraaaft!"

A second voice joined the singer. Villy revealed a barbed, demonic cane, and jammed onto the end of it was a grotesque, singing head: his sidekick and back-up singer, Aleister!

"Zany witchcraaaft!" caterwauled the severed head.

Together, like the Dean Martin and Jerry Lewis of Hell, they sang in strained harmony.

"And although we know this shit is taboo…"

"… when you read from that book to me," sang Villy, *"and threw an ancient spell at me…"*

"… I lost my head and my body, too!" added Aleister's head.

"The devil's in a ditch," Villy crooned, then winked at the tentacled Beast. "Sorry pal!" he offered as an aside. *"It's one that's black as pitch. 'Cause of a Pagan bitch like youuu!"*

Villy pointed at the burning wench at stage right, soliciting a wave of unbearable screams from the flaming victim. "Take it away, boys!" yelled Villy, and the demon orchestra blazed away. As the band swung into the instrumental interlude, Villy held the cane before him and glared at Aleister's head. "You were flat."

"The front of your pants is flat, you fuckin' eunuch!" insisted Aleister. "My tone is pitch perfect.

The problem is that you're sharp. You're *always* sharp!"

"You're going to feel a sharp pain in your ass in a minute," warned Villy.

"Good luck, asshole. You have to find my ass first, and believe me, if you did I'd be the happiest head in Hell!"

Their argument was interrupted by a ground-rattling roar from the abyss. Their bickering had angered the Beast. Villy spun around, putting his back to their dark Lord and bringing his grotesque cane-topper close to his face. "God! Why are you so damned difficult?" He hissed a shouted whisper to his back-up singer. "You're going to get us thrown into the pit again. Why can't you just fuckin' cooperate for once?"

The Beast roared again, shaking the cliff so mightily that Villy nearly lost his footing on the precipice.

"Okay, okay!" growled Aleister. "Come on, turn around. The instrumental is almost over."

Villy spun back around to face the abyss, just in time to come in on the beat.

"*It's witchcraaa…*"

He had spun too quickly. Aleister's head slid off of the cane and shot through the air like a bullet, hitting the Beast directly in his one eye.

"Uh oh," uttered Villy.

The tentacled behemoth roared and writhed hysterically, slamming his tentacles like fists into the black canyon walls around him. Aleister's head bounced off two or three of the slimy, black appendages before getting snatched by a flying demon. He was carried off in the creature's monstrous talons. Nevertheless, Aleister didn't miss a beat. Soaring through the chasm, he yelled, *"Zany witchcraaaft!"* He was screaming and completely out of tune, but really, who could blame him, given the circumstances?

The band knew better than to stop, so they kept right on playing. Villy could see where this was going. He'd been here before, but still, he did his best to keep hope alive. As two hulking demons approached him with sharpened pitchforks, he kept on singing.

"And although we know this shit is taboo…"

Thinking he'd finish the song was a futile bout of optimism. The demons drew closer and simultaneously jabbed him in the posterior. With a great deal of help from barbed metal weapons, Villy sprang off the edge of the cliff—as he'd done a dozen times already that day—and fell for miles into the fiery pit below.

His last line went something like this: *"Oweee!"*

Acknowledgements

My father died when I was four months old. My mother, warned by family members that his children would be made an example of in post-revolution, communist Cuba, bundled my sister and me in a hurry and, when I was only two months short of my first birthday, we emigrated from Havana, Cuba. We settled briefly in Tarrytown, New York. The upstate town had a small Cuban community that struggled to get its footing in a new country. My mother, a young lady with two small children and no working knowledge of English, received public assistance to help feed us as she learned to speak the language. Prohibited from taking money or valuables of any kind out of Cuba, we lived in near squalor. When I was only two or three years old, my widowed mother remarried, primarily out of necessity, and we moved to Newark, New Jersey. My childhood years there in the seventies were as bleak as the city itself. I stood out at my all-black and Hispanic school due to my ghostly pale complexion. Despite explaining again and again to my schoolmates that I was Cuban, and that I was just like them, I remained for the dreadful years that followed, 'the white boy' and was the object of much ridicule and bullying.

One of my only truly magical experiences from those years was the day I learned of the Jersey Devil.

I was in Branch Brook Park when someone (I don't remember anymore who it was) told me the legend of this terrible, fearsome beast. Not having ever seen a forest before, I could easily imagine the Jersey Devil living in the bushes and sparse trees of this inner-city park (a thought that's now ridiculous to my adult brain). While I'm sure the teller of the tale had meant to frighten me, his story had the opposite effect. It lit my imagination on fire!

I experienced this dynamic again at Sunday school at the church I attended briefly. There, in the Bibles, I found images of demons soaring through plasma skies in Hell. Certainly they were there to scare me, to remind me of the dangers of straying from the word of God. But again, they only served to urge my imagination further. They helped me create a world to escape to, a world inside of my own head, full of monsters. But unlike some of the heinous creatures and troubles that surrounded me during those dark years, these monsters were somehow… reassuring. In the years that followed, I became a fan of monsters and became completely obsessed with all manner of monster movies. I was enthralled by the films of Ray Harryhausen and dreamt of becoming a stop-motion animator and maker of monsters, just like him.

When I was in third grade, we moved to the suburbs. I remember looking out the car window as we drove down Pleasant Valley Way. I saw trees and grass and white people walking their dogs on immaculately paved sidewalks. I turned to my sister and excitedly beamed, "We are going to live with the white people!" That euphoria ended on the first day of school.

"Weinstein?" The teacher called out to the class. Her eyes scanned the room. A pasty hand went up. Satisfied, she called the next name on the list. "O'Malley?" Another hand rose. "Severio?" Again a hand shot into the air. And then came my name. "Hernandez?" I raised my hand. The entire class turned and fixed me with their scrutinizing eyes. Then, one of the students cupped his mouth and growled in a low, hateful whisper to the student next to him.

"He's a spic!"

From that day forth, I was no longer white. I was a Hispanic boy surrounded by white people. I was subsequently ridiculed and bullied by a whole new set of people. Apparently, I was too white for Newark and not white enough for the suburbs of New Jersey.

Race was far from my only problem. I wasn't athletic and I made stop-motion monster movies in my basement. In the opinion of many of my peers, that made me a "fag". As I grew into a teenager, I got into New Wave, New Romantic, and Goth music, and that influenced the way I looked. This development was as unpopular at home as it was with my peers at school. The arguments, beatings and bullying were getting too hard to bear. I'd come home from a rough day at school, just to experience more of the same at home.

Eventually, between the hate at school and the troubles at home, the pressure got to be too much and in 1984, at the age of seventeen, I ran away from home. I found my way to Manhattan, where I have spent nearly three decades making monsters in a state of near bliss.

I suppose it should come as no surprise that while my first novel is about New Jersey, it's primarily about the few things in that state that I understand and love: the Jersey Devil and disenfranchised Goth kids.

Big thanks go to the people who made this book possible. First and foremost, thanks go to my editor, Trisha Wooldridge, without whom this book would have been self released. Had she not come to my reading at Dragoncon in 2012 and encouraged me to consider publishing with Spencer Hill Press/Spence City, this book would have come out months earlier but read like it was written by a twelve-year-old. Without her talents and guidance this book wouldn't be half as polished and complete as it is now. It's no hyperbole when I say that she, in essence, taught me to write in one month and I'm extremely grateful for it. My only complaint was her insistence on removing every reference in my book to a "mound of Venus", insisting it's a "bodice ripper" term and something "just plain silly" that people don't really say. Well, apparently I use this term (often) and I will more than make up for it in my next book, *The Neatly Coiffed Mound of Venus of Trisha Wooldridge.*

Thanks to Kate Kaynak and Vikki Ciaffone at Spence Hill Press/Spence City and their dedicated staff for taking a chance on and helping this first time novelist. Thanks to Paul Carrick and Michael Komarck for the gorgeous interior and cover art, respectively.

I might have never thought to write a novel if it weren't for fellow musician and author, Andy Deane, of the band Bella Morte. While on tour, I noticed a book on his merch table with an awesome illustration of a werewolf on the cover. He'd apparently written a novel called *The Sticks*. I read it during the long drives of that tour and thoroughly enjoyed it! Thank you, Andy, for the encouragement!

I would also like to acknowledge my favorite screenwriter, Caroline Thompson. Before *Call of the Jersey Devil* was a novel, it was a screenplay. My first. Ms. Thompson was literally the first person to read it. Having your favorite screenwriter read your work can be… well, really scary. So, when she offered to read it, rather than send it to her, I rewrote it! I felt it was good, but I couldn't send the writer of Edward Scissorhands and The Nightmare Before Christmas "good." I had to send her "great", or at least as close as I was capable of coming to it. When she came back with words of praise and support, well, what can I say? Without that encouragement, it's truly doubtful that I'd be a published novelist today. So from the bottom of my Jack Skellington-shaped heart, thank you, Caroline!

My family deserves a good deal of praise: my son, Mars, for tolerating the fact that I constantly and excitedly quoted from my book all through the writing process, and my loving wife, Jayme, for putting up with my constant disappearing acts. (I tend to write at night at an all-night café).

Lastly, as I rounded the corner of finishing this novel, it crept up on me that it's a story about motherly love—or lack thereof—and how that can effect what kind of person (or monster) you turn out to be. I couldn't in good conscience end this book without thanking my mother, Magali Hernandez. Life is never easy. You've made choices over the years that I know you've regretted. But keep in mind that had you not made them, instead of writing this novel, I'd be cutting sugar cane in a field somewhere, hands covered in blisters, for the glory of the revolution and little more. Despite our disagreements, you were one of the few people in my childhood who nurtured my love in monsters, buying my first stop-motion camera when others deemed this hobby unmanly and worthless. When I was a mere child, you sent me on a bus to New York City to meet my God, Ray Harryhausen! You were the only one who understood what that meant to me. We've had our ups and downs, but I know that when I left, it broke your heart.

Above and beyond everything else, I knew that I was loved. That motherly love was like a torch in the darkness through the very worst of times. I love you and I'm eternally grateful for what you've given me. It's something no one else could have given me, (sadly, something the Jersey Devil never had), a mother's love and...

Self worth.

COPPER GIRL

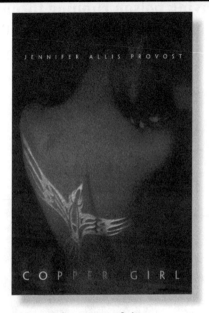

JENNIFER ALLIS PROVOST

COPPER GIRL

Sara had always been careful.

She never spoke of magic, never associated with those suspected of handling magic, never thought of magic, and never, ever, let anyone see her mark. After all, the last thing she wanted was to end up missing, like her father and brother.

Then, a silver elf pushed his way into Sara's dream, and her life became anything but ordinary.

THE LAST IMPERIALS — BOOK ONE
SHERRY D. FICKLIN & TYLER H. JOLLEY

EXTRACTED

An infamous brother and sister have been stolen from history and drafted to opposite sides of a war no one can win—a battle for time itself.

Founded and run by the disembodied head of a mad genius, the Tesla Institute is responsible for locating, retrieving, and training teens with the ability to Rift through time and space. Seventeen-year-old Ember has no memory of her life before being brought to the Institute, but she's made a home there. Just as she's about to officially join the ranks of the Rifters, memories of her bloody past begin to slide through the cracks. Now she's forced to question everyone she loves and everything she's been taught.

Ex still bears the scars from the fire that killed his entire family. The newest member of a group of rogue Rifters known as The Hollows, he thinks he's finally found his place in the world. It's gritty and treacherous and the only place he feels completely free. But his partner and best friend Steinward is dead, and he's to blame. The only chance of saving her is a dangerous mission inside the heart of the Tesla Institute itself. But what he finds there is more than a piece of tech. It's the key to changing his whole life. Now that he understands what's possible, he's willing to break all the rules to put his family back together.

Also available as an ebook • **SPENCER HILL PRESS** • spencerhillpress.com

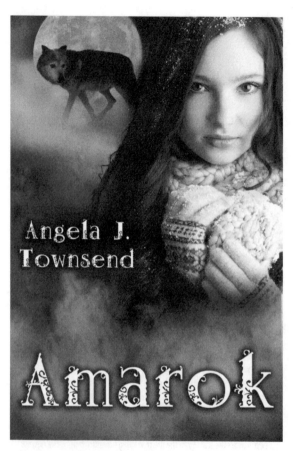

Amarok

Angela J. Townsend

Life has been hell for seventeen-year-old Emma since she moved from sunny California to a remote Alaskan town. Rejected by her father and living with the guilt of causing her mother's death, she makes a desperate dash for freedom from her abusive stepfather. But when her car skids off the icy road, her escape only leads to further captivity in a world beyond her imagining.

~~~~~~~~~~~~~~~~~~~~~~~~~~~~~

Starting college a year early is hard. Starting fae college and learning to protect the world from the Unseelie is harder.

Brielle Reed has always been an over-achiever, but this time she may have bitten off more than she can chew. Between her crash course in faey politics, struggles to control her new mind-reading ability, training sessions with the demanding Dr. Schwartz, and discoveries about the father who is still a mystery to her, Brielle finds herself longing for a chance at a normal life. But she may not get that chance. Or chance at a life at all, for that matter.

Also available as an ebook • **SPENCER HILL PRESS** • spencerhillpress.com

About the Author

Aurelio Voltaire is a media personality and respected authority on all things Gothic, Horror, Sci-fi, Steampunk and involving "geek" culture. He is often referred to as a modern day renaissance man having achieved success in the fields of animation, music, comics, books and toys.

Voltaire's career began in the 1980s as a stop-motion animator and director, creating some of the award-winning, classic MTV and SyFy channel station IDs. He worked in television, animating and directing commercials for nearly twenty years when he realized it was time for him to tell his own stories. Finding comic books to be a vastly more economical tool than feature films Voltaire told his first epic tale, "Chi-chian" in comic book form. This dark, Cinderella story set in Manhattan's future, was published and led to a 14-episode animated web series directed by Voltaire for the SyFy channel's website. His success in comic books also led to several underground hits including the comic book series Oh My Goth!, Human Suck! and most recently Deady. The latter featured collaborations with some of the biggest names in horror and comics including Neil Gaiman, Clive Barker, James O'Barr, Roman Dirge, Gris Grimly and many others. It also spawned a long list of toys including plush toys for Six Flags, Hot Wheels cars for the Japanese market and over a dozen vinyl toy releases including collaborations with Disney and Skelanimals.

In yet another career swerve, 1995 saw Voltaire take the stage at a New York City club where he launched his music career. His songs are a strange brew of murder ballads, tongue-in-cheek exercises in the macabre with just enough bawdy Star Trek and Star Wars songs to keep convention audiences rolling in the aisles. Many in the mainstream know Voltaire as the writer and performer of the songs Brains! and Land of the Dead from the Cartoon Network show, The Grim Adventures of Billy And Mandy. Almost constantly on tour, he has played his music around the world and released eleven full length CDs to date.

Voltaire also wrote the popular books What is Goth? and Paint it Black: a Guide to Gothic Homemaking (Weiser Books) and has appeared on numerous television shows and documentaries as an authority on Goth, Horror and Steampunk. Appearances include Fox News, Biography, MTV News, Fearnet, IFC, PBS and others.

When not touring, writing books or designing toys, Voltaire teaches stop-motion animation at the School of Visual arts and continues to make short films. His "Chimerascope" series of stop-motion shorts are perennial film festival favorites. The five shorts have won a combined 31 awards and feature the voice talents of Deborah Harry, Richard Butler, Gerard Way, Gary Numan and Danny Elfman.

More on Aurelio Voltaire can be found on his official website: www.voltaire.net